Praise for *New York Times* bestselling author

SUSAN MALLERY

"If you want a story that will both tug on
your heartstrings and tickle your funny bone, Mallery
is the author for you!"
—*RT Book Reviews* on *Only His*

"When it comes to heartfelt contemporary romance,
Mallery is in a class by herself."
—*RT Book Reviews* on *Only Yours*

"An adorable, outspoken heroine and an intense hero...
set the sparks flying in Mallery's latest lively, comic and
touching family-centered story."
—*Library Journal* on *Only Yours*

"Mallery...excels at creating varied, well-developed
characters and an emotion-packed story
gently infused with her trademark wit and humor.
One of the Top 10 Romances of 2011!"
—*Booklist* on *Only Mine*

"Mallery's prose is luscious and provocative."
—*Publishers Weekly*

"Susan Mallery's gift for writing humor and tenderness
make all her books true gems."
—*RT Book Reviews*

"Romance novels don't get much better than Mallery's
expert blend of emotional nuance,
humor and superb storytelling."
—*Booklist*

Also available from Susan Mallery and Harlequin HQN

SUSAN MALLERY

A Christmas Bride

HARLEQUIN®
entertain, enrich, inspire™

ISBN-13: 978-0-373-77802-7

A CHRISTMAS BRIDE

Copyright © 2012 by Harlequin Books S.A.

The publisher acknowledges the copyright holder of the individual works as follows:

ONLY US: A FOOL'S GOLD HOLIDAY
Copyright © 2011 by Susan Macias Redmond

THE SHEIK AND THE CHRISTMAS BRIDE
Copyright © 2007 by Susan Macias Redmond

Recycling programs for this product may not exist in your area.

This edition published by arrangement with Harlequin Books S.A.

For questions and comments about the quality of this book, please contact us at CustomerService@Harlequin.com.

® and TM are trademarks of Harlequin Enterprises Limited or its corporate affiliates. Trademarks indicated with ® are registered in the United States Patent and Trademark Office, the Canadian Trade Marks Office and in other countries.

www.Harlequin.com

Printed in U.S.A.

CONTENTS

ONLY US:
A FOOL'S GOLD HOLIDAY

CHAPTER ONE

"POLISH OR NO polish?" Carina Fiore held up two bottles of pet-friendly OPI nail polish. "I think the traditional choices would be best. Fire-Hydrant Red or Bow-Wow Green."

Eight-year-old Kaitlyn McKenzie laughed. "Rina, she's a cat."

"You're saying cats aren't into fashion? I'm not sure I agree. Just last week I caught this one flipping through *In Style* magazine." Rina studied the petite calico sitting on her grooming table. The calico stared back, her expression slightly defiant, as if daring Rina to try polish.

Rina held in a grin. Her plan was to put festive collars on the cats but she loved making Kaitlyn laugh.

The girl chuckled. "Cats can't read."

"You don't actually know that."

"Dad says they can't."

"Oh, well. Sure. Take the word of a veterinarian over me." Rina gave a heavy sigh.

Kaitlyn stepped around the grooming table and

hugged Carina tightly. "We'll do all the dogs' nails. I promise. I'll even help. We want them to look their best."

"Me too."

As much as Rina hated to admit it, cute pets got adopted faster. And as the person in charge of the Fool's Gold Holiday Pet Adoption, she intended to make sure every single animal looking for a home put his or her best foot forward. Or paw or claw or fin. Not that she would be doing anything to groom the fish. Although she was putting little fish-friendly Christmas trees in the tanks.

Her normally tidy grooming space was currently overflowing with cat collars and doggie bandanas in holiday prints. Over the next two weeks, she would be bathing, brushing and clipping until all the pets up for adoption gleamed.

She glanced at the clock on the wall. "We'd better get you home, munchkin."

Kaitlyn looked up at her, her green eyes as dark and beautiful as her father's. "It's Friday."

"I heard that this morning on the news."

The girl's mouth turned up at the corner. "You know what that means."

"That tomorrow's Saturday?"

"Spaghetti."

"Oh, right. I was thinking of something different for dinner."

"Rina!"

"Maybe liver."

Kaitlyn made a gagging sound.

"Brains?"

Kaitlyn clutched her stomach. "I'm going to throw up."

"Swamp soup?"

Giggling, Kaitlyn ran out of the room.

Rina picked up the cat and stroked her. "What do you think about swamp soup?"

The cat purred.

Fifteen minutes later Rina had finished cleaning off her table and washing her brushes. She collected her backpack and walked toward the break room. One of the veterinary assistants stopped her.

"You have to say something," Jesse told her.

"No."

"Soon."

"Did I just say no? I'm sure I heard myself say no."

Jesse, a pretty blonde whom Rina had known since they were both zygotes, raised her eyebrows.

Rina glanced around to make sure they were alone. Even so, she lowered her voice. "I can't."

"You have to. It's been a year, Rina. This is insane. It's the holidays."

"I'm not sure what the time of year has to do with anything."

Jesse sighed. "It's when you want to be with the people you love. You love Cameron. Tell him."

Rina winced. "Don't say that," she whispered as forcefully as she could. "Not here. Someone might hear you."

"It's Friday afternoon. Everyone is gone but us. Cameron's out at the Castle Ranch, checking on one of the goats there." Her friend moved closer and, Carina noticed thankfully, lowered her voice. "You're my best friend and I totally support whatever you decide, but I also know it's time to tell you that you're acting like an idiot."

"You've told me that every day for six months. It's hardly a news flash."

"Then *do* something. If not now, when? Are you going to waste another year being in love with a man who has no idea how you feel?"

Rina opened her mouth, then closed it. She wanted nothing more than to confess her feelings to the man she loved.

She could still remember the first time she'd seen Cameron McKenzie, DVM. He'd bought the practice from the retiring veterinarian with a promise that all the staff would stay. That included her, the practice's resident groomer. He'd requested everyone meet with him on a Saturday afternoon. She'd walked into the building, not sure what to expect. He'd turned, smiled, and she'd been lost.

Seriously, there'd practically been a swell of music and cartoon animals putting ribbons and flowers in her hair.

She wasn't sure what it was about Cameron that got to her. The wavy dark hair and deep green eyes were only the beginnings of his good looks. Still, her feelings weren't all about how handsome he was. It was the way he cared about his work and how he treated his staff. But if she had to guess, she would say her fate had truly been sealed the moment she'd met Kaitlyn.

She adored the little girl and they had become instant friends. Kaitlyn was smart and funny and just as caring as her dad. The only part of their family that didn't make sense was the absence of a mother. Cameron didn't say much about his ex, so all of Rina's information had come from his daughter. Kaitlyn was fairly matter-of-fact about her past, stating her mommy had left shortly after Kaitlyn had been born. Rina could still remember her steady gaze as she'd said, "Babies are a lot of work and my mommy wasn't ready."

Cameron had shared few details, but those he mentioned were in line with what Kaitlyn had said; his wife had walked away from her newborn and husband and had never returned.

Since then, from what she could tell, he'd devoted himself to being a single father and working hard at his practice. He never dated, hadn't once been caught flirting and showed no interest in one woman over another. In a town with a man shortage, he was practically an irresistible force.

Rina had told herself she would get over her crush, that it was just that Cameron was new and shiny. But as time had passed, her feelings had only grown. Now everything was more complicated because of the fact that she took care of Kaitlyn.

Every school day, Rina arrived at the McKenzie household early, made sure Kaitlyn was up and dressed, then fixed her breakfast and walked her to the bus. After school the girl rode the bus to the veterinary practice where she hung out with Rina until it was time to go home.

Back at the McKenzie house, Rina helped her with her homework and started dinner. In the past few months, she'd begun staying to eat with them. Unfortunately, she couldn't remember exactly how that had started. She wanted to say that Cameron had asked, but she suspected the invitation had come from his daughter.

Cameron paid her as a groomer and as the person taking care of his daughter. And, even though he was friendly and considerate, she couldn't be completely sure he'd ever thought of her as more than a friend. Which meant admitting her feelings put a lot on the line. What if he wasn't interested?

What if telling the truth meant losing her friendship with Kaitlyn *and* her job?

"I'd rather have what I have now than not have anything at all," Rina admitted to her friend.

Jesse shook her head. "You're living half a life, Rina, and that's not you. Your parents were crazy about each other until the day they died. Your grandparents are still in love. Don't you want what they have?"

"I'm scared."

"Love is supposed to be scary. If it was easy, everyone would do it."

Rina knew she was right. The thought of having it all, of being able to admit her feelings to Cameron and having him feel the same way, made her ache with longing. She'd known he was the one from the first second they'd met and her feelings had never wavered. But...

"What if he doesn't love me back?"

"Then you hurt and heal and find someone else."

"I don't want anyone else."

"So you'd rather have half of nothing than take the chance? That's not like you."

"I wouldn't just be losing him. I'd lose Kaitlyn, too."

"You wouldn't have to. You could still be friends with her."

Rina was less sure that was possible. Losing

one would be hard enough, but losing them both would be more than she could handle.

CHAPTER TWO

"TINSEL AND GOATS don't mix," Cameron said, looping his stethoscope around his neck. "Not that she'll listen."

Heidi Simpson nodded as she knelt next to her goat. "I swear, Athena has supernatural powers. She's forever getting out of her pen and doing things she shouldn't. I've been so careful with the holiday decorations."

Cameron believed her. Unfortunately a single box of tinsel had fallen out of her shopping bag and Athena had found it. Like most goats, she was willing to eat nearly everything. The tinsel had tangled in her digestive system, but had finally worked its way through.

"She'll be fine now," he said. "Give her a couple of days for her stomach to calm down." He patted the goat resting in the small goat barn, then rose to his feet.

"You've been great," Heidi told him as she stood as well. "You've been here every day. I really appreciate it."

"Part of the job."

"Still. I know Athena is grateful, too, even if she's having trouble articulating her feelings."

Heidi smiled as she spoke.

Cameron collected his medical bag then followed Heidi to his truck. It was late afternoon on the first Friday in December. The skies were dark and threatening, but the temperature wasn't cold enough for snow in town. Further up the mountain, they could get a good dump in the next couple of days.

Holiday decorations brightened the old house that stood on the ranch. The exterior was a little shabby, but the twinkling lights added a welcoming glow. Heidi was friendly enough. Pretty, he thought absently. Single. He should have been interested, maybe ask her to coffee or out for a drink. Only he wasn't the least bit interested.

He'd dated plenty when he'd been younger and had learned he was the kind of man who wanted to settle down. The problem was with whom.

After his daughter had been born, his ex-wife had announced she was leaving. From his point of view, her desire to leave had come out of nowhere, leaving him blindsided and the single father of a newborn. It had taken him a while to realize that whatever made his wife leave was out of his control.

Over the past few years, he'd become aware of a

nagging sense of having missed something. Fool's Gold had plenty of single women and he'd been set up with more than his share. But he hadn't felt the need for further dates with any of them. Maybe the problem was his—he wasn't willing to trust his daughter or his heart with just anyone.

Heidi paused by his truck. "Thanks again."

"You're welcome. You have my cell number. Call me if there are any problems."

"Don't you ever go off duty?"

"No."

"This town is lucky to have you."

He chuckled. "Remind people of that the next time I raise my rates."

"I will, I promise." She smiled. "Don't take this wrong, but I'm hoping not to see you before the holidays. Unless you plan to bring your daughter by for a horse-drawn carriage ride. We're keeping the tradition in place for the holidays."

"We might have to come by for that." He grinned. "But not for anything else. How's that?"

"Perfect. Merry Christmas."

"The same to you, Heidi."

He got in his truck and started the engine. Heidi walked up the porch steps. He watched her go, hoping for a spark or even vague interest in the sway of her hips.

Nothing.

Twenty minutes later Cameron was pulling into

his own driveway. The Christmas lights he'd spent much of the long Thanksgiving weekend putting up glowed in the darkness. Lit wreaths hung in all the front-facing windows, along with flickering candles. Not real candles. Kaitlyn had informed him those weren't really safe around fabric or children. So she and Rina had bought battery-powered ones from the hardware store in town.

Like most homeowners in Fool's Gold, he had an account at the hardware store. Based on all the packages his daughter and Rina had dragged home from various trips, he wasn't looking forward to that bill. But it was worth it to see his baby girl so excited about the holidays.

He parked in the driveway and turned off the engine. Before he could step out, the front door banged open and Kaitlyn flew across the porch.

As always the sight of her made him want to get down on his knees in gratitude for having her in his world. Sure, the first couple of years had been tough as he and his daughter had figured out how to make a single-parent family work. But every second of fear and worry had been worth it. She was the best part of his life.

He left his bag on the passenger seat and stepped into the night. Kaitlyn flung herself at him, wrapping both her arms around his waist and hanging on tight.

"Hey, baby girl," he said softly, touching her cheek.

She looked up at him, grinning. There was a smudge of flour on her cheeks and a mischievous sparkle in her eyes. "We're making cookies. Rina said we could and it's Friday!" As if the cookies were all the more magical because of the day.

"Christmas cookies?" he asked, already knowing the answer.

"Uh-huh. We rolled them out and then used cookie cutters and now they're cooling and after dinner we're decorating and Rina said you could help." She paused to draw breath. "I can't stand waiting, can you?"

"I'll manage."

His daughter released him, then ran around the truck to get his medical bag, something she'd been doing since she was big enough to drag it into the house. Now she carried it more easily. The time might even come when she couldn't be bothered, preferring to spend her time with her friends. But that was for later. Right now, he was a blessed man.

Kaitlyn led the way into the house. The smell of freshly baked cookies mingled with the spice of marinara sauce. Noah, their sheltie, raced to greet him. A female—despite her name—Noah circled around his legs in an attempt to get closer and express her joy about yet another pack member returning.

"Hey, you," he said, scooping up the dog.

Noah bathed his face in ecstatic kisses. When he lowered her to the ground, she ran off to get her ball.

Rina stepped out of the kitchen.

"Hi," she said, her long brown hair pulled back in a ponytail. "Is Athena all right?"

He nodded. "She feels better than Heidi, who's still feeling guilty about what happened. They should both be back to normal by the morning."

Big blue eyes crinkled slightly as she smiled. Cooking had added color to her cheeks, making her look flushed. Her mouth was full and inviting and the way she moved…

Out of long habit, Cameron pushed away "those" kind of thoughts. Sure, Rina was beautiful and funny and great with his daughter. But while he liked her company and liked having her around, he wasn't ready for a long-term relationship. He wasn't going to let something as fleeting and confusing as romantic involvement with Rina get in the way of his daughter's happiness.

He'd thought he loved his ex. She'd stunned him by leaving with no warning. But in the panicked few weeks that had followed her departure, in the reality of caring for a newborn while trying to keep his practice alive, he hadn't had time to miss his wife. Or maybe he hadn't loved her at all. Either way, by the time he'd resurfaced, his life slightly under control, he no longer regretted her leaving.

Lesson learned, he reminded himself. Friendship he could understand and trust. Rina was his friend. One of his best friends. He was going to do everything in his power to make sure that didn't change.

"I told Daddy he could help with the cookies," Kaitlyn said, walking to the sink to wash her hands without being asked.

Rina grinned. "Did you? Do you think he'll do a good job?"

"I have some creative skills," Cameron told her, shrugging out of his jacket.

"Maybe you could audition," Rina told him. "Do one and if we think it's all right, you can do a second."

His daughter burst out laughing. "She's kidding, Daddy. You can decorate as many cookies as you want."

"Thank you, baby girl." He walked by Rina. "I'll deal with you later," he growled in a low voice.

She glanced at him, then looked away. But in the split second when her gaze locked with his, he would have sworn he saw something. A spark. No, bigger than a spark, because whatever it was hit him hard in the gut. It made him think about being alone with her in a dark, quiet room. Just the two of them and all the time in the world. It made him want to hold her in his arms and kiss her. And more.

He shook off the moment, telling himself it was just the season. Holidays were a time for belonging. While Kaitlyn was amazing, she was his kid, not his partner. Maybe it was time for him to start dating.

He went to the sink to wash his hands, then he and Kaitlyn set the table. When the oven timer went off, he removed the garlic bread and put it on a plate. The dance of preparing dinner was a familiar one, formed over the past year. Rina stirred the sauce, while he dumped the cooked spaghetti into a colander. She combined pasta and sauce, then brought the serving bowl to the table while he poured Kaitlyn's milk and a glass of wine for Rina and for himself. Noah settled into her bed in the corner of the kitchen, a dog biscuit held delicately in her teeth.

"Maybe we could get our tree this weekend," Kaitlyn said, her voice faintly pleading.

"It's a little early," Rina told her, passing the garlic bread. "There's a new delivery coming in next Thursday. They'll be fresh. I love that smell."

"Me, too," his daughter said. "You're right. We should wait. If it's fresh, we can keep it up through New Year's."

Conversation flowed around him. A discussion about whether or not there should be more decorations on the lawn. His daughter talking about practicing for the holiday pageant and how she would start taking dance classes in January. That meant next year she would appear in the Dance of the Winter King. There were also not-so-subtle hints about what she would like for Christmas and a recounted conversation in which Rina had threatened to paint a cat's nails.

"How's the adoption program coming?" he asked.

"Good. I've been putting pictures of the pets up online, so people get an idea of what's available. The shelter has been getting lots of calls." She wrinkled her nose. "There's a family interested in the iguana, if you can believe it. Why anyone would want a four-foot-long lizard that can live twenty years is beyond me. But they have a special room prepared for it and everything."

"Having the iguana adopted out will be a big savings," he said.

"I know. Based on the calls we're getting, we have a lot of good prospective owners interested in other animals, too. I'm hoping for a big turnout."

"You've put a lot of work into the project."

Rina smiled. "The animals shouldn't be stuck in a shelter—not even the iguana. Everyone should have a home to be part of, especially over the holidays."

When he'd bought the veterinary practice in

Fool's Gold, he'd wanted to find a welcoming community to raise his daughter. What he'd found was a place to call home. No one simply lived in the town. They became a part of whatever was going on.

"You're not really going to try to paint the cats' nails are you?" he asked.

"You're going to have to wait and see what I do."

They finished dinner and then sat around the table talking. It was close to seven-thirty when they got up to clear the dishes. While Kaitlyn helped Rina load the dishwasher, Cameron walked Noah. When he returned there were boxes of decorations scattered across the coffee table in the living room.

"Just a few more things," Rina said, with a shrug. "We couldn't resist."

"Where am I supposed to store all this?" he asked. "I'll have to add on a second house."

That made Kaitlyn laugh. She spun in a circle, her long hair flowing out behind her, Noah chasing her. Dog and child collapsed onto the floor in a heap. Kaitlyn opened her eyes.

"Daddy, look!"

He followed the direction of her pointed finger and found a small sprig of artificial mistletoe pinned to the door frame.

Turning to Rina he explained, "She read about

mistletoe when she was six. Now she wants me to put it up every year. It's kind of a family joke."

Only Rina wasn't laughing and suddenly he wasn't either. She was standing right under the tacky little plant—she probably hadn't noticed it until his daughter had mentioned it just now. Emotions flashed through her eyes, emotions he couldn't read. They were friends, he reminded himself. Good friends. Kissing would make things awkward between them and that was the last thing he wanted.

"Daddy, kiss her."

It seemed easier to give in than to explain—at least that was what he told himself. He bent forward and lightly brushed Rina's mouth with his own. There was a quick explosion of heat, then she drew back and sidestepped away.

"Now where are we putting those dancing snowmen?" she asked.

Rina had never been much of a believer in signs, but she was starting to rethink her position. Within a few hours of having a conversation with her friend Jesse about telling Cameron how she felt about him, he'd kissed her. Sure, it had been because of mistletoe and in front of his daughter and his dog. Hardly the hot, I've-been-desperately-in-love-with-you-for-months kiss she'd been hoping for, but still. It was a start.

After quietly leaving a sleepy Kaitlyn in her

bed, Cameron and Carina returned to the living room. Before Cameron could offer her a drink or suggest a movie, Rina decided she had to make her move. Telling him how she felt wasn't anything she could imagine doing, but showing him… He'd broken the physical barrier tonight, and she wasn't going to stop the momentum now.

So when he looked at her and started to ask, "Do you want to—" she was ready.

She put her hands on his broad shoulders, raised herself on tiptoe and put her mouth on his.

For a second he didn't react. There was only the ticking of the grandfather clock in the hall and Noah's sigh as she settled back in her bed. Then slowly, his lips moved against hers.

Rina released the breath she'd been holding and allowed herself to relax. She tilted her head and leaned into him. His hands settled on her waist. But the best part was the sparks.

They were everywhere: floating around, dancing against her skin, swirling through her belly and heating the most interesting parts of her body. Loving Cameron meant wanting him. She'd been aware of the desire lurking inside her, but it was a need without substance. She hadn't known if they had that magical chemistry that would add passion to friendship. Until now.

Now she longed for him even more than before. Her breasts ached to be stroked by him. Her thighs trembled and hunger burned. When he brushed his tongue against her lower lip, she parted for him immediately. When he swept inside, she felt herself getting lost in the moment, in the burning need and the taste of him.

Strong hands pulled her closer. She melted against him, curves to his hard planes, female to his male. At last, she thought. They were both in exactly the right place.

CHAPTER THREE

CAMERON FELT DESIRE rising up inside him, threatening to overwhelm him. Reminding himself that his friendship with Rina was more important than any single night didn't seem to be working. While some might say taking things to the next level made sense, he knew better. If he and Rina were friends, he would never lose her. To do more was to risk what they had and he couldn't imagine his life, or his daughter's, without her.

Carefully, he drew back. His resolve nearly crumbled when he saw the passion in her blue eyes and realized her mouth was swollen with his kisses. She was all lush curves and temptation. He could see her breasts rising and falling with every breath and, for a second, he didn't think he was strong enough to hold back. Then he reminded himself what was at stake and he managed to contain himself.

"Sorry about that," he said lightly. "I guess I got carried away."

He hoped that was enough. That she would accept the words and everything could go back to the way it was before. Wishful thinking, he realized when she spoke.

"I kissed you," she told him.

He nodded.

"You kissed me back."

Another nod.

"Cameron, I want more than what we have."

She laid him bare with her words. But what would happen later, to him and his daughter, if she tired of them and walked away? That had been difficult enough for him to go through once. He couldn't risk Kaitlyn, as well.

He drew in a breath. "I like what we have, Rina. We're friends. Good friends. I don't want that to change."

The passion in her eyes bled away, replaced by despair. "Thanks but no thanks?" she asked, her voice low. Tears glistened before she looked down. "Let me guess. I'm not your type."

"You are. It's not that I don't want you, I do. I just want our friendship more. If we started dating then everything would get complicated."

"Dating?" Her voice rose. "Dating? Is that what you think this is about? I'm in love with you, you idiot. I'm here nearly every night, sharing dinner with you, laughing with you, talking about our days. I'm crazy about Kaitlyn. I'm doing everything I can to show you that I'm exactly who you need, who you should love and want and you think I'm interested in a date?"

He couldn't have been more surprised if she'd taken out a baseball bat and hit him on the head. Love? He couldn't begin to figure out what that meant.

Rina stepped back. In a matter of seconds, she was shrugging into her coat and had her purse in hand. And then she was gone. He was left standing in the middle of his living room, not sure what had happened, but knowing it was bad.

Noah raised her head and looked at him questioningly.

"I haven't got a clue," he told the dog. "Not a clue."

Rina spent most of the weekend working with the holiday adoption committee. She was grateful to be running from meeting to meeting, helping write up descriptions and speaking with prospective owners. Being busy kept her from thinking and not thinking was much easier than feeling the burning emptiness. But come Monday morning, life would get much more complicated.

Her weekday started as they always did, with her going over to Cameron's house to get Kaitlyn ready for school. She almost cancelled, but didn't want to disappoint Kaitlyn. Shortly after Cameron and Kaitlyn had moved to town, Kaitlyn had put in an appearance in Rina's grooming salon. She'd thought the girl was charming and Kaitlyn had asked to spend time there...which had led to the official sitting job from Cameron. But Rina rarely thought of it as a job. Kaitlyn had become so much more to her than her boss's daughter.

Still, Rina wasn't looking forward to seeing the man who had rejected her and trampled her dreams with one carefully worded statement.

She let herself into the house, as usual. The smell of coffee filled the warm and welcoming home. After hanging her jacket on the coat hanger by the door and dropping her backpack on the table in the foyer, she squared her shoulders, drew in a breath and walked into the kitchen.

Cameron was already there. He was freshly showered, wearing jeans and a long-sleeved shirt. His gaze was steady, if a little wary, his eyes the perfect color of green.

She wanted to run. Facing him after what she'd said would take more than she had in her. Only she refused to be rejected *and* be a coward.

"I wasn't sure you'd come this morning," he said.

"We have an agreement."

"I know, it's just…"

She poured herself a cup of coffee. At least her hands weren't shaking. "It's what you said," she told him. "We're friends."

Somehow she would figure out a way to make that okay.

"You're not going to disappear?"

"No."

His body relaxed. "Okay. Good. We can get back to where we were, Rina. I know we can."

Then he was more sure than she was. But she would try. Because of his daughter. Because she wasn't the kind of person to run from trouble. And because friendship was better than nothing.

"I have a spelling test on Friday," Kaitlyn said with a sigh later that afternoon. "My computer checks my spelling for me. Why do I have to learn words myself?"

Rina wiped down the grooming table. She'd already finished her last client and was ready to leave. She'd spent most of Monday trying to act normally, all the while avoiding Cameron. A challenging prospect considering her salon was in the middle of his veterinary practice.

"It's important to be able to spell," Rina said, unable to think of a good reason and hoping Kaitlyn didn't ask for one.

The eight-year-old studied her. "Are you sad?"

"No. I'm fine. A little tired. I was busy with adoption-event planning all weekend."

"Maybe you need a boyfriend."

Rina did her best not to wince. "Maybe."

"You can find one on the computer. Daddy's

looking for a girlfriend there. He told me. He was in a chat room yesterday. I told him I wanted you to be his girlfriend, but he said that was out of the question. I never understand when he says that. I didn't ask a question." She continued talking but Rina couldn't hear her over the fury creating a buzz in her ears. Of all the low-life, rat-fink, weasel things to do. Cameron had said they should stay friends and then he'd gone off to some chat room?

She'd been calm. She'd been rational. She'd told herself that if he didn't want her romantically, that was his right and she would have to get over it. She'd taped her shattered heart back together and had shown up that morning because it was the right thing to do and he'd been in some damn chat room?

"Kaitlyn, will you excuse me for a minute?"

The girl nodded.

"I'll be right back and then I'll take you home."

Rina marched out of her salon. A quick glance at the clock told her that unless there was an emergency, Cameron would be in his office, updating patient records. She walked down the short hall, turned left, then stepped into his office and closed the door behind her.

He glanced up and gave her a smile. She knew that smile, knew everything about his face, the way he walked and how vulnerable he looked when he was tired. She understood his moods, had cared for him when he'd had the flu, had even groomed his dog. She'd loved him and his daughter, offering all she had, including her heart. He'd rejected her and then had gone online looking for love?

"I don't think so," she snapped.

The smile faded and wariness invaded his gaze. "What are we talking about?"

They both spoke in low voices. The practice was in an old house and the walls were thin. While Rina wanted to scream, she didn't want everyone hearing every detail of what could be a very humiliating conversation.

"You went online, looking for a girlfriend?"

He tensed. "Kaitlyn told you."

"Of course she told me. She tells me everything. She loves me."

The reality of what she'd just said slammed into her and she had to clutch the bookcase to stay standing. The affection she felt for Kaitlyn went both ways. They needed each other. How was she supposed to fight against that?

"I'm aware of her feelings," Cameron admitted. "What happened Friday got me thinking about a lot of things. I realized that I haven't been fair to either of you. I've let things go along as they were, without making sure everyone understood the rules."

By *everyone* he meant her. Her strength returned and she straightened. And glared.

"So you thought you'd help both of us by looking for a relationship on the computer?" she demanded.

"I thought if I started seeing someone—" He cleared his throat. "—in that way, Kaitlyn would become less attached to you."

She got the truth then. It cut through her cleanly, a sharp blade against her soft heart.

She'd told herself he wasn't ready. That he had suffered through a horrible divorce, after his wife had simply walked away from him and their newborn child. She'd convinced herself that he was wary of relationships and love and that given time he would see they were perfect together. She'd thought that *Let's stay friends* had meant *not now, maybe later.* Instead he'd been telling her no.

It wasn't that Cameron didn't want to be with anyone, it was that he didn't want to be with her.

Rina's eyes burned, but she refused to cry. Not here, not in front of her coworkers and Cameron and most especially not in front of Kaitlyn. Hope and love and dreams battled with cold, hard reality. As much as she wanted to ignore the truth, she couldn't. Not anymore.

"You're wrong," she said slowly. "About finding someone else. I have been there for you all this time. I know you like me and the way you kissed me proves…" She drew in a breath. "But you don't want to go there. Fine. We won't. I told you that

I loved you and the first thing you did was try to go out with someone else."

She linked her hands together in front of her waist and thought about what it would be like once he stopped looking and started dating. Of being at his house in the evening, taking care of his child, knowing he was out with someone else. She couldn't do it.

"I'm leaving."

He stood. "Leaving? Where are you going? What do you mean?"

She wasn't sure, but as she stood there, the answer came to her. "After the first of the year, I'll be moving my business out of here. You'll need to find someone else to take care of Kaitlyn. I want there to be a gradual transition so she's not upset, but you need someone else for daycare."

"You're cutting us out of your life? You said you wouldn't do that. I thought you cared about us."

"You're wrong. I didn't care. I don't care. I love you both." She stared into his eyes. "That's a whole lot more than caring."

"Then stay."

"No. You don't get to have it both ways. I've spent a year waiting for you to realize I was the one. That's enough time wasted."

With that she turned and left. Her heart pounded hard in her chest and she wasn't sure how long she could keep from crying. The sense of emptiness and loss nearly brought her to her knees. But behind the pain and fear and need to turn back and say, "Yes, fine, half a life is good enough for me," was the belief that she'd made the right decision.

It hurt now. It more than hurt. But with time and a little determination, she would recover. And, she thought, a little help from Fool's Gold wouldn't hurt either.

CHAPTER FOUR

Jo's Bar was a gathering place for the women of
Fool's Gold. While the men had a room in back
with a pool table and sports playing on TVs, the
main portion of the bar was dedicated to women.
The walls were painted a skin-flattering mauve,
the large-screen TVs featured shopping channels
and female-friendly reality shows and the menu
included plenty of calorie-light options. During
the day, one corner was turned into a play area for
toddlers. While Friday and Saturday night brought
in the couples crowd, the rest of the time, Jo's Bar
was a place for women to feel comfortable. Or
have a good cry.

"You did the right thing," Jesse said soothingly.
"I know you did."

Rina clutched the tissue in her hand and did her
best to stop the steady stream of tears. At the rate
she was going, she'd be dehydrated and require
emergency medical care within the hour.

"It doesn't f-feel right," she said, her voice

cracking on a sob. "It feels horrible. Everything hurts. I can't do this. I can't go on without him."

Jesse raised her eyebrows, which made Rina laugh. Well, it was more like a hiccup, but still it was an improvement over the crying.

"That made me sound like a stalker," she admitted. "Of course I can live without Cameron." Her humor faded. "I wish I didn't love him. Or that he loved me back. This sucks."

"Yes, it does. It hurts and you feel awful."

Rina looked at her friend and sniffed. "Are you trying to make me feel better? Because it's not really working."

Jesse touched her arm. "Dealing with this will get easier. Once the holidays are over, you can find a place to move your business to and start to cut ties."

Rina nodded and wiped away tears. "You're right. I'm not going to give up seeing Kaitlyn, though. I want to talk to Cameron about working out a schedule. Maybe I can take her a couple of afternoons a week."

"See, you have a plan."

Or at least part of one, Rina thought glumly.

The sound of several women laughing caused her to look to the bar side of the room. At least thirty women were setting up for what looked to be a bridal shower. Rina remembered all three of the Hendrix triplets were getting married over the holidays. Not that she begrudged them their happiness, but ouch.

"This hurts," she admitted. "What a stupid time of year to put it all on the line. I love Christmas. It was always a big thing in my house and I know my grandparents are looking forward to it."

"So you'll be with them and that will be nice."

"I know, it's just…" She swallowed and fought more tears. "We're supposed to go Friday to pick out the tree. That will be hard."

Jesse leaned toward her. "I know it will."

"You're not going to try and talk me out of it?"

"No. If you think you can stand it, you should stick with what's planned. For Kaitlyn. She adores you and getting a Christmas tree is a big deal for an eight-year-old." Jesse studied her. "You've seen him?"

"Since I made my pronouncement yesterday? Briefly. When he came home from work and again this morning when I went to get her ready for school. He hasn't said anything."

This morning he'd simply handed her a cup of coffee and said he would see her at the office. Kaitlyn had been the one to remind her about their date to pick out a tree.

"I'm avoiding him at work," Kaitlyn said. "It's a month, right? I can stand this for a month."

Jesse shifted in her seat. "He came to talk to me this morning."

Rina stared at her. "And? What did he say?"

"That he wasn't online anymore. Looking."

Looking, as in… "Oh. You mean he's not trying to find someone."

"Right."

Rina picked up her glass of wine, then put it down. She was sure it was wonderful, but she'd yet to take a sip. The thought of it made her stomach flip, and not in a good way.

"I wasn't sure if I should tell you," Jesse admitted.

"Don't worry. I'm not going to get my hopes up. Cameron isn't a bad guy. He's stupid, but not evil. I made it pretty clear that rejecting me and going in search of an online girlfriend in the same day was awful and I'm guessing he believed me."

"He did."

"So we'll fake our way through this. After the first of the year, I won't have to deal with him anymore."

The thought should have relieved her but instead she felt sad and empty. Because dealing with Cameron and his daughter had become the best part of her world.

"It's snowing!" Kaitlyn stared up at the sky, her eyes wide, her lips curving into a huge grin.

Tiny, wispy flakes drifted to the ground. Rina knew they wouldn't stick and that in a matter of minutes the snow would stop, but for as long as it lasted, it was beautiful. An unexpected gift designed to remind her life did indeed keep moving on.

She and Kaitlyn walked through the Christmas-tree lot. Holiday music blasted out of battered speakers and plastic reindeer and Santas blinked on and off. The two college-age guys helping customers wore sweatshirts with snowmen on the front.

Kaitlyn clapped her mitten-covered hands together. "They're all so beautiful. How will we decide? Daddy said the ceilings are twelve feet tall, so we can't get anything taller than that."

"We could if we put the tree at an angle."

Kaitlyn laughed. "It would look funny and all the decorations would fall off."

"If you're going to be picky."

The girl wrapped her arms around Rina's waist and squeezed. Rina hugged her back, holding on to the moment, knowing that even if she saw Cameron's daughter a couple of days a week, their relationship would never be the same.

"Daddy!"

Kaitlyn released her and raced to her father. Rina gave herself a second to brace herself, then turned to look at Cameron.

Tiny snowflakes dotted his hair and landed on his leather jacket. His green eyes were more guarded than usual, as if he was unsure of how things were going to be between them. Determined to take the emotional high road, Rina gave him a smile.

"We were discussing tree size," she said cheerfully. "Apparently twelve feet is the limit."

"I'd say ten," he told her. "There's an angel to put on top."

Kaitlyn nodded. "She's beautiful and has wings. I'd forgotten about that."

"Ten feet is still a pretty big tree." Rina held out her hand to Kaitlyn. "Let's walk around and we'll figure out which ones we like."

The girl grabbed her father's hand, then Rina's, walking between them. They'd done this dozens of times before. Rina had always enjoyed the connection, but this time there was also a whisper of pain curling the edges of the moment, a reminder that in a few weeks, she would be moving on, no longer a part of the McKenzie family. Not that she'd ever been a member, but she'd foolishly allowed herself to pretend.

The college guys loaded the chosen tree into the back of Cameron's truck. Rina hovered awkwardly, not sure exactly when she was supposed to leave. Cameron was paying for the tree and Kaitlyn had run into a couple of her friends from school. The three girls were huddled together, laughing about something.

Part of her wanted simply to disappear into the

happy crowds on the street, but ducking out without saying good-bye seemed rude. Cameron was
doing his best to act normal. She should do the
same. Technically, she'd been the one to change
the rules by telling him how she felt. Not that she
regretted being honest, but it seemed the least she
could do was play along.

He pocketed the receipt, then joined her. "She's
going to be a while," he said, nodding at his daughter.

"She has a lot of friends."

"I'm glad. When we first moved here, I worried
that she wouldn't fit in."

"Fool's Gold is very welcoming. My maternal grandparents lived here all their lives. My
mom grew up here. With my dad in the army, we
moved around a lot, but we settled here just before
I started high school." Now she couldn't imagine
living anywhere else.

Cameron studied her. "You must miss your
folks."

She nodded. "It's been six years since they
died, but yeah, I do. Especially now. Christmas
was always a big deal in my house." She smiled,
remembering. "We always got holiday pajamas on
Christmas Eve. My mom tried to find ones that
were exactly alike. Then we wore them on Christmas morning and made breakfast together. It was
wonderful."

"That's what I want Kaitlyn to have. Memories. You've really helped with that. Thanks for being here today."

"You know I care about her. Of course I'm here. And I'm still helping with the holiday pageant." She smiled again, but this time it took a little effort. "You're not getting rid of me completely."

"I don't want to." He stared into her eyes. "Rina, I…"

She was pretty sure he was going to tell her he was sorry or suggest they could go back to what they'd been doing before. Neither of which she wanted to hear.

"What are you favorite Christmas memories?" she asked.

He hesitated as if not sure he was willing to go with the obvious change in subject, then he shrugged. "Things were good when I was younger, but after my mom remarried, they went downhill. My stepdad wasn't a bad man, but he was strict and we didn't get along. I spent one Christmas in juvenile detention."

"No way."

He held up a hand, as if offering an oath. "I did. I'd been messing around with some guys and we set a shed on fire. It was stupid. The whole neighborhood could have gone up in flames. Instead of sending me away, the judge sentenced me to a hundred hours of community service. I was fifteen and it seemed like a lifetime of punishment."

Rina had never heard about his early past. "I can't believe you were that kind of kid."

He smiled. "I turned out okay in the end. That community service changed my life. I got assigned to the local animal shelter. I worked ten hours a week, for ten weeks and by the time I was done, I knew I wanted to be a veterinarian. My stepfather had convinced my mother to send me to boarding school. Rather than fight it, I asked them to pick one specializing in science and math so I could get into a good college. I graduated with honors, got a scholarship and the rest, as they say, is history."

"I'm impressed."

"Don't be. There are a lot of kids who suffered a whole lot more than I did. I acted like an idiot and I was punished. What I'm pleased with is that I learned from my mistake and turned things around."

"Your mom must be proud."

"She is and so's my stepdad. We get along now."

"They live in Florida, right?"

He nodded. "We're going to visit them over spring break. You should come with us." He stiffened. "Sorry. I wasn't thinking."

She ignored the sudden ache in her chest. "No problem. I'm sure you two will have a great time. You can go to Disney World."

"Kaitlyn has already started planning what rides we'll go on first." He shoved his hands into his jeans pockets and looked at her. "Rina, I can't go there."

She knew he didn't mean Florida. "You've explained that."

"No, I haven't. I want you to understand. My wife left. There was no warning. Kaitlyn was two weeks old when she packed her bags and said she was leaving. Said she didn't want to be a mother or married to me. I didn't see it coming." He drew in a breath. "I won't go through that again."

"Someone leaving?"

"Yes. I don't want the uncertainty. Friends are different. You can depend on a friend."

"Meaning you won't trust another woman? If you care about someone, she could leave?"

He shifted uncomfortably. "It's more complicated than that."

She wondered if that was true. Was Cameron's entire problem that he was unwilling to take a chance on being hurt again? She was torn between knocking some sense into him and reacting with compassion. She decided that the latter would speak more highly of her character.

"You need to take a chance. If not on me, then on someone. You can't let one selfish, uncaring person scar you for the rest of your life." She stepped closer. "There's more on the line than your heart. Kaitlyn is going to learn about romantic love from what she sees you doing. If you're afraid to trust, that's what you're teaching her."

"She has other role models. Movies. Books. You."

Rina wasn't sure falling for a guy who was unwilling to trust again was something she wanted to pass on to an eight-year-old girl she cared about.

"You're her father. You are the most important person in her world. She'll do what you do."

CHAPTER FIVE

CAMERON WAS STARTING to feel like the antihero in a bad TV show. He would swear his entire staff was glaring at him behind his back. As he'd yet to catch anyone actually glaring, he knew he was in danger of becoming paranoid. Which would not be his best trait.

It was Rina's fault, he grumbled to himself as he carefully checked the sleeping dog on the operating table. The six-month-old Lab-border collie mix belonged to Max Thurman, the guy who owned K9Rx Therapy Dogs. The dog had been spayed right on time and would later continue her training to be a therapy dog. As he touched her shoulder, she stirred slightly, coming out of the anesthesia.

Jesse noted her vital signs. "She seems to be doing well," she said. "I'll stay with her until she's ready to be moved."

Cameron glanced at the woman, checking for hidden meaning behind her words. He knew Jesse and Rina were friends. Rina was friends with everyone around her, and that made him the bad guy in what was happening, which brought him right back to the paranoia that everyone was glaring at him.

The downside to small-town life, he thought as he gave the dog one last pat.

"Let me know if there are any problems," he said. "I'll be in my office." Where he would update the dog's file and scan the list of appointments he had for the afternoon.

As he walked down the hallway, he instinctively paused outside the grooming area. Rina was wielding clippers with the skill of an artist, trimming a small poodle's feet. She carried on a conversation with the animal as she worked, her voice low and soothing. He was familiar with that voice. He'd heard it when he'd had the flu and Rina had practically moved in to take care of both him and Kaitlyn.

He shook off the memory and continued toward his office. On the main hallway wall were hundreds of pictures of pets, donated by their happy owners. Rina had been the one to suggest the picture wall and it had grown. More than one family brought in a new picture every visit to add to the collection.

The bulletin board in the waiting area had a flyer for the adoption event coming up next weekend. Something else Rina was involved with. In his office, he skirted around a planter full of "kitty grass" Rina insisted they keep for their overnight feline guests.

She was everywhere, and he'd never noticed that before. When he'd first arrived in Fool's Gold, she'd been the one who had given him the list of where to shop and how to avoid trouble with the Gionni sisters by making sure he and Kaitlyn alternated between their hair salons. Rina had chided him into joining the Chamber of Commerce and signed him up to speak on taking care of pets at the local elementary schools. She'd taught his daughter to skate, had baked her a birthday cake and carefully curled her hair for the first day of school.

When Rina disappeared from his life, he would lose far more than simply a babysitter or even a friend. A part of him wanted to be angry at her for changing the rules, but another part of him understood why she wanted more than she had.

Which made him wonder, when she walked away, what would *she* lose?

She said she loved him and he believed her. But, thinking about all she'd done for him and how little he'd done for her, he couldn't help but wonder why. He'd never consciously gone out of his way to be kind. She was someone he liked and enjoyed spending time with. When she'd needed a new-to-her car, he'd helped her pick out the one that suited her needs best and then had given her advice on negotiating. He'd fixed a few things in her apartment. She had a crazy phobia about the dentist, so he literally held her hand during her twice-yearly cleaning. But that's what friends did for each other. It wasn't love.

He crossed to the window. While he paid her to take care of his daughter, he didn't pay her to care. That she had given freely.

The holiday pageant was a celebration of cultures and traditions. The translation of that statement was that it challenged the parents of grade-school-aged children with costume design and construction worthy of Broadway.

Rina had spent nearly a month on Kaitlyn's Christmas princess costume, wanting the girl to be thrilled with the results. The hours of sewing had produced a fairy-tale confection in deep red with ruffles and lace and a few beads thrown in for good measure.

Now Rina carefully removed the hot rollers from Kaitlyn's dark hair and finger-combed the ringlets. The girl stayed completely still, as if willing the transformation.

"This would be better if we had some cartoon forest animals," Rina joked, separating a few curls, then reaching for her can of hairspray. "Okay, deep breath."

Kaitlyn obligingly took a breath and held it. At the same time, she put her hands over her face. Rina carefully sprayed the curls into place, made a few last-minute adjustments, sprayed again, and then announced, "Got it."

Kaitlyn lowered her hands to her side. "How do I look?" she asked.

Rina studied the girl, taking in the green eyes so like her father's and the flush on her cheeks. She was lovely, the structure of her face already hinting at the beauty she would be as she grew up.

An ache began in Rina's chest, the knowledge that she would miss so much about Kaitlyn's daily life.

"Almost perfect," Rina told her. "There's just one thing missing." She reached up for the small diamond heart pendant she always wore. The one her mother had given her for her sixteenth birthday.

After unfastening the pendant, she placed the chain around Kaitlyn's neck. "I think you should wear this tonight. Because every princess needs to sparkle."

Kaitlyn touched the heart, then threw her arms around Rina's neck. "I love you so much."

"I love you, too. Always. Remember that. Whatever happens, I'll be there for you."

Kaitlyn straightened and looked her in the eyes. "I know."

Rina made her way to the front of the auditorium and searched for Cameron. He stood up and waved her over. On cue, her heartbeat increased and her whole body longed for him. She'd heard that falling in love was the best thing that could happen to anyone. She was sure that was true for some, but from her perspective, being in love sucked big-time.

She went around the back of the room and came down the center aisle. She knew most of the people in the auditorium and found her progress slowed by greetings and conversation.

"I've got my eye on that calico cat," Edie Carberry told her. "You make sure you let me know if anyone else seems interested."

"I will," Rina said, pausing to admire the older woman's holiday-themed jogging suit. Both the pants and jacket were green velour and there was a sequined poinsettia on the front by the zipper.

A mom with two kids in the pageant stopped her to ask about a border collie mix and Alice Barns, the police chief, spoke wistfully about a small gray kitten.

"With my boys so busy with their own lives, I could use a little furry something," Alice said. "My husband shocked me the other day when he said he wouldn't mind a cat. Coming from him, that's practically an advertising campaign."

Rina finally made her way to the row where Cameron waited and settled into her seat.

"I think the holiday adoption is going to be a success," she said. "I was worried it was a dumb idea, but I'm getting plenty of people interested. Now if only they show up and take the pets they say they're interested in."

"They will."

She braced herself, then glanced at him. His steady gaze locked with hers, making her feel warm inside. He'd always had the ability to make her believe she was safe around him. Too bad that had turned out not to be the truth.

"You can't know that for sure," she told him.

"Yes, I can. This is Fool's Gold and the people here take care of their own."

"Do you mean me or the pets?"

"Both."

The lights dimmed before she could respond.

The production had the usual mishaps. A couple of the kindergarteners were frightened by the bright lights and began to cry. A boy in Kaitlyn's class knocked over a tree and about half the kids forgot their lines. But Cameron didn't care about that. As he watched the skits and listened to the songs, he was once again grateful that he'd decided to move to Fool's Gold.

Kaitlyn looked like the fairy princesses she adored and he knew Rina was the reason. He'd seen the dress in pieces, but not since it had been assembled and it was everything a little girl could want.

"You didn't have to do that," he whispered,

leaning toward Rina. "I never meant for you to spend so much time on her costume."

"I wanted to."

In the dark, it was difficult to read her expression, but he could inhale the sweet scent of her body and feel the heat that tempted him.

For a second, he allowed himself to wonder what it would be like if he permitted himself to give in. To share her feelings and to take what she offered. To touch her and taste her, to let her the rest of the way into his life.

He couldn't risk that, but maybe he could keep the part of her that mattered to him most.

She turned to him. "What?" she asked in a whisper.

"Later," he promised.

After the program had ended, everyone stood up and collected their coats.

"They're serving the kids cupcakes and punch before releasing them back to their families," Rina said with a grin. "Because they're not already wound up from their performances, right? The teachers want to seal the deal with a little sugar rush?"

Cameron knew he should laugh or at least smile, but he couldn't. He grabbed her hand and pulled her to the middle of the rapidly emptying row.

"We need you," he said urgently. "Kaitlyn and

I. We're friends. You said it yourself. Don't go. We can keep things the way they were."

The light slowly faded from her blue eyes. Her mouth straightened.

"You mean give up what I want because having me around is convenient? What do I get out of it, Cameron? Aside from a check every week? A family? Someone to love who loves me back? You want the best of what I have without risk. Without having to share yourself. That's not going to happen. You can buy childcare, but you can't buy me. Not anymore."

"I didn't mean it like that. You can still have a life. Date."

She flinched. "Right. Because seeing me with another man wouldn't bother you at all. Don't you understand that's the best reason for me to leave?"

They were supposed to get Kaitlyn together, to go home and celebrate with popcorn. Put up the last of the decorations. But Rina drew back.

"I'm going to tell Kaitlyn I have to go."

Cameron reached for her, but she was too far away. "Wait."

"No. I'm done waiting. I'm moving on."

CHAPTER SIX

"WHY CAN'T RINA get me ready for school?" Kaitlyn asked, the following Thursday morning.

Cameron carefully brushed his daughter's hair. "She's busy with the pet adoption this coming Saturday and she has a lot to do."

He knew Rina was avoiding him, but he wasn't going to say that. Whatever was going on between him and Rina had nothing to do with Kaitlyn.

"We haven't talked about what we're getting her for Christmas," his daughter informed him. "I don't want to get her a sweater. Rina loves us. We need to give her a present that says we love her, too."

There was a conversation he didn't want to have, he thought grimly. "Love is complicated," he began, but his daughter shook her head.

"It's not. It's simple. Love is when we care more about somebody else than we do ourselves. It's like with Mommy. She didn't love us and that's why she left. Because if she'd loved us, she would have wanted to stay. People who love you want to be with you. And we want the people we love to always be around."

He put down the brush and turned his daughter so she faced him.

"I'm sorry about your mother."

"I know, but it's not your fault." She wrinkled her nose. "Sometimes I get sad about her leaving, but mostly I don't think about it." She beamed at him. "You shouldn't either because we have Rina." Her eyes widened. "I know! Make Rina your girlfriend. Then she would be real instead of an internet girlfriend."

He stared at his daughter, not sure where to start. "I'm not looking for an internet girlfriend."

"You were."

"It was a bad idea."

"What about Rina? We already love each other."

"It's different."

"Why?"

"It just is."

She sighed and mumbled something that sounded a lot like "No, it's not," but he let the comment go. This wasn't a fight he could win.

Kaitlyn turned her back so he could start on her braid. "Rina's pretty."

"Yes, she is."

"She makes our favorite dinners a lot and we laugh together."

"I know."

"You liked kissing her."

That truth kicked him in the gut. He had liked kissing her. A lot, as his daughter would say. But he couldn't get involved with Rina that way.

"Kaitlyn…" he began.

She sighed. "I'll be quiet now."

"Thank you."

Cameron went through a busy morning of appointments. Simon Bradley, a local surgeon, brought in CeCe for her quarterly checkup. These days the small toy poodle was no longer a full-time therapy dog, having been adopted by Simon and his fiancée.

Cameron always enjoyed watching a big, powerful man reduced to cooing over a tiny dog. Not that he would say that to Simon. As CeCe still did some work at the hospital, working with children who had burns, she had to be checked more often to make sure she wasn't carrying any parasites or had the beginnings of an infection.

"You know Rina's not in today," Cameron said as he finished checking CeCe's heart. Usually the poodle was left in the salon for a grooming on her check-up days.

"I know. She told me when she called."

"Rina called you?"

Simon nodded. "To switch appointment days. She mentioned she's relocating her business. That she needs more room to expand."

Cameron nodded. That was the story she'd come up with. He knew she'd decided on the almost-truth to protect Kaitlyn as much as him. Announcing to the world she was forced to move because the man she loved was too stupid or selfish to love her back wouldn't play well. At least not for him. Which she wouldn't want.

He swore under his breath. Why did she have to be so damned good?

"What?" Simon asked anxiously. "Is everything okay with CeCe?"

"Yes. Sorry." Cameron straightened. "She's fine. It's something else. Woman trouble."

"I know what that feels like," Simon admitted with a grin. "Although in my case, it was all my fault."

The grin faded. "Montana put her heart on the line and I walked away. Or tried to. I told myself not being in a relationship was easier than risking losing it. Because then I was in control." He shook his head. "What a crock. There's no control when it comes to the heart. I hate to think about how pathetic I sounded, trying to be brave when I was really terrified. I could have lost everything. For what it's worth, if she's half as amazing as Montana, you should suck it up, apologize for what you did wrong and beg her to take you back."

"Interesting advice."

"Good advice," Simon corrected.

Later that afternoon, when Cameron returned to his office to catch up on paperwork, he found himself unable to stop thinking about what Simon had said about losing what mattered most. The problem was, to risk everything not to do that would mean he couldn't protect himself or Kaitlyn. They could both...

He leaned back in his chair and closed his eyes. Who was he kidding? Protect himself from what? Having Rina in his life? Having her integrated into every moment of his day? Missing her? It was too late for that. Too late for him to protect Kaitlyn from another maternal loss. She might not remember her mother but she would remember Rina. She loved Rina. And as his eight-year-old had wisely pointed out, he loved Rina, too.

He stood, not sure what to think or what to do next. The truth flooded through him. He loved Rina. That's why he'd been so freaked by her confession, why he hadn't wanted to change their relationship. If he loved her, she could hurt him. His ex-wife leaving had been a shock, but he'd gone on. Looking back, he hadn't missed her nearly as much as he should have. But if Rina left, he would be destroyed and so would his daughter.

That's what he'd been afraid of. Losing her. So rather than risk it, he'd pushed her away. As Simon had done with Montana. He had felt that if he decided the course of the relationship, he had the illusion of control.

He shrugged out of his white coat and grabbed his jacket, then stopped. He couldn't just track Rina down and blurt out that he'd changed his mind. That now he wanted her. He'd hurt her and made her feel small. He'd tossed aside what she had offered and then made things worse by trying to keep her around as some kind of on-call child-care staff.

She was the woman he loved, he woman he wanted to be with for the rest of his life. He needed to prove himself to her, to win her. Which meant he needed a plan. A way to apologize and prove to her that she was all he'd ever dreamed about. A tough road, considering how he'd acted.

He started toward the door. He was lucky, he reminded himself. With the pet adoption, Rina wouldn't have had time to go looking for someone else or even to start falling out of love with him. What he had to do was convince her he was worthy. Someone she could trust to be there, no matter what. And he knew exactly how to do it.

The noise in the Fool's Gold Convention Center was nearly deafening. The cement-and-block-wall construction had originally been meant for a big-box store that had never come to town. About eleven years ago, the city had taken over the property and turned it into a convention center, which meant the acoustics weren't perfect. Especially when nearly thirty dogs were barking, kids were running around yelling and a spate of angry hisses came from the kitty corner.

Through it all, Rina smiled, answered questions and confirmed that the paperwork for the adoptions had been filled out correctly.

Holiday decorations brightened their small section of the huge structure, the paper and plastic carefully hung out of dog-reach. She and her volunteers wore cheerful, red, long-sleeved T-shirts with bright letters proclaiming Adopt a Pet, with a cartoon cat and dog under the words. The real dogs wore painted nails and bandanas, the cats, festive collars. She'd left the iguana unadorned.

A crowd had been waiting when the event had begun and adoptions were steady. What confused her were the snippets of conversation she overheard.

"Dr. McKenzie came by yesterday afternoon," Edie Carberry was telling a friend, while holding a carrier containing her new cat. "He made sure I understood the best way to take care of Marilyn." The seventy-something grinned. "I named her after Marilyn Monroe. They have the same eyes."

A family with a beagle mix on a leash stopped by to thank Rina. "We love him," the oldest boy, who was all of ten or eleven, said earnestly. "Dr.

McKenzie talked to us about responsibility. We'll take good care of him. We promise."

Their mother sighed. "He was impressive. Oh, and that certificate for a free exam in six months was great."

"I don't understand," Rina said. "He came to see you?"

The woman nodded. "From what I understand, he went to see everyone who had already expressed interest in a specific pet. He wanted us to be prepared for the first few days of settling in and talked about food and exercise. That was more than enough, but then he offered a free exam. What a great guy."

"I heard that," her husband told her.

The woman laughed.

Rina chatted with the family a few more minutes, then went to find Jesse.

"What do you know about Cameron visiting prospective adoptive families?"

Jesse handed Rina a cloth bag that she started filling with cat food. Each pet was being sent home with a month's worth of food.

"You didn't know?" she asked, sounding surprised. "He spent part of Thursday afternoon and most of yesterday out talking to people who'd said they were interested in adopting. He didn't tell you?"

Rina shook her head. "No. He's offering a certificate for a free exam, too."

Jesse smiled. "He wants your holiday pet adoption to be a success. You should be happy."

"I am, of course. It's just strange."

He hadn't said a word. Not that she'd seen him in the past few days. She'd had the excuse of being busy. Now she just had to get through the holidays, and then she could start forgetting she'd ever fallen in love with him.

Jesse took the full bag of food. "It's a good thing. Maybe you should just accept that."

Rina nodded and got back to work.

By three in the afternoon, all the pets had been adopted, the pet food was distributed and more than a couple of the decorations had started to droop. Rina had accepted help for cleanup and then had sent everyone home. There were only a few chairs left to stack and she could handle that on her own.

She'd just collected her backpack to head to her car when the side door opened.

She opened her mouth to tell the people that the event was over, only to realize they weren't prospective pet owners. Instead, Cameron and Kaitlyn walked toward her.

She hadn't seen either of them in three days and it felt like years. She wanted to rush forward and hug Kaitlyn, be hugged by Cameron and taken home. She wanted to revel in the affection and laughter she always found in their house. But that wasn't to be.

"I heard all the pets got adopted," Cameron said as he approached. "Congratulations."

"You had a big part in that," she said, hoping she was looking friendly rather than desperately in love. "Thank you for your help."

"It's the least I could do." He raised his chin slightly. "I like your shirt."

She glanced down at the Adopt a Pet graphic. "I thought they were festive. It made the volunteers feel special and—"

As she'd been speaking, Cameron and Kaitlyn had started removing their coats. Now she saw they wore similar shirts, only the phrase was a little different. Cameron's T-shirt said Adopt a Vet and Kaitlyn's read Adopt a Vet's Daughter. Instead of a drawing of a cat and dog, there was a picture of the three of them, taken at the end of the summer festival earlier that year.

Hope blossomed. Fragile, brave hope that grew inside her. "I don't understand," she whispered.

Cameron stepped toward her. "Rina, I'm sorry. I was blind and stupid and afraid. I wasn't looking to fall in love, so I didn't recognize it when it happened. I couldn't see the beautiful, special, wonderful woman standing right in front of me."

She drew in a breath. "It happens," she managed.

He took another step and reached for her hands, taking them in his. His steady gaze was full of promise.

"When I kissed you that night, I felt all the possibilities and they terrified me. I was afraid loving meant losing and I couldn't bear to lose you. You are strong and kind and the most giving person I know. I trust you with my heart. More important, I trust you with my daughter."

Rina glanced at the girl, who was practically dancing in place. She'd obviously promised to be quiet, but was having trouble keeping her promise. As Rina smiled at her, Kaitlyn slapped a hand over her mouth and spun in a circle.

"I'm sorry I didn't accept what you offered," he continued, drawing her attention back to him. "I'm sorry I couldn't see what you did for us. But I do know, and I hope you'll give me a chance to prove myself. Kaitlyn and I love you." He smiled at his daughter. "We want to marry you and be a family together."

"Like we are now!" The words burst from Kaitlyn, who rushed toward them.

Then the three of them were holding on as if they would never let go. Rina felt the pain draining away, replaced by the knowledge that dreams really do come true. Loving Cameron and his daughter had been the best part of her. It would continue to be so…forever.

CHAPTER SEVEN

CHRISTMAS MORNING CAME early. Rina found herself being gently shaken a little before six. She opened her eyes and saw Kaitlyn staring down at her.

"You were awake, right?" the girl asked anxiously. "Daddy said I wasn't to wake you."

Rina laughed. "I was awake enough."

"Good. There are presents and it's snowing! I know it won't stick, but there's snow on Christmas! Come on. Get up!"

Rina sat up and stretched. She was wearing red and white candy-cane pajamas, just like the ones Kaitlyn had on. Somewhere in the house, Cameron had on a pair, too. An early Christmas present from her fiancé.

As she got out of bed, her diamond engagement ring caught the light and sparkled. Another early Christmas present that Cameron had given her last night. And after Kaitlyn had gone to bed, things had gotten even better.

Usually she went home after dinner. They had agreed it would be better for her not to spend the night until after they were married in a couple of weeks. Then Kaitlyn had begged for Rina to sleep over on Christmas Eve and sometime around two in the morning, Rina had reluctantly left Cameron's bed to spend the rest of the night in the guest room.

Noah trotted into the room, her nails clicking on the hardwood floor. Cameron followed, looking both handsome and silly in his Christmas pajamas.

"Merry Christmas," he told her. "I have coffee brewing."

"And hot chocolate for me," Kaitlyn said. "And she was already awake. Sort of."

"Give me five minutes," Rina said, smiling at them both. "Then I'll be right out."

She used the bathroom and brushed her teeth, then stepped into slippers and joined Cameron and Kaitlyn in the kitchen. Outside, snow fell. A light dusting covered the deck and backyard. Only Noah's pawprints disturbed the pristine beauty.

Before handing Rina her coffee, Cameron pulled her close and kissed her. Then he held out his arm so Kaitlyn was included.

"Group hug," the girl said with a contented sigh. "Daddy, I'm really glad there are presents, but this is the best one."

"For me, too," Rina said.

"For all of us," Cameron agreed.

Kaitlyn looked up at them and smiled. "See. I told you. We had to give Rina something so she knows we love her. And we gave her us."

* * * * *

THE SHEIK AND THE
CHRISTMAS BRIDE

PROLOGUE

"THIS IS AN impossible situation," King Mukhtar of El Deharia announced as he paced the width of his private chambers.

Princess Lina watched her brother, thinking it would be impossible for him to pace the *length* of his chambers—the room was so big, she would probably lose sight of him. Ah, the trials of being king.

Mukhtar spun back unexpectedly, then stalked toward her. "You smile. Do you find this amusing? I have three sons of marriageable age. *Three!* And has even one of them shown interest in choosing a bride and producing heirs? No. They are too busy with their work. How did I produce such industrious sons? Why aren't they out chasing women and getting girls pregnant? At least then we could force a marriage."

Lina laughed. "You're complaining that your sons are too hardworking and that they're not playboys? What else is wrong, my brother? Too much money in the treasury? Do the people love you too much? Is the royal crown too heavy?"

"You mock me," he complained.

"As your sister, it is not just my privilege, it's my duty. Someone needs to mock you."

He glared at her, but she was unimpressed. They had grown up together. It was hard to find awe in the man when one had seen the boy with chicken pox.

"This is serious," he told her sternly. "What am I to do? I must have heirs. I should have dozens of grandchildren by now and I have not a single one. Qadir spends his time representing our country to the world. As'ad deals with domestic issues so our people have a thriving economy. Kateb lives his life in the desert, celebrating the old ways." Mukhtar grimaced. "The old ways? What is he thinking?"

"Kateb has always been a bit of a black sheep," Lina reminded the king.

Her brother glared at her. "No son of mine is a sheep. He is powerful and cunning like a lion of the desert or a jackal."

"So he is the black jackal of the family."

"Woman, you will not act this way," Mukhtar roared in a fair imitation of a lion.

Lina remained unimpressed. "Do you see me cowering, brother? Have you ever seen me cowering?"

"No, and you are poorer for it."

She covered her mouth as she pretended to yawn.

His gaze narrowed. "You are intent only on your own amusement? You have no advice for me?"

"I do have advice, but I don't know if you'll like it."

He folded his arms across his chest. "I'm listening."

Not according to his body language, Lina thought humorously. But she was used to her brother being imperious. Having him ask for her advice was a big step for him. She should go with it.

"I have been in communication with King Hassan of Bahania," she said.

"Why?"

She sighed. "This will go much faster if you don't interrupt me every thirty seconds."

Mukhtar raised his eyebrows but didn't speak.

She recognized the slightly stubborn expression. He thought he was being protective and concerned, making sure she was kept safe from the evilness of the world. Right. Because the very handsome king of Bahania was so likely to swoop down and ravish her forty-three-year-old self.

Not that she would say no to a little ravishing, she thought wistfully. Her marriage had ended years before when her beloved husband had died unexpectedly. She'd always meant to remarry and have a family, but somehow that had never happened. She'd been busy being an aunt to Mukhtar's six boys. There had been much to do in the palace. Somehow she'd never found the time…or a man who interested her.

Until Hassan. The widower king was older, but vital and charming. Not to mention, he was the first man who had caught her attention in years. But was he intrigued by her? She just couldn't tell.

"Lina," her brother said impatiently, "how do you know Hassan?"

"What? Oh. He and I spent time together a couple of years ago at a symposium on education." She'd met the king formally at state events dozens of times, but that had been the first occasion she'd had to speak with him for more than five minutes. "He also has sons and he has been very successful in getting them all married."

That got her brother's interest. "What did he do?"

"He meddled."

Mukhtar stared at her. "You're saying…"

"He got involved in their personal lives. He created circumstances that brought his sons together with women he had picked. Sometimes he set up roadblocks, sometimes he facilitated the relationship. It all went well."

Mukhtar lowered his arms to his sides. "I am the king of El Deharia."

"I know that."

"It would be inappropriate for me to behave in such a manner."

Lina held in a smile—she already knew what was coming. "Of course it would."

"However, you do not have my restrictions of rank and power."

"Isn't that amazing."

"You could get involved. You know my sons very well." His gaze narrowed. "You've been thinking about this for some time, haven't you?"

"I've made a few notes about a couple of women I think would be really interesting for my nephews to get to know."

He smiled slowly. "Tell me everything."

CHAPTER ONE

PRINCE AS'AD OF El Deharia expected his world to run smoothly. He hired his staff with that expectation, and for the most part, they complied. He enjoyed his work at the palace and his responsibilities. The country was growing, expanding, and he oversaw the development of the infrastructure. It was a compelling vocation that took serious thought and dedication.

Some of his friends from university thought he should use his position as a prince and a sheik to enjoy life, but As'ad did not agree. He didn't have time for frivolity. If he had one weakness, it was his affection for his aunt Lina. Which explained why he agreed to see her when she burst into his offices without an appointment. A decision, he would think many weeks later, that caused him nothing but trouble.

"As'ad," Lina said as she hurried into his office, "you must come at once."

As'ad saved his work on the computer before asking, "What is wrong?"

"Everything." His normally calm aunt was flushed and trembling. "There is trouble at the orphan school. A chieftain is in from the desert. He's demanding he be allowed to take three sisters. People are fighting, the girls don't want to go with him, the teachers are getting involved and one of the nuns is threatening to jump from the roof if you don't come and help."

As'ad rose. "Why me?"

"You're a wise and thoughtful leader," Lina said, not quite meeting his gaze. "Your reputation for fairness makes you the obvious choice."

Or his aunt was playing him, As'ad thought, staring at the woman who had been like a mother to him for most of his life. Lina enjoyed getting her way and she wasn't above using drama to make that happen. Was she this time? Although he couldn't imagine why she would need his help at a school.

She bit her lower lip. "There really *is* trouble. Please come."

Theatrics he could ignore, but a genuine request? Not possible. He walked around his desk and took her arm to lead her out of his office. "We will take my car."

Fifteen minutes later As'ad wished he'd been out of the country when his aunt had gone looking for assistance. The school was in an uproar.

Fifteen or so students huddled in groups, crying loudly. Several teachers tried to comfort them, but they, too, were in tears. An elderly chieftain and his men stood by the window, talking heatedly, while a petite woman with hair the color of fire stood in front of three sobbing girls.

As'ad glanced at his aunt. "No one seems to be on the roof."

"I'm sure things have calmed down," she told him. "Regardless of that detail, you can clearly see there *is* a problem."

He returned his gaze to the woman protecting the girls. "She doesn't look like a nun," he murmured, taking in the long, red hair and the stubborn expression on her face.

"Kayleen is a teacher here," his aunt said, "which is very close to being a nun."

"So you lied to me."

Lina brushed away the accusation with a flick of her hand. "I may have exaggerated slightly."

"You are fortunate we have let go of the old ways," he told his aunt. "The ones that defined a woman's conduct."

His aunt smiled. "You love me too much to ever let harm befall me, As'ad."

Which was true, he thought as he walked into the room.

He ignored the women and children and moved over to the tall old man.

"Tahir," he said, nodding his head in a gesture

of respect. "You do not often leave the desert for the city. It is an honor to see you here now. Is your stay a long one?"

Tahir was obviously furious, but he knew his place and bowed. "Prince As'ad. At last a voice of reason. I had hoped to make my journey to the city as brief as possible, but this, this *woman*—" he pointed at the redhead still guarding the children "—seeks to interfere. I am here because of duty. I am here to show the hospitality of the desert. Yet she understands nothing and defies me at every turn."

Tahir's voice shook with outrage and fury. He was not used to being denied and certainly not by a mere woman. As'ad held in a sigh. He already knew nothing about this was going to be easy.

"I will defy you with my dying breath, if I have to," the teacher in question said, from her corner of the room. "What you want to do is inhuman. It's cruel and I won't allow it." She turned to As'ad and glared at him. "There's nothing you can say or do to make me."

The three girls huddled close to her. They were obviously sisters, with blond hair and similar features. Pretty girls, As'ad thought absently. They would grow into beauties and be much trouble for their father.

Or would have been, he amended, remembering this was an orphanage and that meant the girls had no parents.

"And you are…" he asked, his voice deliberately imperious. His first job was to establish authority and gain control.

"Kayleen James. I'm a teacher here."

She opened her mouth to continue speaking, but As'ad shook his head.

"I will ask the questions," he told her. "You will answer."

"But—"

He shook his head again. "Ms. James, I am Prince As'ad. Is that name familiar to you?"

The young woman glanced from him to his aunt and back. "Yes," she said quietly. "You're in charge of the country or something."

"Exactly. You are here on a work visa?"

She nodded.

"That work visa comes from my office. I suggest you avoid doing anything to make me rethink your place in my country."

She had dozens of freckles on her nose and cheeks. They became more visible as she paled. "You're threatening me," she breathed. "So what? You'll deport me if I don't let that horrible man have his way with these children? Do you know what he is going to do with them?"

Her eyes were large. More green than blue, he

thought until fresh tears filled them. Then the blue seemed more predominant.

As'ad could list a thousand ways he would rather be spending his day. He turned to Tahir.

"My friend," he began, "what brings you to this place?"

Tahir pointed at the girls. "They do. Their father was from my village. He left to go to school and never returned, but he was still one of us. Only recently have we learned of his death. With their mother gone, they have no one. I came to take them back to the village."

Kayleen took a step toward the older man. "Where you plan to separate them and have them grow up to be servants."

Tahir shrugged. "They are girls. Of little value. Yet several families in the village have agreed to take in one of them. We honor the memory of their father." He looked at As'ad. "They will be treated well. They will carry my honor with them."

Kayleen raised her chin. "Never!" she announced. "You will never take them. It's not right. The girls only have each other. They deserve to be together. They deserve a chance to have a real life."

As'ad thought longingly of his quiet, organized office and the simple problems of bridge design or economic development that awaited him.

"Lina, stay with the girls," he told his aunt. He pointed at Kayleen. "You—come with me."

Kayleen wasn't sure she could go anywhere. Her whole body shook and she couldn't seem to catch her breath. Not that it mattered. She would gladly give her life to protect her girls.

She opened her mouth to tell Prince As'ad that she wasn't interested in a private conversation, when Princess Lina walked toward her and smiled reassuringly.

"Go with As'ad," her friend told her. "I'll stay with the girls. Nothing will happen to them while you're gone." Lina touched her arm. "As'ad is a fair man. He will listen." She smiled faintly. "Speak freely, Kayleen. You are always at your best when you are most passionate."

What?

Before Kayleen could figure out what Lina meant, As'ad was moving and she found herself hurrying after him. They went across the hall, into an empty classroom. He closed the door behind them, folded his arms across his chest and stared at her intently.

"Start at the beginning," he told her. "What happened here today?"

She blinked. Until this moment, she hadn't really seen As'ad. But standing in meant she had to tip her head back to meet his gaze. He was tall and broad-shouldered, a big, dark-haired man who made her nervous. Kayleen had had little to do with men and she preferred it that way.

"I was teaching," she said slowly, finding it oddly difficult to look into As'ad's nearly black eyes and equally hard to look away. "Pepper— she's the youngest—came running into my classroom to say there was a bad man who wanted to take her away. I found the chieftain holding Dana and Nadine in the hallway." Indignation gave her strength. "He was really holding them. One by each arm. When he saw Pepper, he handed Dana off to one of his henchmen and grabbed her. She's barely eight years old. The girls were crying and struggling. Then he started dragging them away. He said something about taking them to his village."

The rest of it was a blur. Kayleen drew in a breath. "I started yelling, too. Then I sort of got between the chieftain and the stairway. I might have attacked him." Shame filled her. To act in such a way went against everything she believed. How many times had she been told she must accept life as it was and attempt change through prayer and conversation and demonstrating a better way herself?

Kayleen desperately wanted to believe that, but sometimes a quick kick in the shin worked, too.

One corner of As'ad's mouth twitched. "You hit Tahir?"

"I kicked him."

"What happened then?"

"His men came after me and grabbed me. Which I didn't like, but it was okay because the girls were released. They were screaming and I was screaming and the other teachers came into the hall. It was a mess."

She squared her shoulders, knowing she had to make As'ad understand why that man couldn't take the girls away.

"You can't let him do this," she said. "It's wrong on every level. They've lost both their parents. They need each other. They need me."

"You're just their teacher."

"In name, but we're close. I live here, too. I read to them every night, I talk to them." They were like her family, which made them matter more than anything. "They're so young. Dana, the oldest, is only eleven. She's bright and funny and she wants to be a doctor. Nadine is nine. She's a gifted dancer. She's athletic and caring. Little Pepper can barely remember her mother. She needs her sisters around her. They *need* to be together."

"They would be in the same village," As'ad said.

"But not the same house." She *had* to make him understand. "Tahir talks about how people in the village are *willing* to take in the girls. As if they would be a hardship. Isn't it better to leave them here where they have friends and are loved? Where they can grow up with a connection to each other and their past? Do you know what he would do to them?"

"Nothing," As'ad said flatly, in a voice that warned her not to insult his people. "He has given them his honor. They would be protected. Anyone who attacked them would pay with his life."

Okay, that made her feel better, but it wasn't enough. "What about the fact that they won't be educated? They won't have a chance. Their mother was American."

"Their father was born here, in El Deharia. He, too, was an orphan and Tahir's village raised him. They honor his memory by taking in his three daughters."

"To be servants."

As'ad hesitated. "It is their likely fate."

"Then he can't have them."

"The decision is not yours to make."

"Then you make it," she told him, wanting to give him a quick kick to the shins, as well. She loved El Deharia. The beautiful country took her breath away every time she went into the desert. She loved the people, the kindness, the impossible blue of the skies. But there was still an expectation that men knew better. "Do you have children, Prince As'ad?"

"No."

"Sisters?"

"Five brothers."

"If you had a sister, would you want her to be taken away and made a servant? Would you have wanted one of your brothers ripped from his family?"

"These are not your siblings," he told her.

"I know. They're more like my children. They've only been here a few months. Their mother died a year ago and their father brought them back here. When he was killed, they entered the orphanage. I'm the one who sat with them night after night as they sobbed out their pain. I'm the one who held them through the nightmares, who coaxed them to eat, who promised things would get better."

She drew herself up to her full five feet three inches and squared her shoulders. "You talk of Tahir's honor. Well, I gave my word that they would have a good life. If you allow that man to take them away, my word means nothing. I mean nothing. Are you so heartless that you would shatter the hopes and dreams of three little girls who have already lost both their parents?"

As'ad could feel a headache coming on.

Kayleen James stated her case well. Under other circumstances, he would have allowed her to keep the children at the school and be done with it. But this was not a simple case.

"Tahir is a powerful chieftain," he said. "To offend him over such a small matter is foolish."

"Small matter? Because they're girls? Is that it? If these were boys, the matter would be large?"

"The gender of the children is immaterial. The point is Tahir has made a generous gesture from what he considers a position of honor. To have that thrown in his face could have political consequences."

"We're talking about children's *lives*. What is politics when compared with that?"

The door to the classroom opened and Lina stepped inside. Kayleen gasped. "He has the girls?"

"Of course not. They've gone back to their rooms while Tahir and his men take tea with the director." Lina looked at As'ad. "What have you decided?"

"That I should not allow you into my office when you do not have an appointment."

Lina smiled. "You could never refuse me, As'ad. Just as I could never send you away."

He held in a groan. So his aunt had taken sides. Why was he not surprised? She had always been soft-hearted and loving—something he had appreciated after the death of his own mother. But now, he found the trait inconvenient.

"Tahir is powerful. To offend him over this makes no sense," he said.

Lina surprised him by saying, "I agree."

Kayleen shrieked. "Princess Lina, no! You know these girls. They deserve more."

Lina touched her arm. "They shall have more. As'ad is right. Tahir should not leave feeling as if his generous offer has been snubbed. Kayleen, you may not agree with what he's trying to do, but believe me, his motives are pure."

Kayleen looked anything but convinced, yet she nodded slowly.

Lina turned to As'ad. "The only way Tahir can save face in this is to have the children taken by someone more powerful who is willing to raise them and honor the memory of their father."

"Agreed," As'ad said absently. "But who would—"

"You."

He stared at his aunt. "You would have me take three orphan girls as my own?" It was unbelievable. It was impossible. It was just like Lina.

"As'ad, the palace has hundreds of rooms. What would it matter if three girls occupied a suite? You wouldn't have to deal with them. They would have your protection as they grew. If nothing else, the king might be momentarily distracted by the presence of three almost-grandchildren."

The idea had merit, As'ad thought. His father's attempts to marry off his sons had become unbearable. There were constant parades of eligible young women. An excuse to avoid the events was worth much.

As'ad knew it was his duty to marry and produce heirs, yet he had always resisted any emotional involvement. Perhaps because he knew emotion made a man weak. His father had told him as much the night the queen had died. When As'ad had asked why the king did not cry, his father explained that to give in to feelings was to be less of a man.

As'ad had tried to learn the lesson as well as he could. As a marriage of convenience had never appealed to him, he was left with the annoyance of dealing with an angry monarch who wanted heirs.

"But who would care for the girls?" he asked. "The children can't raise themselves."

"Hire a nanny. Hire Kayleen." Lina shrugged. "She already has a relationship with the girls. They care for her and she cares for them."

"Wait a minute," Kayleen said. "I have a job. I'm a teacher here."

Lina looked at her. "Did you or did you not give the girls your word that their life would get better? What are you willing to do to keep your word? You would still be a teacher, but on a smaller scale. With three students. Perhaps there would even be time for you to teach a few classes here."

The last thing As'ad wanted was to adopt three children he knew nothing about. While he'd always planned on a family, the idea was vague, in the future, and it included sons. Still, it was a solution. Tahir would not stand in the way of a prince taking the children. And as Lina had pointed out, it would buy time with his father. He could not be expected to find a bride while adjusting to a new family.

He looked at Kayleen. "You would have to be solely responsible for the girls. You would be given all the resources you require, but I have no interest in their day-to-day lives."

"I haven't even agreed to this," she told him.

"Yet you were the one willing to do anything to keep the sisters together."

"It would be a wonderful arrangement," Lina told Kayleen. "Just think. The girls would be raised in a palace. There would be so many opportunities for them. Dana could go to the best university. Nadine would have access to wonderful dance teachers. And little Pepper wouldn't have to cry herself to sleep every night."

Kayleen bit her lower lip. "It sounds good." She turned to As'ad. "You'd have to give your word that they would never be turned out or made into servants or married off for political gain."

"You insult me with your mistrust." The audacity of her statements was right in keeping with what he'd seen of her personality, but it was important to establish control before things began.

"I don't know you," she said.

"I am Prince As'ad of El Deharia. That is all you need to know."

Lina smiled at her. "As'ad is a good man, Kayleen."

As'ad resented that his aunt felt the need to speak for his character. Women, he thought with mild annoyance. They were nothing but trouble.

Kayleen looked him in the eye. "You have to give your word that you'll be a good father, caring more for their welfare than your own. You'll love them and listen to them and not marry them off to anyone *they* don't love."

What was it with women and love? he wondered. They worried too much about a fleeting emotion that had no value.

"I will be a good father," he said. "I will care for them and see that they are raised with all the privileges that go with being the daughter of a prince."

Kayleen frowned. "That wasn't what I asked."

"It is what I offer."

Kayleen hesitated. "You have to promise not to marry them off to someone they don't care about."

Such foolish worries, he thought, then nodded. "They may pick their own husbands."

"And go to college and not be servants."

"I have said they will be as my daughters, Ms. James. You test my patience."

She stared at him. "I'm not afraid of you." She considered for a second.

"I can see that. You will be responsible for them. Do as you see fit with them." He glanced at his aunt. "Are we finished here?"

She smiled, her eyes twinkling in a way that made him wonder what else she had planned for him. "I'm not sure, As'ad," she told him. "In a way I think we're just beginning."

CHAPTER TWO

KAYLEEN WOULDN'T HAVE thought it was possible for her life to change so quickly. That morning she'd awakened in her narrow bed in a small room at the orphanage. If she stood in the right place and leaned all the way over, she could see a bit of garden out of her tiny window, but mostly the view was a stone wall. Now she followed Princess Lina into an impossibly large suite in a palace that overlooked the Arabian Sea.

"This can't be right," Kayleen murmured as she turned in a slow circle, taking in the three sofas, the carved dining table, the ornate decorations, the wide French doors leading out to a balcony and the view of the water beyond. "These rooms are too nice."

Lina smiled. "It's a palace, my dear. Did you think we had ugly rooms?"

"Obviously not." Kayleen glanced at the three girls huddled together. "But this stuff is *really* nice. Kids can be hard on furniture."

"I assure you, these pieces have seen far more

than you can imagine. All will be well. Come this way. I have a delightful surprise."

Kayleen doubted any surprise could beat a return address sticker that said El Deharian Royal Palace but she was willing to be wrong. She gently pushed the girls in front of her as they moved down the hallway.

Lina paused in front of a massive door, then pushed it open. "I didn't have much time to get things in order, so it's not complete just yet. But it's a start."

The "start" was a room the size of a small airport, with soaring ceilings and big windows that let in the light. Three double beds didn't begin to fill the space. There were armoires and desks and comforters in pretty pastels. Big, fluffy stuffed animals sat on each bed, along with a robe, nightgowns and slippers. Each of the girls' school backpacks sat at the foot of her bed.

"Laptop computers are on order for the girls," Lina said. "There's a big TV back in the living room, behind the cabinet doors. There are a few DVDs for the girls, but we'll get more. In time, we can move you to a different suite, one with a bedroom for each of the girls, but for now I thought they'd be more comfortable together."

Kayleen couldn't believe it. The room was perfect. Bright and cheerful, filled with color. There was an air of welcome, as if the space had been hoping for three girls to fill it.

Dana turned around and stared at her. "Really? This is for us?"

Kayleen laughed. "You'd better take it, because if you don't want it, I'll move in."

It was the permission they needed. The three girls went running around the room, examining everything. Every few seconds one of them yelled, "Look at this," because there was so much to see.

A ballerina lamp for Nadine, a throw covered with teddy bears for Pepper. Dana's bed had a bookcase next to it. Kayleen turned to Princess Lina.

"You're amazing."

"I have resources and I'm not afraid to use them," her friend told her. "This was fun. I don't get to act imperious very often and send servants scuttling to do my bidding. Besides, we all enjoyed pulling this together in a couple of hours. Come on. Let's go see where you'll sleep."

Kayleen followed Lina past a large bathroom with a tub big enough to swim in, to a short hallway that ended in a beautiful room done in shades of green and pale yellow.

The furniture was delicately carved and feminine. The bedcovering was a botanical print that suited her much better than ruffles and frills. The attached bathroom was more luxurious than any she'd ever seen.

"It's silk," she whispered, fingering the luxurious drapes. "What if I spill something?"

"Then the cleaners will be called," Lina told her. "Relax. You'll adjust. This is your home now that you're a part of As'ad's life."

Something else that just plain wasn't right, Kayleen thought. How could she be a part of a sheik's life? Make that a sheik *prince?*

"Not a happy part," she murmured. "He didn't want to help."

"But he did and isn't that what matters?"

Kayleen nodded, but her head was spinning. There was too much to think about. Too much had happened too quickly.

"Our bags! Kayleen, hurry! Our bags are here."

Kayleen and Lina returned to the main room to watch as their suitcases were unloaded. The pile had looked so huge at the orphanage, but here it seemed small and shabby.

Lina lightly touched her arm. "Get settled. I'll have dinner sent up. Things will look better in the morning."

"They look fine now," Kayleen told her, almost meaning it. "We live in a palace. What's not to like?"

Lina laughed. "Good attitude." She held out her arms and the sisters rushed to her for a hug. "I will see all of you in the morning. Welcome to the palace."

With that, she was gone. As the door to their suite closed behind her, Kayleen felt a whisper of unease. A palace? How could that be home?

She glanced at the girls and saw fear and apprehension in their eyes. It was one thing for her to worry, but they shouldn't have to. They'd already been through so much.

She glanced at her watch, then looked back at the girls. "I think we need to give the new TV a test drive. Here's the deal. Whoever gets unpacked first, and that means putting things neatly in the armoire, not just throwing them, gets to pick the movie. Start in five, four, three, two, one. Go!"

All three sisters shrieked and raced for their bedroom.

"I can go fastest," Pepper yelled as she crouched down in front of her suitcase and opened it.

"No way," Dana told her. "I'm going to win because you'll pick a stupid cartoon. I'm too old for that."

Kayleen smiled at the familiar argument, then her smile faded. Dana was all of eleven and in such a hurry to grow up. Kayleen suspected the reason had a whole lot to do with being able to take care of her sisters.

"That's going to change," she whispered, then returned to her room to unpack her own suitcases.

Lina had promised that Prince As'ad could be trusted. He'd given his word that he would raise the girls as his own. That meant they were safe. But, after all they'd been through, how long would it take them to feel that way?

The evening passed quickly. Dinner was sent up on an elegant rolling table and contained plenty of comfort foods for lost, lonely children. Kayleen piled everyone on the largest sofa and they watched *The Princess Diaries,* then compared the differences in the movie castle and the real-live palace they'd moved into. By nine all three of them were asleep and Kayleen found herself alone as she wandered the length of the beautiful suite.

She paused by the French doors leading onto the balcony, then stepped out into the warm night.

Lights from the shoreline allowed her to see the movement of the waves as they rolled onto the beach. The inky darkness of the water stretched to the horizon. The air was warm and salty, the night unexpectedly still.

She leaned against the railing and stared into the sky. What was she doing here? This wasn't her world. She could never in a million years have imagined—

The sound of a door opening caused her to turn. She saw a shadow move and take the shape of a man. Fear gripped her then, as quickly as it had come, faded. But she *should* be afraid, she told herself. He could be anyone.

But he wasn't, she realized as he stepped into the light. He was Prince As'ad.

He was as tall and broad as she remembered. Handsome, in a distant sort of way. The kind of man who intimidated without trying. She wondered if she should slip back into her own rooms before he saw her. Perhaps she wasn't supposed to be out here. Then his dark gaze found her.

"Good evening," he said. "You and the girls are settled?"

She nodded. "Thank you. The rooms are great. Your aunt thought of everything to make us feel at home." She looked up at the imposing structure of the palace. "Sort of."

He moved toward her. "It's just a really big house, Kayleen. Do not let the size or history intimidate you."

"As long as none of the statuary comes alive in the night and tries to chase us out."

"I assure you, our statuary is most well-behaved."

She smiled. "Thanks for the reassurance. No offense, but I doubt I'll sleep well for the next couple of nights."

"I hope that changes quickly." He shrugged out of his suit jacket. "If you find my aunt forgot something, let someone on the staff know."

"Sure." Because every palace had a staff. And a king. And princes. "What do we call you? The girls and I. Your Highness? Prince As'ad?"

"You may all use my first name."

"Really? And they won't chop off my head for that?"

One corner of his mouth twitched. "Not for many years now." He loosened his tie, then pulled it free.

Kayleen watched for a second, then looked away. He wasn't undressing, she told herself. The man had the right to get comfortable after a long day of…of…being a prince. This was his balcony. She was the one who didn't belong.

"You are uneasy," he said.

She blinked. "How did you figure that out?"

"You are not difficult to read."

Great. She had the sudden thought she wanted to be mysterious and interesting. Mostly interesting. Like *that* was going to happen.

"A lot has changed in a short period of time," she told him. "This morning I woke up in my usual bed in the orphanage. Tonight I'm here."

"And before you lived in El Deharia? Where did you sleep?"

She smiled. "In the Midwest. It's very different. No ocean. No sand. It's a lot colder. It's already November. Back home the leaves would be gone and we'd be bracing for the first snowfall. Here, it's lovely."

"One of the great pleasures of the most perfect place on earth."

"You think El Deharia is perfect?"

"Don't you think the same of your birthplace?"

Not really, she thought. But they came from very different circumstances. "I guess," she murmured, then felt awkward. "I was a teacher there, too," she added, to change the subject. "I've always loved children."

"Which makes your employment more enjoyable," he said. "I would imagine a teacher who dislikes children would have a difficult time."

Was he being funny? She thought he might be, but wasn't sure. Did princes have a sense of humor? She'd assumed being royal meant being serious all the time.

"Yes, that was a joke," he said, proving she was as readable as he said. "You are allowed to laugh in my presence. Although I would suggest you are sure I'm being humorous. To laugh at the wrong time is a grave mistake most people only make once."

"And we're back to the head-chopping. You're not like anyone I've ever met."

"Not many princes in the Midwest?"

"No. Not even rock stars, which in my country are practically the same thing."

"I have never been fond of leather pants on a man."

That did make her laugh. "You could be considered fashion forward."

"Or foolish."

"You wouldn't like that," she said without thinking, then covered her mouth. Oops.

Something flickered in his gaze. He folded his arms. "Perhaps a safer topic would be the three sisters you insisted I adopt."

"What about them?" Had he changed his mind? She would hold him to his promise, no matter how nervous he made her.

"They will have to change schools. The orphanage is too far away. The American School is closer."

"Oh. You're right." She hadn't thought that part through. "I'll get them registered in the morning." She hesitated. "What do I tell the administrator?"

"The truth. They are my adopted daughters and are to be treated as such."

"Bowing and scraping?"

He studied her. "You're an interesting combination of rabbit and desert cat. Fearful and fearless."

She liked the sound of that. "I'm working to be all fearless. I still have a ways to go."

He reached out and before she realized what he intended, he touched a strand of her hair. "There is fire in your blood."

"Because I'm a redhead? I think that's just an old wives' tale." She'd always wanted to be a cool blonde, or a sexy brunette. Well, maybe not sexy. That wasn't her style.

"I know many old wives who are wise," he murmured, then released her. "You will be responsible for the girls when they are not in school."

She nodded, wishing they were still talking about her being brave and that he was still touching her hair. Which was strange. Prince As'ad was nothing more to her than her employer. A very handsome, *powerful* employer who could trace his lineage back a few thousand years. She didn't even know who her father was.

"What are you thinking?" he asked.

She told him the truth.

"And your mother?"

Kayleen regretted the change in topic. "I, um, don't really remember her. She left me with my grandmother when I was a baby. She took care of me for a few years, then left me at an orphanage." She gave a little shrug as if the rejection hadn't mattered. "She was older and I was a handful."

In the darkness it was difficult to read As'ad's expression. She reminded herself there was no reason to be ashamed of her past—she hadn't been able to control it. Yet she felt as if she were being judged and found wanting.

"Is that the reason you defended the girls so fiercely?" he asked. "Your own past?"

"Maybe."

He nodded slowly. "They live here now. As do you. You are all to consider the palace your home."

If only. "Easier said than done," she murmured.

"It will be an adjustment. Although it would be best if they did not roller-skate down the hallways."

"I'll make sure of that."

"Good. You will want to learn about the palace. There is much interesting history here. Perhaps you and the girls should take one of the daily tours."

She stared at him. "Tours? People come here and take tours?"

"Only of the public rooms. The private quarters are off-limits. There are security people on duty. You are safe here."

She wasn't worried about being safe. It was the idea of living somewhere grand enough to have tours that made her mouth go dry.

"What does your family think of this?" she asked. "Will anyone be angry?"

He seemed to grow taller. "I am Prince As'ad of El Deharia. No one questions my actions."

"Not even the king?" she asked.

"My father will be pleased to see me settling down. He is anxious for his sons to start a family."

Kayleen had a feeling adopting three American sisters wasn't exactly what King Mukhtar had in mind.

"You said you have brothers," she said.

"I am one of six," he said. "They are in and out of the palace. Kateb lives in the desert, but the others keep rooms here."

Six princes, one princess, one king and her. What was wrong with this picture?

"You will be fine," he said.

"Would you stop knowing what I'm thinking? It's not fair."

He shrugged. "I am gifted. It can't be helped."

"Apparently not." He also seemed to have no problems with his ego. What would it be like to grow up so confident, so sure about everything, including his place in the world?

"Kayleen, you are here because of me," he said, his voice low and mesmerizing. "My name is all the protection you require. It can be used as a shield or a weapon, however you prefer."

"I can't imagine using it as either," she admitted.

"It is there for you. Know that. Know no harm can befall you while you are under my care." He looked at her. "Good night."

Then he turned and was gone.

Kayleen stared after him, feeling as if she'd just had a close encounter with a character from a book or a movie. Who said things like "My name is all the protection you require"? Yet, he was telling the truth. She believed that down to her bones.

No one had ever taken care of her before. No one had ever protected her.

Oh, sure, the nuns had always made sure their charges were safe, but that was different. This was specific.

She hugged her arms across her chest, as if feeling the comforting weight of his protection. As if feeling the strength of the man himself.

It felt good.

As'AD WALKED INTO the king's offices the next day and nodded at Robert, his personal assistant.

"Go right in, sir," Robert said with a smile. "The king is expecting you."

As'ad walked through the double doors and greeted his father.

"I hear you have taken in a family," his father said from his seat behind his impressive desk. "Lina tells me you are to adopt three orphans. I did not know you cared for such causes."

As'ad took one of the chairs opposite the desk and shook his head. "It is all Lina's doing. She insisted I go to the orphanage to prevent a nun from jumping off a roof."

"A what from what?"

"Never mind. There was no nun. Only a teacher."

A small kitten who had spit in fury and out-rage. He smiled at the memory of Kayleen's de-termination.

"Three American girls were there," he said. "Their father was born here. When their mother died, he brought them back and then he was killed. Tahir heard of their situation and wanted to take them back to his village."

"Admirable," the king said. "Three orphaned girls would be of no value. Tahir is a good man."

"Yes, well, their teacher didn't share your ad-miration. She insisted the girls could not be sep-arated, nor could they give up their education to be servants."

"Without family, what choice did the girls have? Tahir would have given them the honor of his name."

"I agree," As'ad said. "Yet that, too, was lost on their teacher. She attacked Tahir."

The king's eyebrows rose. "She lives?"

"She's small and apparently did him no harm."

"She is lucky he didn't insist on punishing her."

"I suspect he was pleased to find a way out of the situation."

"So you solved the problem by taking the girls."

"Yes, and their teacher, who will be responsi-ble for them." He looked at his father. "They are charming girls," he said, hoping it was true. "Al-most like granddaughters for you."

The king stroked his beard. "Then I will visit them and their teacher. As'ad, you did the right thing. This pleases me. Obviously you are settling down as you grow older. Well done."

"Thank you, Father."

As'ad kept his voice respectful. Lina was right. Now As'ad would be spared the royal matchmaking for a while.

"What is she like, this teacher?" the king asked. "Is she of good character?"

"Lina thinks so." He was nearly convinced himself. Her sad history could have made her hard or bitter. Instead she led with her heart.

"Have you any interest in her yourself?"

As'ad stared at his father. "In what way?"

"As a wife. We already know she likes children and is willing to face a chieftain to protect her charges. Is she pretty? Would she do for one of your brothers?"

As'ad frowned. Pretty? Kayleen? "She is not unattractive," he said slowly, remembering how she'd looked the previous night with her long hair glowing like fire. "There is a spark in her. A pureness."

Pureness? Where had *that* thought come from?

"I wonder what she thinks of the desert," the king mused. "Perhaps she would do for Kateb."

"She would not," As'ad said sharply, suddenly irritated, although he could not say why. "Besides,

I need her to care for my daughters. Find my brothers' brides elsewhere."

"As you wish," the king said easily. "As you wish."

AS'AD STARED AT the three bridge proposals in front of him. While each provided the necessary access, they couldn't be more different. The cheapest bid offered a utilitarian design while the other two had an architectural element that would add to the beauty of the city. There were—

His phone buzzed. He stared at it a second, then pushed the intercom. "I said I was not to be disturbed."

"I understand, sir. Your orders were very clear." His normally calm assistant sounded...flustered. "It's just, there's someone here to see you. A young woman. Kayleen James. She says she is the nanny for your children?"

The slight rise in Neil's voice probably came from the fact that he wasn't aware As'ad *had* any children.

"I'll explain it all later," As'ad told him. "Send her in."

Seconds later Kayleen walked into his office. As she moved across the open space, he took in the plain brown dress that covered her from the neck to down past her knees, and the flat, sensible shoes. She'd pulled her hair back in a braid.

Her pale skin looked bare, and although her eyes were large, she did nothing to enhance her features. Even her earrings, tiny gold crosses, provided little adornment.

He was used to women who took the time and made the effort to be as beautiful as possible. Women who dressed in silk, who showed skin, who smelled of enticing perfumes and glittered with diamonds. Did Kayleen not care for such adornments or had she not had the opportunity to dress that way?

She could, he acknowledged, easily transform herself into a beauty. The basics were already in place—the perfect bone structure in her face, the large eyes, the full mouth.

Without meaning to, he imagined her wearing nothing at all. Pale and soft, covered only by her long hair, a naked temptress who—

"Thank you for seeing me," Kayleen said, interrupting the erotic image that had no place in his head. "I guess I should have made an appointment."

"Not at all," he said as he came to his feet and motioned toward a sofa in the corner. "How can I help you?"

She sat down. "You're very polite."

"Thank you."

She smoothed the front of her dress. "The palace is really big. I got lost twice and had to ask directions."

"I can get you a map."

She smiled. "For real or are you teasing?"

"Both. There is a map of the palace. Would you like one?"

"I think I need it. And maybe a computer chip implant so security can find me." She looked uneasy as she glanced around the room. "This is nice. Big, but I guess that comes with being a prince."

He couldn't tell if she was just nervous or stalling. "Kayleen, is there a reason for your visit?"

"What? Oh. Right. I enrolled the girls in the American School this morning. It all went well. I used your name."

He smiled. "Bowing and scraping?"

"Some. Everyone was very eager to help. And to have me tell you they helped. That part is weird. You're probably used to it."

"I am."

"The school is great. Big and modern with a real focus on academics. Not that the orphan school is terrible. If they had more funding…" She sighed. "Asking about that is probably inappropriate."

"Will knowing that stop you from asking?"

She considered for a second. "Not really."

"I will see if funds can be made available."

Her eyes widened. "Just like that?"

"I have made no promises. But I'm sure a few dollars could be found."

"That would be great. We're not working with a big budget over there, so anything would help. Most of the teachers live in, which means the salaries aren't huge."

He doubted they would ever be huge. Teachers didn't choose their profession in an effort to amass a personal fortune. He frowned.

"Why did *you* become a teacher?" he asked.

"Because I couldn't be a nun."

An answer he never would have expected. "Did you want to be a nun?"

Kayleen nodded slowly. "Very much. The orphanage my grandmother took me to was run by nuns. They were wonderful to me. I wanted to be just like them. But I don't really have the right personality."

"Too outspoken?"

"Too…everything. I'm opinionated, I have a temper, I have trouble with the rules sometimes."

She seemed so quiet and mousy in her baggy brown dress, but there was something in her eyes, a spark that told him she was telling the truth. After all, she had attacked Tahir.

He'd never met an almost-nun before. Why would a pretty woman want to lock herself away from the world?

"Our Mother Superior suggested I go into

teaching," Kayleen continued. "It was a great idea. I love it. I love the children. I wanted to take a permanent position there, but she insisted I first see the world. That's how I ended up here. Eventually, I'll go back."

"To the convent school?"

She nodded.

"What about a husband and a family?"

Kayleen ducked her head, but not before he saw her blush. "I don't really expect that to happen to me. I don't date. Men are... They don't think of me that way."

He recalled his earlier fantasy about seeing her naked. "You would be surprised," he murmured.

She looked up. "I don't think so."

"So there has never been anyone special?"

"A boyfriend?" She shook her head. "No."

She was in her mid-twenties. How was that possible? Did such innocence truly exist? Yet why would she lie about such a thing?

He found himself wanting to show her the world she'd been avoiding. To take her places.

Ridiculous, he told himself. She was nothing to him. Only the children's nanny.

CHAPTER THREE

KAYLEEN BACKED OUT of the kitchen, her hands up in front of her, palms out. "No really. I mean it. Everything we have is terrific. I love the food. I've gained three pounds."

When she could no longer see the head chef's furious expression, she turned and hurried to the closest staircase, then ran up to a safer floor.

She'd only been offering to help, she told herself. But her offer of assistance had been taken as an insult.

With the girls gone all day and a kindly worded but clear letter from the orphan school saying it would be too awkward to have her teaching there, now that she was under Prince As'ad's "protection," Kayleen had nothing to do with her time. Sitting around was boring. She needed to keep busy with *something*. She couldn't clean the suite she and the girls lived in. There wasn't even a vacuum in the closet.

She wandered down the main hallway, then

paused to figure out where she was. The wide doorways looked familiar. Still, what would it hurt to have a few "you are here" maps to guide newcomers?

She turned another corner and recognized the official royal offices. In a matter of minutes she was standing in front of As'ad's assistant, Neil.

"I really need to see him," she said.

"You do not have an appointment."

"I'm his nanny." It was a bluff. She was staff and she had a feeling that all staff needed an appointment.

"I'm aware of who you are, Ms. James. But Prince As'ad is very particular about his schedule."

Neil was British, so the word sounded like "shed-ule."

The door to As'ad's office opened. "Neil, I need you to find—" He saw Kayleen. "How convenient. You're the one I'm looking for."

Guilt flooded her. "Is it the chef? I didn't mean to insult him. I was only trying to help."

His gaze narrowed. "What did you do?"

She tucked her hands behind her back. "Nothing."

"Why don't I believe you? Come inside, Kayleen. Start at the beginning and leave nothing out."

She glanced longingly at the exit, but followed As'ad into his office. When they were both seated, he looked at her expectantly.

She sucked in a breath. "I went down to the kitchen. I thought I could maybe help out there. I didn't mean anything by it. I'm bored. I need to do *something.*"

She stopped talking and pressed her lips together to hold in a sudden rush of emotion. *Need*—there was the word that mattered. She had to be needed.

"You have your three charges," he said. "Many would find that enough."

"Oh, please. They're in school for hours at a time. Someone else cooks, cleans and I'm guessing does our laundry. So what do I do the rest of the time?"

"Shop?"

"With what? Are you paying me? We never discussed a salary. Are there benefits? Do I have a dental plan? One minute I was minding my own business, doing my job, and the next I was here. It's not an easy adjustment."

One corner of his mouth twitched. "If I remember correctly, you assaulted a chieftain. Not exactly minding your own business."

She didn't want to talk about that. "You know what I mean."

"I do. Tell me, Kayleen. What did you teach?"

"Math," she said absently as she stood up and crossed to the window. As'ad's view was of a beautiful garden. She didn't know anything about plants, but she could learn. Maybe the gardener needed some help.

"Advanced?"

"Some."

"You're comfortable with statistical analysis?"

"Uh-huh." What were the pink flowers? They were stunning.

"Then I have a project for you."

She turned. "You want me to do your taxes?"

"No. I want you to work with the education minister. While many girls from the rural villages are graduating from high school and going on to college, the number is not as great as we would like. For El Deharia to grow as a nation, we must have all our citizens educated and productive. I want you to find out which villages are sending the most girls to college, then figure out what they're doing right so we can use that information to help the other villages. Does that interest you?"

She crossed back to the sofa. "You're serious? You're not just offering me this to keep me busy?"

"You have my word. This is vital information. I trust you to get it right."

He spoke with a low, steady voice that seemed to pull her closer. There was something in his eyes that made her want to believe him.

Excitement grew inside of her. It was a project she could throw herself into, and still have plenty of time for the girls. It would be challenging and interesting and meaningful.

She rushed toward him. "I'd love to do it. Thank you."

She leaned forward impulsively, then stopped herself. What was the plan? To hug him? One did not idly hug a prince and she didn't go around hugging men.

She straightened and took a step back, not sure if she should apologize or pretend it never happened. As'ad rose and crossed to his desk. Apparently he was going to ignore what she'd almost done. Or he hadn't noticed.

"Then we are agreed," he said. "You'll report your progress to me in weekly meetings." He opened a desk drawer and pulled out a credit card. "Use this to get yourself a laptop and printer. Your suite already has Internet access."

She hesitated before taking the card. No one had ever offered her a credit card before. She fingered the slim plastic. "I'll, um, make sure I get a bargain."

"You don't have to. Kayleen, do you have any idea how wealthy I am?"

"Not really," she admitted.

"You don't need to shop for a bargain."

But she would. She would be responsible with his money, even if he didn't care.

"Okay. I'll get right on ordering one."

He studied her for a moment. "You may also use that to shop for yourself and the girls."

"We don't need anything."

"You will. Clothes wear out. Even my limited knowledge of children tells me they grow and require new clothes."

"You're right." She stared at the card. "You're also very kind."

"I am not. My daughters deserve the best because of who I am."

"You don't have a self-esteem crisis, do you?" she asked, both amused and envious.

"No. I am clear on my place in the world."

Must be nice, she thought longingly.

"You belong here, as well," he told her.

Because he was once again reading her mind? "Not really."

"If I say it is so, it is."

"Thank you" seemed the right response. He was being kind. The truth was, she didn't belong here at all. She was just staff and easily replaceable.

She turned to leave, but he called her back.

"I'll get you information on your salary and benefits," he said. "I should have taken care of that before."

She smiled. "You're a prince. I guess you're not into details."

"You're very understanding. Thank you."

"You're welcome."

His dark gaze caught hers. She told herself it was okay to go now, that they were done. But she couldn't seem to pull away. She felt a powerful need to move closer, to…to… She wasn't sure what, but *something*.

The phone rang. He glanced down and she was able to move again. As much as she wanted to stay, she forced herself to walk out of the office.

"WE'RE MAKING PROGRESS," Lina said as she curled up on her bed and held the phone close.

"There is no 'we,'" Hassan told her. "You are in this on your own."

"That's not true. This was all your idea. You're in this as deeply as I am."

"You're a very difficult woman."

"I know." She smiled. "It's part of my charm."

"You *are* charming."

She squeezed her eyes shut and did her best not to scream. Not only wasn't it fitting her position, but she was forty-three. Forty-three-year-old women didn't go around screaming because a handsome man flirted with them on the phone. Even if that handsome man was the king of Bahania.

"Kayleen really likes As'ad," she continued. "She's having a little trouble adjusting to the palace, but who wouldn't? Still, she's doing well. He came and talked to me about making sure she had a salary and benefits. He wants to be generous. That's something."

"You may be reading too much into what he says."

"I hope not. She would be good for him. He always holds back his emotions. I blame his father for that."

"How refreshing," Hassan said dryly. "One usually blames the mother."

She laughed. "Speaking as a woman, I would say that needs to change."

"This is my favorite part of our conversations. The sound of your laughter."

Her heartbeat went from normal to hyperdrive in two seconds. Good thing she was lying down— otherwise, she would have fallen.

"It is as beautiful as the rest of you." He paused. "Have I startled you with my confession?"

"Um, no. It's fine. I mean, thank you."

He sighed. "How much of this awkwardness is because I am a king and how much of it is because I am so much older?"

"None of it is because you're the king," she said without thinking.

His short "I see" had her backpedaling.

"No, no. It's not about your age. I just wasn't sure... We've never really talked about... I thought we were friends."

"We are. Do you wish us to be more?"

Oh, my. Talk about putting it all out there.

Lina clutched the phone and told herself to keep breathing. She was terrified to tell the truth, to admit that she thought about him a whole lot more than she should. What if he wanted to know so he could let her down gently?

"Hassan," she began, then stopped.

"I would like us to be more than friends," he said. "Does that information make things easier or harder for you?"

She exhaled. "Easier. A lot easier. I want that, too."

"Good. I did not expect to find you, Lina. You are a gift for which I will always be grateful."

"Thank you," she whispered, not sure what else to say. "I'm intrigued, as well."

"Intrigued," he repeated. "An interesting choice of words. Perhaps we should explore all the possibilities."

As'ad walked into his suite at his usual time in the early evening. But instead of quiet, dark rooms, he found the living area bright and loud. Dana and Pepper were stretched out on the floor, watching a show on his large television. Nadine swirled and danced by the window and Kayleen stood at the dining room table, arranging flowers.

She looked up when he entered. "Oh, good. You're here. I called Neil to ask him what time you'd be home. He didn't want to tell me." She wrinkled her nose. "I don't think he likes me."

"Perhaps he is just trying to protect me."

"From us?" She asked the question as if it were a ridiculous possibility. "I wanted to have dinner ready, which it is. I have to say, this calling down to the kitchen and ordering food is really fun. We each picked a dish. Which may not have been a good idea. The menu is fairly eclectic."

She paused for breath, then smiled. "We wanted to have dinner with you."

She wore another dress that was ugly enough to be offensive. The dull gray fabric sucked the life from her face and the bulky style hid any hint of curve. Yet when she smiled, he found his mood lifting. He wanted to smile back. He wanted to pull her close and discover the body hidden beneath.

Heat stirred, reminding him how long he had lived only for his work.

He ignored the need and the wanting, the heat that forced blood south, and set down his briefcase. He even ignored that, given her past, Kayleen had probably never been with a man, and instead focused on the fact that she and the girls were in his room.

He had made himself extremely clear. She was to keep the children away from him. They had their own suite and everything they could possibly want or need. He had only taken the sisters to keep them from a less desirable fate. Yet when he started to remind Kayleen of that, he could not seem to bring himself to say the words.

Perhaps because she looked so hopeful as she smiled at him. He did not want to squash the light in her eyes.

"I'll get some wine," he said, moving to the small wine rack tucked in a cabinet. Something stronger might make the evening go more quickly, but he only had wine in his rooms. He did not, as a rule, drink here. Of course he did not, as a rule, have a woman and three children to contend with.

Nadine danced over to him. "Hi, As'ad," she said, her eyes bright with happiness, her mouth smiling. "Did you have a good day? I got every word on my spelling test except one and it was really hard. My new teacher says I'm a good speller. I'm good in all my subjects, except math, and Kayleen is gonna help me with that."

Pepper ran over and pushed in front of Nadine. "Hi! I'm in school, too, and I'm good at math." She stuck out her tongue at her sister, then smiled back at him. "I made a picture and I brought it for you, but you don't have a 'frigerator, so where are we gonna put it?"

Dana stood and joined them. "He doesn't want

your picture," she said, then sighed, as only an older sibling can. "She's not a very good artist."

Pepper stomped her foot. "I'm an *excellent* artist. You're just a butthead."

Dana gasped, Nadine looked worried and Pepper slapped her hand over her mouth. Terror darkened her blue eyes and she glanced between him and Kayleen. Apparently saying "butthead" was not allowed.

As'ad rubbed his temple.

Kayleen walked over and looked at Pepper. "You know that's wrong."

Pepper nodded frantically, her hand still over her mouth.

"You need to apologize to Dana."

Pepper, a tiny girl with long, curly blond hair, turned to her big sister. "I'm sorry I called you that."

Dana put her hands on her hips. "That's not good enough. You always call people—"

Kayleen cleared her throat. Dana hunched her shoulders.

"Thank you for apologizing," she grumbled.

Kayleen touched Pepper's shoulder. "Now you help me think of a suitable punishment. What is appropriate for what you did?"

Pepper's eyes filled with tears. "No story tonight?" she asked in a whisper.

Kayleen considered. "That's a little harsh. What

if you have to give up your choice on movie night? Dana gets two choices instead."

Pepper shivered slightly, then nodded. "Okay."

"Good." Kayleen smiled at As'ad. "We're healed. You ready to eat?"

He opened the bottle of wine and joined them at the table. When he was seated, before he could pour, Kayleen reached for Pepper's hand and his. He stared at her.

Pepper leaned toward him. "We have to say grace."

"Of course."

He took Kayleen's hand and Nadine's, then lowered his head while Kayleen offered brief thanks for their meal. While she served, he poured two glasses of wine and passed her one.

Kayleen handed him a plate. "I've never been much of a drinker."

"Neither have I." Although under the circumstances, he just might be starting.

This was too much, he thought. More than he'd expected or wanted. There were children at his table. And a woman he did not know and was not going to sleep with, and having sex with her would be the only acceptable reason to have her here. Yet he saw no easy way to escape.

"We go around the table and talk about our day," Kayleen said as she passed Dana her plate.

"Everyone has to say one good thing that happened. I hope that's okay."

And if it was not?

He glanced down at the plate in front of him. Lasagna, mashed potatoes, macaroni and cheese and a salad.

"Perhaps some kind of menu would be helpful," he told Kayleen.

"I know. I'll get one made up. But the girls really wanted to order you their favorites."

Dana talked about how she'd finished her homework early and had found a collection of medical texts in the palace's main library. Nadine mentioned her dance class and how well she'd done.

"I hit a boy," Pepper announced cheerfully. "He was teasing these three girls. He's kinda big, but I wasn't scared. So I hit him. The teacher didn't like it but because I'm new, she said she was going to let it go this one time. I heard this other teacher saying that boy needed a good beating and maybe I'm the one to give it to him." She beamed. "That was fun."

Kayleen quickly covered her mouth with her napkin. As'ad saw the humor in her eyes and knew she was hiding a smile. He took a sip of wine to keep from laughing. He liked Pepper—she had the heart of a lion.

"Perhaps hitting boys is not the best plan," he

said as he set the glass down. "One day one of them might hit you back."

"I'm tough," she said.

"Still. Violence is a poor strategy."

"What's a better one?"

He hesitated, not sure what to say.

Kayleen grinned. "We're all waiting to be dazzled by your strategy."

"Perhaps you would like to offer a suggestion?" he asked.

"Not really. Go ahead."

Privately he agreed with Pepper's approach, but he doubted it would be successful as she grew.

"We'll talk later," Kayleen said, rescuing him. "I know hitting a bully seems like a good idea, but it's going to get you into a lot of trouble. Not only with the teachers and with me, but as As'ad mentioned, you could get hurt."

"All right," Pepper grumbled. "But sometimes boys are really stupid."

Dana looked at As'ad. "What good thing happened to you?"

"I decided on a bridge. There is to be a new one over the river. After much planning and discussion, a choice was made. I am pleased."

All three girls stared at him. "You're going to build a bridge?" Nadine asked.

"No. I have given my approval and told them what to do. Now they will do it."

"Cool," Dana breathed. "What else can you tell people to do?"

"Can you throw them in the dungeon?" Pepper asked. "Can I see the dungeon?"

"One day."

Her eyes widened. "There's a real one? Here? In the palace?"

"Yes, and sometimes children who do not behave are sent to it."

They all went silent.

He chuckled. "So, Kayleen, what was your one good thing for today?"

This, Kayleen thought as she tried not to stare at the handsome man at the head of the table. This dinner, this moment, with the girls having fun and As'ad acting like they were all part of the same family.

It wasn't real—she knew that. But all her life she'd wanted to be a part of something special, and here it was.

Still, she had to say something. "There are stables nearby," she told the girls. "I found them when I was out walking."

All three of them turned to him. "Horses? You have horses?" Dana asked.

"We love horses," Nadine told him.

"I can ride." Pepper paused, as if waiting for As'ad to be impressed. "I've had lessons."

He turned to Kayleen. "At the orphanage?"

"A former student left several horses to the school, along with the money to pay for them. Many of the children ride."

"Do you?"

There was something about his dark eyes, she thought, knowing she could stare into them for hours and never grow tired of the effect of the changing light.

"Badly," she admitted. "The horse and I never figured out how to talk to each other."

"That's because horses don't talk," Pepper told her, then turned to As'ad. "Kayleen falls off a lot. I try not to laugh, because I don't want her to hurt herself, but it's kinda funny."

"For you," Kayleen murmured.

The main door to the suite opened and a tall, gray-haired man strode into the suite.

"As'ad. There you are. Oh. You're having dinner with your family."

"Father," As'ad said as he rose.

Father? Something nagged at the back of Kayleen's mind, before bursting free. Father? As in the king?

She jumped to her feet and motioned for the girls to do the same. Once they were standing she didn't know what to do next. Bow? Curtsy?

As'ad glanced at her, then the girls. "Father, this is Kayleen, the girls' nanny." Then he introduced each of the sisters. "Ladies, this is my father, King Mukhtar."

Three mouths dropped open. Kayleen kept hers shut by sheer force of will.

The king nodded graciously. "I am delighted to meet all of you. Welcome to the royal palace of El Deharia. May you live long, with happiness and health in abundance. May these strong walls always protect you and provide solace."

Kayleen swallowed. As greetings went, it was a really good one.

"Thank you so much for your hospitality," she murmured, still trying to accept the fact that she was in the presence of a real live king. Which meant As'ad really was a prince.

She knew he held the title, but she didn't think of him as royal or powerful. Yet he was.

The king motioned to the table. "May I?"

Kayleen felt her eyes widen. "Of course, Your Highness. Please. We weren't expecting you, so the meal isn't exactly…traditional."

The king took a seat. As'ad motioned for them to resume theirs. Mukhtar studied the various serving bowls, then scooped some macaroni and cheese onto a plate.

"I haven't had this in years."

"It was my pick," Pepper told him. "It's my favorite. They make it really good here. Sometimes, at the orphanage, Kayleen would sneak us into the kitchen and make the kind in a box. That's good, too."

The king smiled. "So my chef has competition."

"Not really," Kayleen told him. "His food is amazing. I'm honored just to eat it."

As'ad looked at his father. "In an effort to fill her day, Kayleen went down to the kitchen and offered to help. It did not go well."

Kayleen felt herself flush. "He was a little insulted. There was a crash. I'm guessing he threw stuff."

"Was that the night my soufflé was burned?" the king asked.

"I hope not," Kayleen told him.

He smiled. "So what conversation did I interrupt?" he asked.

"We were talking about horses," Nadine told him. "We rode and took lessons at the orphanage."

The king looked at his son. "Horses. I believe we have a stable, do we not?"

As'ad glanced at the girls. "The king is teasing. The palace stables are world famous."

Dana leaned toward him. "Do you have horses that go fast?"

"Faster than would be safe for a novice rider."

She wrinkled her nose. "If we took more lessons, we would be experts."

"Exactly," As'ad told her.

The king nodded. "I agree. All young princesses should know how to ride. I will speak to the head groom myself and arrange lessons." He glanced at Kayleen. "For all of you."

"Thank you," she murmured, because it was expected.

"You do not look excited," As'ad whispered to her.

"Pepper wasn't kidding about me falling. It happens all the time."

"Perhaps you need more personal instruction."

She stared into his eyes as he spoke and found herself getting lost in his gaze. It was as if he had an energy field that pulled her closer. She had the oddest feeling he was going to touch her—and she was going to like him touching her.

"Riding is an enjoyable way to get exercise," the king said.

"Has anyone asked the horse about that?"

She spoke without thinking—something that had often gotten her in trouble back at the convent. There was a moment of silence, then the king laughed.

"Very good," he said. "Excellent. I like her, As'ad. This one may stay."

"I agree," As'ad said, still looking at her in a way that made her thighs feel distinctly weak. "She will stay."

Would she? Kayleen wasn't so sure. She still

had her life plan to fulfill and that included leaving El Deharia in a matter of months. A situation complicated by As'ad and her promise to the girls.

CHAPTER FOUR

AFTER THE KING left and dinner was finished, Kayleen sent the girls back to their suite while she lingered behind to speak with As'ad.

"There are just a couple of things I need to discuss with you," she told him when they were alone.

"I'm learning that with you, there always are."

She wasn't sure what he meant by that, so decided to ignore the comment. "It's only about six weeks until Christmas," she said. "We have to start planning. I don't know what happens here at the palace, but this is the girls' first Christmas without either of their parents. We have to do something."

He studied her for a long time. "El Deharia is a very open country. All faiths are celebrated here. No one will object if you wish to set up a tree in your suite."

"It's more than that," she said, telling herself there was no reason to be afraid, even though As'ad was much taller than her and having to look up to meet his gaze gave her a crick in her neck. "You need to participate."

He looked shocked. "I do not."

She'd had a feeling he would be difficult.

"You've always had family," she pointed out. "Your brothers, your aunt, your father. These girls have no one. The holidays are going to be sad and scary and they're going to feel so alone."

Kayleen spoke from experience. She still remembered waking up on Christmas morning and feeling an ache in her chest. No matter how many presents had been donated to the orphanage, no matter how the nuns tried, there hadn't been *family*.

She hadn't even had the dream that a wonderful couple would find her and want to adopt her. She had plenty of relatives—just no one who wanted her.

"They need traditions, both old and new," she continued. "They need to feel welcome and loved."

His expression tightened. "Then you will take care of that."

"But you're their father now."

"I am someone who agreed to let them live here. Kayleen, these girls are your responsibility, not mine. Do not cross this line with me."

"I don't understand. You were so great with them at dinner. Are you telling me that was just an act? That you don't care?"

"I have compassion. I have honor. That will be enough."

Was he kidding? "That's not enough. It will never be enough. We're talking about children, As'ad. Lost, lonely children. They deserve more. They deserve to be loved." She wasn't just talking about the children—she was talking about herself. The difference was she'd already given up her dreams.

"Then they will have to find that love in you."

She took a step back. Her throat tightened and her cheeks were hot. "You're saying you don't plan to love them?"

He might as well have said he was going to kill them in their sleep!

"I will honor my responsibilities. In doing so, it is necessary for me to be strong. Emotion is weakness. You are a woman—I don't expect you to understand. Just trust me, it is so. I will see to the girls' needs. You can take care of their hearts."

She didn't know what to say or where to begin to argue with him. "That's the craziest thing I've ever heard," she told him. "Love isn't weakness. It's strength and power. The ability to give means you can be more, not less."

He actually smiled at her. "Your passion is a testament to your caring. That's excellent."

"So it's okay for me to have emotions, but not you? Because you're a man?"

"More than a man," he reminded her. "A prince. I have responsibilities for others. It is my duty to stay strong, to not be swayed by something as changeable as feelings."

"Without compassion, there can be no judgment," she snapped. "Without feelings, you're only a machine. A good ruler feels for his people."

"You cannot understand."

"And you can't mean this."

"I assure you, I do." He took her arm and walked her to the door. "Celebrate Christmas however you wish. You have my permission."

"Can I have your head on a stick instead?" she muttered as she jerked free and walked out into the hallway.

Of all the stupid, annoying things she'd ever heard. He wasn't going to feel anything because he was a prince? But it was okay for her because she was a woman?

"No way," she told herself as she headed back to her own rooms. "Something is going to change around here and it isn't going to be me."

"IT's SO EGOTISTICAL," Kayleen ranted the next morning as she paced the length of her living room. "So two hundred years ago. He gets to be in charge because he's a man? What does that make the rest of us? Chattel? I'm so angry, I want to throw him in the dungeon until he begs. I'm smart. I'm capable. And I have a heart. Why can't he see that emotions give us depth? They define us. Are all men so stupid? I have to tell you, Lina, the more I see of the world, the more I long for the convent."

Her friend smiled at her. "Is it possible your energy and intensity on this topic is one of the reasons you *weren't* called to serve in that way?"

"That's what I was always told when I was growing up. I was too passionate about things. Too willing to go my own way. It's just when I see an injustice, I can't stop to think. I act."

"As you did with Tahir."

Kayleen remembered the tall chieftain who had wanted to take the girls. "Exactly."

"Life does not always move on your timetable," Lina said. "You need to be patient."

"Don't act impulsively," Kayleen said, knowing she'd heard the same advice a thousand times before.

"Exactly." Lina patted the seat next to her. "As'ad is a product of his world. His father taught all his sons to avoid emotion. To think logically. While my brother grieved after his wife died, he chose not to show that to the boys. In front of them, he went on, as if unmoved by her passing. In my opinion it was the wrong lesson."

Kayleen agreed. "Because of that, As'ad won't care?" She didn't wait for an answer. "He's not stupid. Why can't he see the truth all around him?"

"He has been trained for a specific purpose. His is a life of service, in a way, but with ultimate power and ego. You haven't met his brothers, but they are all like him. Strong, determined men who see little virtue in love. It's probably why none of them have married."

"But love is strength and a great gift," Kayleen said as she sat on the sofa. "He has to love the girls. They need that. They deserve it. He would be better because of it. Happier. Besides, there's a ticking clock here."

Lina frowned. "You're still leaving?"

"I can go back on my twenty-fifth birthday. That's less than four months away."

"But you have the girls now."

"I know." Kayleen hadn't worked that part out. "They'll get settled and then As'ad can bring in someone else."

She spoke bravely, but the words sounded a little feeble, even to her.

"I'm surprised," Lina admitted. "When you asked As'ad to adopt the girls, I thought you were taking on the responsibility with him. This isn't like you, Kayleen. To retreat from the world."

"The world isn't always a fun place. I want to go back to where I belong." Where she'd grown up. It was the only home she'd ever known. "I can teach there." That was the deal. She had to stay away until she was twenty-five. Then she could return to the convent school forever.

"You can be a mother here."

"Not really. It's just a game. When the girls are older, As'ad will have no use for me. Besides, if he doesn't want to get involved, maybe I can take them with me."

"I assume my nephew doesn't know about your plan to leave."

"I haven't mentioned it."

"When will you?"

"Soon. It's not as if he'll miss me or anything."

Kayleen had always wondered what it would be like to be missed by someone. By a man. To be cared for. Loved, even.

"Things change," Lina told her. "You have a responsibility to the girls."

"I know."

"Would you walk away from them so easily?"

Kayleen shook her head. "No. It won't be easy. Sometimes I do think about staying." She didn't know what was right. Her plan had always been to go back. Being here with the three sisters had changed everything.

Was Lina right? Did she, Kayleen, have a responsibility to the children? Should she give up her dreams for them? Could she go back later? When the girls were older?

Three weeks ago, she'd known all the answers and now she knew none. Her instinct was to go talk to As'ad about all this. But that made no sense. He was a man who didn't listen to his heart and she had always believed the truth could be found there.

"My head is spinning. Enough about this. Let's change the subject."

"All right." Lina smiled slowly. "Hassan is coming here."

Kayleen stared at her friend. "The king of Bahania? The one you've been talking to all this time?"

"I can't believe it, either. I just… We were talking and he said he liked the sound of my laughter and now he's coming here."

Kayleen hugged her. "That's wonderful. I'm so happy. You've been shut up in this palace for years. Good for you."

"I'm scared," Lina admitted. "I thought my life was all planned out. I helped my brother raise his sons, I have my charity work. I was waiting to be a great-aunt. Suddenly there's this wonderful man offering me something I thought I'd lost. There are possibilities. Am I too old for possibilities?"

"Never," Kayleen said fiercely. "The heart is never too old. At least it isn't in all those romantic movies."

"I hope not. I married young and I was so in love. Then he was killed and I never planned to love again. I'm the sister to the king. It's difficult to date. After a while, I stopped wanting to. Then Hassan and I started talking and suddenly I'm alive again." Lina took Kayleen's hands. "I want this for you. I at least experienced falling in love when I was young, but you've never had that."

Kayleen squirmed. "I'm not good with men."

"You don't try. How many dates did you go on before you gave up? Five? Six?"

Kayleen cleared her throat, then pulled her hands free. "One and a half."

"You're too young to lock yourself away in that convent school of yours."

"Because I would meet so many men here at the palace?"

"You'd meet some. More than you would there. There are many young men in the palace. I would be happy to introduce you to one or two of them."

"I don't know…. I work for As'ad. As nanny to his children."

"Why would he mind you dating?"

"He wouldn't." Not that she enjoyed admitting that truth.

"Then think about what I said. Wouldn't it be wonderful to fall in love?"

As'ad looked up as his brother Qadir walked into his office. "I must speak with Neil about keeping out people who don't have appointments."

Qadir ignored that. "I am back from Paris, where the city is still beautiful, as are the women. You should have come with me. You have been locked up here working for far too long."

As'ad had spent two sleepless nights unable to rest for the need burning inside. Worse, when he closed his eyes, the woman he saw satisfying his ache was Kayleen. An impossible situation. The nanny and a virgin?

"You are right, my brother," he said as he rose and greeted Qadir. "I should have gone with you. There have been changes since you were last here."

"I heard." Qadir settled on a corner of his desk. "Three daughters? What were you thinking?"

"That I had been placed in an impossible situation and this was the easiest way out."

"I find that hard to believe. There had to be another solution."

"None was presented."

Qadir shook his head. "To raise children that are not your own. At least they are girls."

"There is the added advantage of our father now believing I am occupied with my new family and therefore cannot be expected to look for a wife."

"Lucky bastard."

"Indeed. Perhaps now he will focus more of his attention on you."

"He has already begun," Qadir grumbled. "There is to be a state function in a few weeks. Several likely candidates are to be paraded before me, like very attractive cattle."

As'ad grinned. "I, of course, will be busy with my family."

As'ad turned the corner to walk to his rooms and saw all three girls huddled by his door. They wore riding clothes and boots. When they saw him they ran to him.

"You have to help!" Dana told him.

"It's terrible. Please!" Nadine begged.

Pepper simply cried.

He stared at the three of them. "What happened?"

"We went riding," Dana told him, her blue eyes wide and filled with fear and guilt. "We might have been gone longer than we were supposed to, but we were fine. We were only a little late. But Kayleen got worried and came after us, even though we had a groom with us. She went out by herself and she's not back yet."

Pepper brushed her hand across her face as she tugged on the bottom of his suit jacket. "She's not a very good rider. She gets thrown a lot. What if she's hurt and it's all our fault?"

As'ad's first thought was that he regretted that whoever had let Kayleen go out by herself could not be flogged. Sometimes he missed the old ways. His second was the low-grade worry at the thought of a defenseless young woman alone in the desert. It was not a place to be traveled lightly.

The girls crowded close, as if seeking comfort from him. Although he had no time for this, he resisted the urge to push them away and instead awkwardly patted them on their shoulders.

"All will be well," he told them. "I will find Kayleen and return her to you."

"Promise?" Pepper asked, her lashes spiky from her tears.

He crouched down until he could look her in the eye. "I am Prince As'ad of El Deharia. My word is law."

Pepper sniffed. "Promise?"

He gave her a slight smile. "I promise."

Ten minutes later the girls were settled with Lina and he was in the garage, sliding into an open Jeep. The desert was a vast space and in theory, Kayleen could be anywhere. But in truth, an inexperienced rider would stick to trails and not get far. Unless she had been thrown.

He did not allow himself to consider that option. He would find her and if she were hurt, he would deal with the situation as it arose.

He found the riding trail easily. He had been taking it all his life. As it bent to the left, he considered how far Kayleen might have traveled, then accelerated. A mere ten miles into the desert was the permanent outpost of a local tribe. If Kayleen kept to the trail, she would end up there.

He drove slowly, checking the area for signs of any accident, or a woman walking without a horse, but found nothing. At the outskirts of the outpost he saw a cluster of people gathered around a petite woman with flaming red hair. She was holding on to a horse and gesturing wildly.

As'ad eased the Jeep to a stop and picked up the satellite phone. When he was connected with his aunt, he informed her he had found Kayleen and that she appeared fine.

"Will you be coming right back?" Lina asked.

As'ad considered. "I believe we'll stay for dinner."

"That's fine. I'll put the girls to bed. Thanks for letting me know. They were worried."

He disconnected the call and parked, then walked toward the crowd.

Kayleen saw him and excused herself from the group, then raced toward him. When she was close enough, she launched herself at him.

He caught her and held her against him as she trembled in his embrace.

"You came," she breathed. "It's the girls. They're gone. They were late and we had no way to get in touch with them and I was so worried, so I took a horse out myself. I found this village, but no one speaks English and I can't tell if they've seen the girls. What if something happened to them? I'll never forgive myself."

She was distraught and panicked and surprisingly beautiful. Her hazel eyes darkened with emotion and her cheeks were flushed. Impulsively, he bent down and lightly brushed her mouth with his.

"They're fine," he told her. "All three of them returned unharmed. You are the one who is missing."

"What?" She drew in a breath. "They're all right?"

"Perfectly fine, although suffering from guilt for causing you distress. Kayleen, the girls are good riders. The head groom took them out himself to confirm that. They also had someone with them. Why did you feel it necessary to go rescue them yourself?"

"I don't know. I was worried and I acted."

"Impulsively."

She glanced down. "Yes, well, that's an ongoing problem."

"So it seems."

She looked around and noticed the villagers gathered close. "Oh." She pulled back.

As'ad let her go, but only reluctantly. She had felt good in his arms. He wanted to kiss her again—but thoroughly and without an audience. He wanted to push aside her unattractive clothing and touch the soft skin beneath. Instead he stepped back and turned to greet Sharif, the village chieftain.

"She is your woman?" Sharif asked.

Kayleen spun toward the old man. "You speak

English? You stood there, pretending not to understand and you speak *English?*"

"They don't know you," As'ad told her. "They
were being cautious."

"What about desert hospitality? What about
claiming sanctuary or asylum or something?"

"Did you?" he asked.

Kayleen pressed her lips together. "No. I was
asking if they'd seen the girls. They wouldn't answer and they weren't speaking English."

As'ad glanced at Sharif. "She is mine."

"Then you are both welcome. You will stay and
eat with us?"

"It is an honor."

"Arrangements will be made."

"Arrangements?" Kayleen asked. "What arrangements? And what's all this about being your
woman? I'm your nanny. There's a really big difference."

He took her by the elbow and led her to the
Jeep. "It makes things easier if they think you belong to me. Otherwise you would be fair game for
every man here. You're very exotic. They would
find that tempting."

Kayleen didn't know what to say to that. She
was so far from exotic that if they put her picture
on that page in the dictionary, it would have a circle with a line drawn through it over her face. She
couldn't imagine a man ever being tempted by her.

It was the hair, she thought with a sigh. Bright red hair tended to call attention to itself.

"Fear not," As'ad told her. "I have claimed you. You are safe."

She shivered slightly, but not in fear. It was more from the memory of the brief kiss he'd given her when he'd first arrived. An unexpected and warm touch of his lips on hers. She'd been shocked by the contact, but not in a scary way. More surprised, but pleased.

"We're staying for dinner," he said.

"I got that."

"It's the polite thing to do."

She looked around at the tidy camp. "I don't mind. I like it here, out in the desert. Although it would be nice if they didn't pretend not to understand me."

"They are private people. You rode in from nowhere, babbling about missing children. They were cautious."

She narrowed her gaze. "I do *not* babble."

He raised an eyebrow.

"Not often," she amended. "I was scared. I thought the girls were lost."

"You were not equipped to find them, yet you went after them."

"Someone had to."

"Perhaps one of the grooms. Or you could have called me."

Oh. Right. "I didn't think of that. I'm not used to having resources."

"Perhaps next time you will consider that you do."

It would take some getting used to. "You came after me yourself," she said. "*You* could have sent one of the grooms."

"The girls were most distressed to think they were the cause of your being gone. Coming after you myself seemed the quickest way to allay their fears."

"It was a little impulsive. You have resources, too."

"You mock me?"

"Maybe."

"A dangerous path."

"I'm not afraid."

Something flashed in his eyes. Something dark and primitive that made her heart flutter. She didn't know if she should throw herself at him or run into the desert, so she stood her ground.

"So what do you think is for dinner?"

THE WOMEN OF the village prepared a rich stew with lots of vegetables and a flat bread that smelled so good it made Kayleen's mouth water. She did her best to be friendly and polite, helping with the cooking as much as the women in the camp would let her.

Zarina, Sharif's oldest daughter, was the only one who would speak to her in English.

"Am I really that scary?" Kayleen asked quietly as she stirred the stew.

"You are different. From the city and from another country. You do not know our ways."

"I could learn."

Zarina, a dark-haired beauty with a flashing smile, laughed. "Give up your comforts to roam the desert? I do not think so."

"Comforts don't matter to me," Kayleen told her. She would give up many things to belong somewhere.

"Yet you live in the palace with the prince."

"It's a long story and I don't live with him. I take care of…" She shook her head. "It's a really long story."

Zarina glanced at As'ad where he sat with the leaders of the tribe. "The prince is handsome. If I were not happily married, I might try to steal him from you."

Kayleen started to say he wasn't hers to steal, but figured there was no point. "He's nice."

Zarina laughed. "Not nice. No man worth having is nice. As'ad is a desert warrior. He takes what he wants, but then he protects those he claims. He is a strong man. A powerful husband. You have chosen well."

A lion of the desert? As'ad? He was strong and

powerful and he did seem to take care of those around him. His presence here was proof of that. But a dangerous animal? She didn't believe that. As for her choosing him…as if.

He looked up and met her gaze, then rose and approached. "What troubles you, Kayleen?"

"Nothing. I was just thinking. Zarina says it's good she's happily married, otherwise she would steal you from me."

He laughed. "She is a beautiful woman."

Kayleen didn't like that answer. "You and I don't have that kind of relationship."

"So you would not mind if she and I…"

"No," Kayleen said carefully, even as a knot formed in her stomach. It was hard and hot and made her feel uncomfortable. "You have a family now. You should be with someone."

"You suggest Zarina?"

"She's already married."

"I am Prince As'ad of El Deharia. I can have whomever I choose."

How annoyingly arrogant. "I don't think so. You're just a man. There are women who would say no to you."

He moved closer. "Who would that be?"

She stood at straight as she could, tilted her head back and glared at him. "Me, for one. I'm not interested."

His smile was slow, sexy and confident beyond measure. "You think so."

"Absolutely."

"I see."

He reached toward her. Before she knew what he intended, he pulled her close and kissed her.

CHAPTER FIVE

KAYLEEN HAD ALMOST been kissed once in her life, on a date with a young man in college. He had been nice enough, but she was so inexperienced that just being around him had made her nervous. At the end of their awkward evening, he'd moved in for a kiss and she'd bolted for the safety of her dorm room.

But there was no bolting from As'ad. With his arms around her, she had nowhere to go. Not to mention the fact that she didn't want to run.

She'd wondered about kissing, had wondered if she was the last innocent in a world where even twelve-year-olds seemed to know more about men and sex than she did. She'd wondered how it was possible to enjoy someone being so close, pressing his mouth against hers. Worse, using his tongue in some intimate way.

Would she feel trapped, uncomfortable, violated?

The short answer was no, she thought as As'ad moved his mouth gently against hers, teasing, caressing, but not taking. Even though his arms were around her, she didn't feel trapped. Instead she felt protected and wanted.

The wanting was new, as was the odd hungry sensation inside of her. She needed to be closer, although she couldn't say why.

She put her hands on his shoulders, feeling the strength and heat of him. As'ad would keep all in his world safe, she thought, distracted by the pressure of his lips. It would be nice to feel safe.

She inhaled the masculine scent of him, liking the fragrance. She enjoyed the feel of his body so close to hers. She grew bolder and slipped her arms around his neck, bringing her front in contact with his.

He increased the pressure of his mouth on hers. His strong hands traveled up and down her back. When he stroked his tongue against her bottom lip she gasped in shock, then felt the soft, erotic touch of his tongue against hers.

Fire shot through her. The unexpected heat made her tremble as she almost expected to go up in flames. Sensations exploded everywhere, especially in places that were usually without them. Her breasts ached in a way they never had before. Her legs felt funny—trembly and weak. She stood frozen, unsure, awkward, yet willing him to keep on kissing her.

Fortunately As'ad seemed more than capable of

reading her mind. He explored her mouth with his tongue, making her tingle and want to lean into him. She ached, but couldn't say for what. She clung to him, and at last, tentatively, slowly, carefully, touched her tongue to his.

A low, masculine groan burst from him. The sound filled her with a sense of sensual power she'd never experienced before. She touched his tongue again and felt a reaction in her own body. A clenching. A wanting. A hunger.

She let herself get lost in the touching, the intimate kiss. It was heaven. She could do this for hours. She liked how her body turned to liquid. She liked everything about kissing him.

But instead of reading her mind again, he put his hands on her shoulders and eased her away from him.

"What?" she breathed.

"Perhaps another time," he said calmly. "When we are alone."

Alone? What was he...

Kayleen bit her lower lip and turned her head. While much of the village had gone about their business, there were still several obviously interested people observing their kiss. As she looked at them, they grinned. A couple waved. A few of the women laughed knowingly.

"Now no one will question that you are mine," he told her.

THEY ARRIVED BACK at the palace shortly after ten. Kayleen met Lina in the suite she, Kayleen, shared with the girls.

"We're back," she said. "Thanks for staying with them."

"It was fun," Lina told her. "So how was your evening?"

Kayleen did her best not to blush, although she could feel heat on her cheeks. "It was fine. Good. I really liked meeting everyone in the village. They're wonderful people. Dinner was good. They let me help a little with the cooking. Everyone was friendly." She realized she was babbling and pressed her lips together, then blurted, "Nothing happened."

Lina slowly raised her eyebrows. "Excuse me?"

"Nothing happened. With As'ad. In case you were, you know, wondering. Nothing happened."

"I see." Lina smiled. "You're protesting an awful lot, especially when you consider I never asked if anything happened."

"Oh." Kayleen shifted. She needed to stop talking now or Lina would find out about the kiss. Not that Kayleen regretted it—on the contrary, it was a delicious secret she wanted to keep to herself.

Lina waited another few seconds, then walked to the door. "I'll see you later, then."

"Uh-huh. Thanks again for staying with the girls."

"Anytime," Lina said, and then left.

When she was alone, Kayleen tiptoed into the girls' bedroom. All three of them were asleep. She smoothed covers, adjusted the nightlight, then went into her own room. When she had shut the door behind her, she sighed with happiness, spun in a slow circle, then sank onto the bed.

She'd been kissed. Really kissed and it had been wonderful. Better than she could have imagined.

She'd liked everything about kissing As'ad... the taste of him, the heat, the way he'd held her. She wanted to kiss and be kissed again. Unfortunately, it wasn't the sort of thing she could simply ask him to do. Worse, she wasn't sure *why* he'd kissed her. Had he wanted to, or had he just been proving a point in the village? And why did it suddenly matter which?

SEVERAL DAYS LATER As'ad returned to his rooms to find Kayleen sitting at his dining table in front of a sewing machine. Fabric covered every available surface. She'd pulled over a floor lamp for additional light and didn't notice his arrival.

His reaction was as powerful as it was instantaneous. Not about the fact that she'd once again ignored his request that she take care of all things involving the girls. Instead his body recognized the woman who had most recently brought him to his knees with a single kiss.

A virgin's kiss, he reminded himself, still annoyed and aroused at the sight of her. What should have been meaningless, done only to prove a point, had instead started a fire within him that still burned hot and strong. He'd been hungry before kissing her—now he was starved.

He hadn't been able to sleep for wanting Kayleen. The kiss had shown him potential where he'd seen very little. She'd felt right in his arms—all soft curves and innocence. Yet there had been heat in her, an instinctive passion that had matched his own.

The event should have meant nothing. He should have been able to walk away without thinking of it again. Instead it was all he could do not to cross the room, pull her to her feet and kiss her over and over until she surrendered. He wanted her wet, naked and begging. He wanted all of her.

She looked and saw him. "As'ad." She smiled. "You're back." She stood and held up both hands. "I know what you're going to say. This is a big mess. I'm sorry. I meant to get it cleaned up before you got home. I lost track of time."

Her mouth. He couldn't seem to look away from it. The shape, the hint of white teeth and nimble tongue. His brother Qadir was right—he *should* have gone to Paris and spent the week mindless in an unknown woman's bed. Now the opportunity was lost. He had a bad feeling it would be some time before he could use someone else to forget the appeal of Kayleen.

"What are you doing?" he asked, pleased his voice was so calm. Nothing of his turmoil must show.

"Making costumes for the Christmas pageant. All three girls are in it. I want the costumes to be a surprise."

"The school will not provide them?"

"I suppose they could. They asked if some of the parents could help out. I said I would. Lina found this machine for me. It's fabulous and practically sews on its own. You should see the instruction manual—it's as thick as a dictionary. But I'll figure it out."

He fingered a length of fabric. "I am sure there are employees in the palace who could do this for you."

She looked as if he'd slapped her. "But I like sewing. Besides, it'll matter more if I make the costumes for the girls."

"As you wish."

"I'm going to guess you're not into crafts."

He allowed himself a slight smile. "No."

"I learned to sew in the orphanage. I could make more clothes for a lot less. You probably don't do anything like that here."

"We do not."

She tilted her head and her long, red hair tumbled over her shoulders. His fingers curled toward his palms as he ached to touch her hair, to feel it in his hand, dragging along his chest, across his thighs.

"Did your mother sew?" Kayleen asked, jerking him back to the present.

"I don't know. She died when I was very young. I don't remember her."

The light faded from her eyes. "Oh. I'm sorry. I knew she was gone. I didn't know how old you were when it happened. I didn't mean to remind you of that."

"It is of no consequence."

"But it's sad."

"How can it be sad if the memory is gone?"

She frowned. "That is the loss of what should have been."

"I am not wounded, Kayleen. Share your concerns with someone who needs them."

"Because you feel nothing?" she asked. "Isn't that what you told me? Emotion makes you weak?"

"Exactly." Any emotion. Even passion. His current condition proved that.

"What about trust?" she asked.

"Trust must be earned."

"So many rules. So many chances to turn people away. It must be nice to have so many people in your life that there are extras."

She sounded wistful as she spoke, which made him want to pull her close and offer comfort.

Kayleen, who wanted to belong, he thought, realizing her concern for the girls came from having lived in an orphanage herself. She was all heart and would bruise easily in a harsh world. Their backgrounds couldn't be more different.

"It is a matter of control," he told her. "To need no one is to remain in charge."

She shook her head. "To need no one is to be desperately alone."

"That is not how I see it."

"That doesn't make it any less true. There's nothing worse than being alone," she told him. "I'll get this cleaned up now, and get out of your way."

KAYLEEN WALKED THROUGH the palace gardens. While she loved the beauty of the rooms inside, they were nothing when compared with the opulence of the lush gardens that beckoned just beyond her windows.

She chose a new path that twisted and turned, and once again reminded herself that she wanted to find a book on flowers in the palace library. She'd grown up gardening, but in the convent, all extra space had been taken up with vegetables. With money tight and children to feed, the nuns had not wasted precious earth on flowers.

Kayleen plucked a perfect rose and inhaled the

sweet scent, then settled on a stone bench warm from the sun. She needed a moment to close her eyes and be still. Maybe then the world would stop turning so quickly.

So much had happened in such a short time. Meeting As'ad, moving here with the girls, getting ready for the holidays, kissing As'ad.

The latter made her both sigh and smile. She longed for another kiss from him, but so far there had been no opportunity. Which made her wonder if the kiss had been as interesting and appealing to him. Maybe he'd found her inexperience disgusting. Maybe he'd been disappointed.

Did it matter? There shouldn't be any more kissing between them. She had her life plan and As'ad had his. They wanted opposite things—she needed to connect and he claimed connection didn't matter. She just wasn't sure she believed him.

She heard footsteps on the path and turned toward the sound. She expected to see one of the many gardeners. What she got instead was the king.

"Oh!" Kayleen sprang to her feet, then paused, not sure what she was supposed to do.

King Mukhtar smiled. "Good afternoon, Kayleen. I see you are enjoying my garden."

"I enjoy wandering," she said with a slight bob she hoped would pass for a curtsy and/or bow. "Have I stepped into off-limits space?"

"Not at all. I welcome the company. Come, child. Walk with me."

It didn't sound like a request.

Kayleen fell into step beside the king and waited for him to start the conversation. She was just starting to sweat the silence when he said, "Are you settled into the palace? Does it feel like home?"

She laughed. "I'm settled, but I'm not sure anywhere this magnificent will ever feel like home."

"A very politically correct answer," he told her. "Where did you grow up?"

"In an orphanage in the Midwest."

"I see. You lost your parents at an early age?"

She shrugged. "I don't know anything about my father. My mother had me when she was really young. She couldn't handle a baby so she left me with her mother. When that didn't work out, I went to the Catholic orphanage, which turned out to be a great place to grow up."

She was used to telling the story in a upbeat way that avoided making anyone feel awkward. There was no reason for the king to know that her mother had abandoned her and that her grandmother hadn't wanted to be stuck with another child to raise. No reason to talk about what it had felt like to be left on the doorstep of an orphanage on her fifth birthday, knowing no one in her family wanted anything to do with her. King Mukhtar wouldn't know what it felt like to never belong anywhere.

"So you don't remember your mother at all?" he asked.

"No." Which was fine with Kayleen.

"Perhaps you'll meet again one day," the king said.

"I would like that very much," Kayleen lied, knowing it was what the king wanted to hear.

Growing up, she'd been taught that it was her duty to forgive her mother and grandmother for abandoning her. She'd made peace with what had happened, but that didn't mean she wanted to be close now. Perhaps there *were* circumstances that, if explained, would help her understand. In truth, she wasn't interested enough to find out.

"So your past is the reason you were so against the three sisters being split up," the king said.

"Absolutely. They only have each other. They need to stay together."

"Because of you, they will."

She smiled. "Actually As'ad gets all the credit. He's the one who saved them. I'll always be grateful to him."

The king glanced at her. "I heard you rode into the desert and met with some of the villagers who live there."

"I did. I liked them a lot. It's an interesting way of life. Carrying one's roots wherever one goes."

"Most young women would be more interested in the elegant shops on our boulevards than in the desert."

She wrinkled her nose. "I'm not much into shopping." She'd never had the money for it to be serious sport and she doubted the stores the king spoke of had much in the way of bargains.

"Perhaps As'ad will take you one day," the king said.

"That would be fun, but it's not necessary. He's given me so much already."

"So you like my son?"

"Of course. He's a wonderful man. Charming and kind and patient." And a great kisser, but she wasn't going to mention *that* to the king.

"I am pleased to hear you are getting along," King Mukhtar told her. "Very pleased."

CHAPTER SIX

KAYLEEN WAVED AT Neil, As'ad's assistant, and when the man didn't lunge for her, walked past him and into the prince's office.

As'ad glanced up from his computer. "You have so intimidated my assistant that he has given up trying to stop you."

She laughed. "If only that were true. I won't stay long, I just…" She walked to the desk, started to sit down, then stopped. "I spoke with the king."

As'ad looked at her as if waiting for her point.

"Your father is a king," she said.

"Yes, I know."

"I don't. I can't be speaking with a king. That sort of thing doesn't happen to people like me. It doesn't happen to anyone. It's not normal."

"You live in the royal palace. What did you expect?"

"Not to be living here," she admitted. "It's too crazy. You're a prince."

"Again, information I have already obtained."

She sighed and sank into a chair. "You're not taking me seriously."

"You have given me no reason to. My father and I are who we have always been."

She nodded slowly. He'd grown up this way. It was impossible for him to grasp the incredibleness of the situation for her.

"I shouldn't have made you take the girls," she told him. "I didn't think the whole thing through. How they would change things for you."

He rose and walked around the desk until he was standing in front of her and she had to look way, way up to meet his gaze.

"You did not *make* me do anything."

She waved that away. "You know what I mean."

"Indeed, I do not. I was aware that adopting three American sisters would make things different and still I went forward."

Which made her wonder why he hadn't just dismissed her like an annoying gnat. Isn't that what princes did?

"I don't belong here," she told him. "I'm not used to this sort of thing."

He took her hand and pulled her to her feet. "I say who belongs and who does not."

"Off with my head?"

"That is not what I had in mind."

She knew he was going to kiss her even before he bent toward her and brushed his mouth against hers. She couldn't say how she knew, only that anticipation tightened her stomach and she forgot to breathe. Nothing else mattered but the feel of his lips on hers and the nearness of his body. He put his arms around her and drew her close.

It was like going home. The sense of belonging and safety. She'd never experienced that before and the sensation was so sweet, so perfect, she never wanted to be anywhere else. Then his mouth was moving on hers and she got lost in the kiss, the feel of his hands moving up and down her back. The heat of them. The way they pressed against each other, her body melting into his.

She put her hands on his upper arms and explored his muscled strength. When the pressure on her lips increased, she parted and was rewarded by the sensual sweep of his tongue across hers.

Somewhere along the way she must have remembered to breathe again because she moaned low in her throat. She felt tense and relaxed at the same time. She wanted this to never stop and she wanted more.

Without thinking, she rose on tiptoe, so she could press herself against him more fully. She tilted her head and kissed him back, teasing his tongue with hers.

His hands moved more urgently. One slipped to her rear, where he squeezed her curves. The contact shocked her, but excited her, too. Instinctively she arched forward, bringing her lower body in contact with his. He squeezed again, then moved his other hand to her waist before sliding it higher.

Anticipation chased away any hint of apprehension. His large hand settled on her breast with a confidence that allowed her not to be afraid. She broke the kiss so she could lean her forehead against his shoulder while he cupped her breast in his hand.

His touch was gentle and slow, but more wonderful than anything she'd ever experienced before. It was as if he knew the best way to touch her, to stroke her. When he moved his fingers across her nipple, she gasped and clung to him.

He moved his free hand to her chin, raised her head, then kissed her again. She held on to him as the room began to spin faster and faster. When he finally stepped back, she wasn't sure she could stay standing.

His eyes were dark as night, but bright with a fire that burned as hot as the one flaring inside of her. She'd never seen sexual need on a man's face before, but she recognized it now. Recognized it and knew that somehow she had caused it.

He wanted her. It was magic and filled her with delight and wonder and a sense of feminine power. Now if only she knew what to do with it.

"Kayleen."

He'd spoken her name dozens of times before,

but never with his voice so heavy and rumbling. She wanted this, she thought happily. She wanted this and so much more.

Somewhere in the distance she heard people talking. She remembered they were in his office and she had interrupted his day. The realization made her unsure of what to do next.

"I should, ah, probably go," she told him, wondering if he would ask her to stay.

"Do not worry about the king," he said instead. "My father is very pleased with you."

"How do you know? Have you talked to him?"

"I have no need. You are exactly what he wants you to be."

What? But before she could ask for an explanation, As'ad's phone rang. He glanced at his watch. "A teleconference with the British foreign minister."

"Right. Okay. I'll see you later."

She walked back to her room, wondering what it all meant. The kiss, the intimate touch, As'ad's comment that she was what the king wanted her to be. Did that mean a good nanny? A tidy guest?

Yet more reminders that this was a foreign world and not one she was likely to be comfortable in. She should be eager to escape. Yet there was a part of her that wouldn't mind staying for a very long time.

"YOU SUMMONED ME?" Lina asked as she breezed into the room. "And don't say you didn't. There was a definite command in your message."

"I won't deny it," As'ad told her, motioning to the sofa in the corner and joining her there.

"Am I to be punished?" she asked, a twinkle in her eye.

"You are my aunt and the woman who raised me. I have great respect for you."

"So I'm in *serious* trouble."

She didn't sound worried, but then why should she? He would never do anything to hurt her. Despite what she'd done, he had trouble being angry with her. Not that he would let *her* know that.

If he was annoyed with anyone, it was with himself for being too blind to see what was happening. It had been obvious from the beginning and he hadn't noticed.

"Shall you go first or shall I?" Lina asked.

"I called you here."

"I know, but that doesn't mean I don't have an agenda."

He nodded. "Please. Begin."

"I spoke with Zarina the other day. You claimed Kayleen as your own."

"For the moment. She created a stir in the village. I did not wish things to get awkward."

"You kissed her."

That damn kiss, he thought grimly. It had created nothing but trouble. The second kiss had been worse. Now he knew the passion between them had not been brought on by too many nights alone. It flared as bright and hot as the sun. He ached to claim Kayleen's body. But her innocence and position in his household made the situation complicated.

"To make a point," he said with a casualness he didn't feel.

"So that explains it," Lina murmured. "You have no feelings for her yourself."

None that he would admit to. "No."

"So if I wanted to introduce her to a pleasant young man, you would be agreeable?"

"I would," he lied, picturing himself ripping off the man's head. "But it will not be an issue."

"You're saying I don't know any young men, but you are wrong. I know several. One is an American. I mentioned Kayleen to him and he thought he would like to meet her. Did you know it's nearly Thanksgiving?"

"Nearly what?"

"Thanksgiving. It's an American holiday. I had forgotten myself, but the young man in question mentioned getting together with Kayleen that evening. They would both be missing home and could connect over that."

Missing home. Kayleen would, he thought, and

so would the girls. They would miss the traditional dinner.

"I will arrange it," he told his aunt.

"Kayleen's date?"

"Of course not. Thanksgiving dinner for her and the girls. A traditional meal. I'll speak with the head chef right away." He turned his attention back to his aunt. "As for your young American, I doubt he exists."

"Of course he does."

"Perhaps, but he is not intended for Kayleen. You have other plans for her."

"I have no idea what you're talking about. But while we're on the subject, Kayleen is lovely, isn't she? I met her the first time I volunteered at the orphanage. She'd been here all of two weeks and yet had already settled in. I was impressed by her intelligence and her dedication to the children. She has many fine qualities."

"I will not marry her."

Lina narrowed her gaze. "No one has asked you to." Her voice was level enough, but he saw the temper in her eyes.

"You would not ask," he told her. "But you have gone out of your way to throw her in my path. Tell me, was Tahir a part of your plan? Did you arrange for him to come to the orphanage and set the events in motion?"

"I have no idea what you're talking about, but if I did, I would point out Kayleen would be a good mother. Her sons would be strong. You have to marry someone. Why not her?"

Why indeed? A case could be made for his aunt's logic. Kayleen may not have been born royal, but sometimes that was an advantage. She had an inner strength he respected—it was her heart that made him wary.

"She cares too much," he told his aunt. "She is too emotional."

"She's a woman."

"She leads with her heart. She deserves someone who can appreciate that."

Lina studied him for several seconds, then nodded. "All right. That's the one answer I can respect. It's too bad. I think she would have been good for you. Then we'll just have to find her someone else."

"She is the children's nanny."

"She deserves more than just a job. You were right, there's no young American man, but I'll find her someone." She rose and smiled. "Don't worry, As'ad. While I'm finding Kayleen a husband, I'll find you another nanny. You won't be inconvenienced."

Those should have been the words he wanted to hear, but something about them bothered him.

Something he couldn't define but that created a knot in the middle of his chest.

"WHAT IS IT?" As'ad asked, staring at the thick, flat cutout.

Dana grinned. "It's a turkey."

He eyed the layers of paper. "It is a turkey that has met with some unfortunate circumstances."

She giggled, then pulled the top over, creating a three-dimensional paper turkey. "It's a decoration," she told him. "They delivered a whole box of 'em. We can put them on the table and hang them from the ceiling." She glanced up at the curved, fifteen-foot ceiling. "Okay, maybe not the ceiling. But we'll put them all around."

"This is tradition?" he asked.

"Uh-huh. Along with the leaves."

The box with the flat paper turkeys had also included festive garlands in fall colors, along with silk leaves in red, brown and gold.

Pepper leaned over and grabbed a handful of leaves. "I'll put these on the table. We can make a line down the center of the tablecloth. It'll be pretty."

Nadine trailed after her younger sister, picking up the leaves that drifted to the floor. As'ad took a length of garland and followed them to the table.

"This will go on top of the leaves?" he asked.

Pepper grinned. "Uh-huh. And we need to have candles. Really tall ones. They're the prettiest." She set down her leaves, put her hands on her hips and looked at him. "How come you don't know this?"

"We don't celebrate Thanksgiving here."

Her blue eyes widened. "But you have to."

"They weren't discovered by pilgrims," Nadine told her. "America was the new world. It had to be found."

"It was lost?" Pepper asked.

"In a manner of speaking," As'ad said. "It's a celebration unique to your country. Although I believe the Canadians also celebrate Thanksgiving, but on a different day."

He waited while the two girls straightened out the leaves, then he set the garland on top. It was attractive, he thought. Very festive. Kayleen would like it. The surprise would make her happy.

He imagined her throwing herself at him, and him pulling her close. Then the vision shifted and changed so they were both naked and he was pushing his way inside of her as they—

"As'ad, what traditions do you have here?" Dana asked.

He forced his attention back to the present. This was not the time to explore sexual fantasies with the girls' nanny.

"We have many celebrations. There is the day the El Deharian armies defeated the Ottoman Empire. We also celebrate Christmas, although it is not as big a holiday here as it would have been for you back in the States."

Pepped sighed. "I worry about Santa being able to find us here."

"He'll find you and he'll enjoy the large fireplace in your room," As'ad told her. "It won't be so hard for him to get inside."

Her eyes widened. "Santa comes to the palace?"

"Of course."

"So I can write him a letter? I've been very, very good this year."

"Yes. You can write a letter. We'll arrange to have it sent through the royal post office, so it gets priority treatment."

The little girl beamed at him.

"Will there be snow at Christmas?" Dana asked as she set yet another paper turkey on the bookcase.

"We do not get snow here."

"I didn't think so." She shrugged. "I miss snow. We grew up in Michigan and we always had a white Christmas. We used to made snowmen and snow angels. Mom always had hot chocolate and cookies waiting."

"I don't remember her much," Pepper said in a whisper.

"Sure you do," Nadine told her. "She was tall and pretty, with blond hair."

There was a wistful, sad quality to her voice. It tugged at something in As'ad. Like Pepper, he had minimal memories of his mother. Perhaps his older brothers had more. He had never asked. Instead he'd been raised by a series of nannies when he'd been young and tutors when he was older. Then he'd been sent away to school. It was the expected life of a prince.

"I don't remember her," Pepper insisted, her eyes filling with tears.

He crouched in front of her. "You remember snow, don't you?"

She nodded slowly. "It's cold and white and it makes my nose red. I want snow for Christmas."

"It seems unlikely," he told her. "We live in the desert, on the edge of the ocean. This is not a cold climate. But it can still be very beautiful."

"We'll be fine," Dana told him bravely. "You'll see. It's just the change. Change is hard. For all of us."

"Agreed, but you are here now. This is where you will stay. Didn't Kayleen tell you?"

The girls exchanged glances, then looked at him.

"We don't know what we're going to do," Pepper told him. "We're supposed to stay here, with you, but what happens when Kayleen leaves?"

He straightened. "What are you talking about? She's not going anywhere."

"Yes, she is. She told us a long time ago." Dana drew in a breath. "She'll be twenty-five soon. When she's twenty-five she gets to go back to teach at the convent school where she grew up. It's what she always wanted. What we don't know is if we go with her or stay here with you."

LINA HOVERED BY the front of the palace, not an easy thing to do when there were tour groups lining up, official visitors arriving and she was well recognized. She supposed it would make more sense to wait in her rooms until she was notified that King Hassan was in residence. But she couldn't stand the thought of being confined right now. It was far easier to walk the length of the entryway—a distance of about two hundred feet—than walk back. If nothing else, she was getting her exercise for the day.

Part of the problem was she hadn't slept for a week. She'd barely dozed the previous night and had been wide awake at four in the morning. It had taken nearly a half hour with chilled gel packs on her eyes to reduce the puffiness. Then there had been the issue of what to wear.

She'd gone through her considerable wardrobe

more than once over the past few days. A dress seemed too formal, slacks too casual. In the end she'd settled on a black skirt and a silk blouse. She'd fussed over her makeup, her hair, her jewelry. It was like being sixteen again, but with all the baggage that comes with middle age. It was exhausting.

As she paced, smiled at visitors and did her best not to be recognized by the tour group moving into the palace, she told herself it was ridiculous to be so nervous. Officially she'd known King Hassan for years. But this was the first time he was coming to El Deharia to see *her*.

"It's not a date," she murmured to herself, grateful the vast entryway was finally almost empty. "It's a...a..." She sucked in a breath, not sure what his visit was.

A large SUV drove into the courtyard, followed by a dark Mercedes. Another SUV parked behind it.

Guards stepped out, looking stern in their business suits and sunglasses. One of them moved to the rear of the Mercedes and opened the passenger-side door.

Lina walked toward the car, telling herself to be calm, to smile and speak with at least the pretense of intelligence. King Hassan stepped out into the afternoon.

He was a man of medium height and strong

build. His hair was gray, as was his neatly trimmed beard. He had handsome features and an air of confidence and power about him. There were no outward symbols of his rank, yet just looking at him, it was easy to guess he wasn't like everyone else.

Lina hesitated. Normally she curtseyed when she greeted a monarch, yet that now seemed strange. Still, protocol and her upbringing won out.

But before she could offer the gesture of respect, Hassan stepped toward her, took both her hands in his and smiled at her.

"My dear Lina. You are more beautiful than I remember."

He gazed into her eyes. She stared back, seeing pleasure and humor, along with something very much like interest. Her stomach continued to flop around, but the reason changed from nerves to anticipation. A warmth stole through her and she smiled.

"Welcome, sir. All of El Deharia is pleased at your visit. Me, most of all."

He pulled her close and tucked her hand into the crook of his arm. "Hassan," he said. "You must call me Hassan. Do you forget how you mocked me in your e-mails? You can't be formal now."

They walked into the palace. "I never mocked

you," she told him, liking the feel of being next to him, close to him.

"You called me a crazy old man who was too concerned about his cats."

She laughed. "I did not. You're making that up."

"Perhaps."

He smiled at her, making her heart beat wildly and her throat get dry. It had been so long since any man had affected her, she thought happily. So long since she'd let herself notice a smile, a voice, a touch.

They walked along the main corridor, toward the elevators that would take them up to the guest floors.

"How is your first project coming?" he asked. "Has As'ad noticed the lovely Kayleen?"

"Absolutely." Lina grinned. "She got lost in the desert and ended up with some local tribesmen. As'ad went after her and claimed her for his own. He says it was to keep her safe, but I think there was more to it than that. When they got back, Kayleen specifically told me nothing had happened. She was so intent on telling me that, I knew something had."

"So you are a success."

"Not yet, but I hope to be soon."

They rode up three floors and exited onto a wide, open hallway.

"Your suite is just down here," Lina told him. "It is the one you stayed in before."

When they reached the double doors, she opened one and led the way in. The rooms were large, elegantly furnished and only used for kings and heads of state.

Fresh flowers filled several vases and a large fruit basket sat on the dining room table.

"I thought we could go out to dinner tonight," she said. "There are a couple of really nice restaurants in the city with private rooms. I can give the names to your head of security so he can check them out in advance. There are a few plays we could take in and a visiting European symphony, depending on what interests you most. My brother would be delighted if you would care to ride any of his horses and I—"

Hassan crossed to her and pressed his finger to her mouth. "You can stop talking now."

She drew in a breath, then pressed her lips together. "All right."

"I am not here to be entertained or to go riding. I am here to spend time with you. You have charmed me, Lina. I had not thought that would happen again in my lifetime and I am delighted to be wrong. I sense many possibilities."

Oh, my. The man had simply put it out there. Of course, he was a king and that could have something to do with his confidence level. If only she could say the same about herself.

"I, ah…" She swallowed. "Me, too."

He laughed, then pulled her close. "So let us see where this all leads."

And then he kissed her.

CHAPTER SEVEN

As'ad watched as several members of the kitchen staff set up the dinner. There was a large turkey, along with dishes of stuffing, yams, vegetables, mashed potatoes, gravy and several pies.

"I'm starving," Pepper whispered to Dana. "Can I have just a bite?"

"No," her sister told her. "We're waiting for Kayleen, remember? It'll just be a few more minutes."

Kayleen had phoned to say she'd received the message telling her to come to As'ad's room for dinner and would be right up.

As'ad did his best to focus on the girls, on how Pepper kept sniffing the air and how Nadine gracefully danced from foot to foot in impatience.

His plan had worked perfectly—the room was decorated, the meal prepared and Kayleen would be able to celebrate her country's holiday. Yet despite the success, he couldn't shake the deep sense of outrage that stirred within him.

She was leaving in a few months? Just like that?

She hadn't said anything to him, hadn't hinted.
He had hired her to be nanny to the three girls
she had insisted he adopt and now she was going
to disappear?

Equally insulting was the fact that Dana said
she didn't know if the sisters were staying or going.
As if it was their decision to make. He was Prince
As'ad of El Deharia. *He* decided who would stay
and who would leave. How dare Kayleen think she
could simply walk away without speaking to him.

He took out his anger on the bottle of Chardon-
nay he'd chosen for their dinner, jerking out the
cork with more force than necessary.

Did Kayleen think it was acceptable to leave
the girls so soon after bringing them to the palace?
Did she think they could bear another upheaval in
their lives? What about him? Was he to raise them
on his own?

He didn't know what annoyed him more—the
fact that she'd been making plans without consult-
ing him or the reality that she'd been considering
leaving in the first place. Not that he personally
cared if she went. His outrage was all for the girls,
and perhaps for the violation of her position. She
was the nanny. She reported to *him*.

Apparently she was not impressed enough with
his position and power. Obviously he needed to
show her what it meant to deal with someone in
the royal family.

He poured himself a glass of wine and drank it down. Even more annoying was her desire to cut herself off from the world. She did not belong in drab clothes, teaching at a convent school. What would happen to her there? Her bright spirit and fresh beauty would wither and die. She would grow old before her time.

It was up to him to change that. As her employer, he had a duty to protect Kayleen, even from herself. He knew best. At least here, in the palace, she would *live* her life. So how to convince her that she must stay, must serve him and be nanny to the girls?

He could order her, he thought as he poured a second glass of wine, then dismissed the idea as quickly as it formed. It pained him to admit the truth, but Kayleen was not one to take orders well, even from a prince. So he must convince her another way. He must make her see that there was more to her future than the high walls of a convent school. That there was much she would miss.

It would be one thing if she wanted to leave to live, he told himself. Perhaps to marry, although the idea of her with another man was irritating. Who would be good enough for her? Who would be patient with the unexpected virgin? Who would teach her the—

The thought formed. A solution. Perhaps unorthodox, but workable. He considered the possibilities and knew that it would be successful. A sacrifice, he thought, but not a hardship.

In time, she would thank him.

KAYLEEN WALKED INTO As'ad's rooms with her mind still on her work. She'd been making a lot of progress on the report he'd requested and had found out a lot of interesting information about the various reasons why some villages sent a lot of young women to college and some didn't. She wanted to discuss it all over dinner after they—

She paused, noting the room was especially dark, which didn't make sense. There had been lights in the corridor. Had she accidentally gone into the wrong room?

She reached for a switch on the wall, only to have all the lights come on, the three girls jump out from behind furniture and yell, "Surprise!"

Kayleen took a step back. "What are you up to? What's the surprise?"

And then she saw the paper turkeys covering every surface in the room. The festive fall garland, the leaves decorating the perfectly set table.

"It's Thanksgiving," Pepper said, rushing up and grabbing her hand. "We're having a real Thanksgiving dinner."

As'ad appeared. "The kitchen staff have done their best. They have never had a Thanksgiving dinner, so they apologize in advance if they didn't get everything exactly as you would have it."

Thanksgiving? Here? She'd willed herself not to think about the holiday, but it had been difficult and much of the day she'd felt sad. To walk into this was more than she could have imagined.

Dana and Nadine moved next to her. Kayleen crouched down to hug all three girls. Still holding them close, she looked up at As'ad.

"Thank you," she said, delighted by the surprise and feeling oddly emotional. "You're very thoughtful."

"I cannot take all the credit. Lina reminded me of the holiday and the girls helped with the preparations. Are you pleased?"

She rose and smiled at him. "Very. Thank you."

She'd never expected the gesture. As'ad wasn't who or what she'd expected. There was a kindness in him, a caring and sensitivity she hadn't thought possible. He was the classic handsome prince, yet he wasn't indifferent or selfish. He could have chosen to spend his life going to parties and hanging out with models and stars. Instead he worked hard and took in orphans.

It occurred to her that he was a good man, the sort of man she admired. The kind of man the Mother Superior had told her to look for when she left for college. Kayleen hadn't found anyone remotely fitting that description during her four

years away. How odd she should find him now…
here in El Deharia.

As'ad poured her a glass of wine as the girls
dragged her to the table. "What are you thinking?"
he asked, passing her the glass.

"That you're very unexpected."

"I could say the same about you."

His low voice made her insides quiver.

They served themselves from the buffet and
then settled at the table. Kayleen said grace, then
took her first bite of turkey.

"It's delicious. Dana, what do you think?" She
looked at the girl and was surprised to see tears
in her eyes. "What's wrong?"

"Nothing. This is nice. Thank you." A tear
rolled down her cheek.

Pepper was crying, as well, and Nadine was
sniffing into her napkin.

"I miss my mom and dad," Nadine whimpered.
"I want to go home and be with them."

"Me, too," Dana said, and turned her gaze to
As'ad. "You're the prince. Can't you do something?"

Kayleen felt helpless. What could she possibly
say to make the situation better? She felt awful
for the girls, because she understood what they
were going through. Holidays were always a mixed
blessing—she'd loved the specialness of the day,

but it had also reminded her of how alone she was. How she had no family, no one who loved her best.

As'ad put his arm around Dana, then kissed the top of her head. "If only I could," he said quietly. "I know your pain and can tell you with time, it will get better."

"You can't know that," the preteen told him, her voice thick with bitterness. "You can't know anything about it."

"I lost my mother when I was very young. Kayleen grew up with no family. We understand exactly what you are feeling."

Dana seemed to deflate. "That doesn't help. I know it should, but it doesn't. I want to go home."

As'ad stared at her for a long moment, then said, "When I was about your age, I ran away. I was angry at my father for not recognizing that I was growing up, practically a man. I was tired of being sent away to school every year, of being different. A prince. You'll find that out as you grow. To be royal defines one."

"I'm not royal," Dana told him.

He smiled at her. "You are now. You are my daughter."

Dana fiddled with her fork. "What happened when you ran away?"

"I decided to become a camel dealer."

All three of the girls stared at him. Kayleen tried not to laugh. "Really?" she asked.

"Yes. I thought I could make a good living selling camels. I took several from the royal stable, thinking I would use them to start my business."

Her lips twitched, but she was determined to be serious. "There's a royal camel stable?"

His dark gaze settled on her, seeming to caress her with a warm, tender touch. "Of course. There is a royal everything."

Pepper took a bite of turkey and chewed. "Can I see the royal camels?"

"Certainly."

"Do they look different than regular camels?" Nadine asked.

"They wear very small crowns."

Dana grinned. "They do not."

As'ad laughed. "You're right. But they are a special breed. And they are extremely stubborn. I did not know this when I first took them, but soon they were leading *me* into the desert, rather than the other way around."

Nadine giggled. Dana joined in. "What happened?" she asked.

As'ad wove a funny tale about a boy and four stubborn, angry camels, a lost night in the desert and many disasters. By the time he was done, all three sisters had finished their dinner, gotten seconds and were eyeing the pie. The tears were gone, as were the bad memories.

This is what they would remember about their

first Thanksgiving in El Deharia, Kayleen thought as she tucked them in and kissed them good-night. As'ad's story would be a part of their history and they would remember it and him for the rest of their lives.

He'd escorted them down to their suite and had waited while they got ready for bed. As she walked back into her living room, she saw he'd started a fire in the fireplace and made himself at home on the large sofa across from the flickering flames.

"It's not exactly chilly outside," she told him, knowing it made sense to sit next to him, but suddenly feeling shy.

"I thought you would appreciate the ambience. More memories of home, but happy ones I hope."

She walked over to the sofa and sat down at the far end. "There are a lot of happy ones," she said, then turned to him. "Thank you for tonight. For the surprise and for helping the girls through a difficult time. This is their first holiday season without their parents and it's going to be hard for them."

"They will need both of us to get through," he said.

"I agree." She was a little surprised that he saw it that way, though. "I didn't think you wanted much to do with them."

"They are charming girls with much potential. I find I enjoy spending time with them."

"I'm glad."

"And you?" he asked, his dark gaze seeming to see into her soul. "What do you think of them?"

"I adore them. Why do you ask?"

"Because you plan to leave them."

She opened her mouth, then closed it. Embarrassment made her stare at the fire. She battled guilt, as if she'd done something wrong. She knew she should have talked to him before—so he learned of her plans from her and not someone else. But she'd been afraid of what he would think of her.

"They told you," she murmured.

"Dana said you planned to return home on your twenty-fifth birthday. That you would lock yourself away and teach at the convent school."

When he said it, her dreams seemed small and pointless. "As you say, it's my home."

"A place we cannot always return to. What of your commitment to the girls?"

"I don't know," she admitted. "I haven't really thought anything through. This was planned a long time ago. I didn't expect to be their nanny."

"You are the one who insisted I adopt them. You *are* the most stable adult presence in their lives. Would you subject them to more upheaval by leaving them so soon after they came to be here? Are they nothing to you?"

"No. Of course not." She hated what he was saying. "I don't know what I was going to do. Of course I'd help you hire someone else. Someone to replace me."

"Would you? Or was your plan to take them with you?"

She ducked her head. "I thought of that, too."

"Did you think that would be allowed? This is El Deharia. No one may take royal children from the country without their parents' permission. I will not give it."

Kayleen could only stare at him. Of course. Thanks to her, he *was* their father and his rules applied. She hadn't thought that part through, either.

"It's all a mess."

"No decision has to be made now," he said. "We will find a solution together. Do you have any other secrets you are keeping from me?"

"What? No. Never. And I would have told you about leaving." She leaned toward him. "As'ad, I wasn't trying to trick you about anything. I was desperate for Tahir not to take the girls back to his village."

Somehow he wasn't at the far end of the sofa anymore, she thought as he reached out and lightly stroked her cheek. "I believe you."

"Good, because it's true. I just…" She had a hard time stringing words together. His touch was very distracting. "I love your country. It's beautiful. I love the modern city and the wildness of the desert. I love your people, the kindness of them.

You were right about Tahir only wanting to do the right thing, even if I don't agree with him. I've been learning so much about the villages while researching my project for you. This is an amazing place."

"But it is not home?"

She shook her head slowly. "I feel safe at the convent. That probably sounds stupid to a man like you."

"Feeling safe is important, especially when one did not grow up with that benefit. But there is so much more for you to experience than what you will find behind the convent walls."

"I like the convent walls."

"They lock you in."

"They shelter you."

He smiled gently. "From life. That is not a good thing."

Getting back had been her goal from the moment she'd been told she must leave and live in the world. Those words had broken her heart. It was like being thrown out of her home.

"Those walls protect me," she told him.

He looked at her intently. "*I* will protect you."

Then he leaned in and kissed her.

It was as if she'd been waiting for his kiss all her life. The second his mouth touched her, she felt both relief and an odd tension.

His lips were warm and firm, asking rather than

taking, making her want to give all that he asked
and more. He brushed against her, exploring, remembering perhaps. She remembered everything
about their heated kiss in the desert. The feel of his
body against hers, the hard planes and strength of
him. The way he'd held her so tenderly, the taste
and heat of him.

Those memories combined with the wonder of
his kiss to make her strain forward, as she eagerly
waited to experience it again. She parted without
being asked and was rewarded when he licked her
bottom lip before slipping inside.

He kissed her deeply, exploring all of her. She
put her hands on his shoulders, as much to steady
herself as to touch him, then kissed him back,
stroking, dueling, dancing. It was magical, something more wondrous than she'd ever imagined.
It was as if she were melting from the inside out.

Again and again he kissed her, taking his time,
making her feel as if the magic could go on forever.
He stroked her back, moving up and down. Oddly,
that touch made her want to squirm in place. If
only he would touch her breasts again, she thought
hazily. If only he would put his hands there, like
he had before.

And because that's what she wanted and because she trusted him fully, she let him ease her
onto the sofa, until she was nearly lying down.

He pulled back and stared into her eyes. "You

are so beautiful," he murmured before kissing her cheekbones, her nose, her forehead, then her jaw.

Beautiful? Her? She'd seen her reflection a thousand times. Sometimes she thought she might be pretty, but other times, she knew she was just like everyone else.

"Your skin is so soft and pale," he continued as he nibbled his way down her jaw to her neck. It both tickled and aroused, so she stayed very still, wanting him to continue forever.

"Then you blush and the fiery color delights me."

"I'm a redhead," she whispered. "Blushing comes with the package."

"It is a glorious package." He touched her hair. "So cool to the touch. I have fantasies about your hair."

"Seriously?"

"Seriously."

He kissed her again and she kissed him back, but all the while she was wondering what fantasies he could have about her hair? It was just hair, wasn't it? Long and wavy and very red.

He kissed her chin, then trailed down her neck. She'd never thought about a man's lips on her neck and was unprepared for the electric sensations that shot through her, making her toes curl and her insides tighten.

He put his hand on her belly. Even through the

layers of clothing, she felt the warmth and each individual finger. He moved up slowly, so slowly. Her breath caught in anticipation.

Touch me there, she whispered to herself, closing her eyes and waiting until he finally settled his palm on her breast.

The feeling was exquisite. She wanted more of that, but didn't know how to ask. He kissed her ear, which was a distraction, then nipped her earlobe, which was delicious. Everything felt so good that she barely noticed when he unbuttoned the front of her dress and eased the fabric open.

She supposed her first instinct should have been to cover herself, but she didn't want to. She wanted to know what it would feel like to have his hand there, on her breast, with only her bra between them.

And then she knew. He touched her gently, almost teasing, fingers lightly brushing her skin. He moved against her tight nipple. She groaned. It wasn't a sound she'd ever made before and she wanted desperately to have reason to make it again.

He explored both breasts, then reached behind her to unfasten her bra. He eased his hand under the cup and touched her again. This time bare skin on bare skin.

It was amazing, she thought, her body practically shaking. She hadn't known she was capable of such sensations. More. She wanted more.

More touching, more naked, more kissing, more everything.

As'ad drew back and stood. She opened her eyes and wondered what she'd done wrong. Why was he stopping? Then he bent down and picked her up in his arms. He cradled her against him and kissed her, even as he began to walk across the rug toward the bedroom.

It was the most romantic moment of her life. As they stepped into the darkness of her bedroom, she knew that she wanted to be with him, to experience making love with him. Perhaps there should have been questions or fears, but her mind was free of both. She only knew that her body seemed to recognize him and welcome him. He made her tremble and feel and she wanted more of that.

He lowered her to her feet, then closed the door behind them and turned on a bedside lamp. The light was dim, which was probably better, because as much as she wanted more, she was a little nervous about being naked. People did get naked when they made love, didn't they?

She thought about asking, but then he was kissing her again and speaking seemed really unimportant. His hands were everywhere, gently easing her dress from her shoulders so it puddled at her feet, then removing her bra.

Even as he stroked her tongue with his, he put both his hands on her breasts, cupping the curves and teasing her nipples with his thumbs. It was good—better than good. It was amazing.

Her body was suddenly a great unknown to her. She didn't have any idea about what she would experience next, but she wanted it all.

When he bent his head down and took her breast in his mouth, she gasped, then grabbed him to help herself stay standing. Fire roared through her, settling between her legs where the heat grew.

She knew the mechanics of what went on between a man and a woman, but she'd never imagined it could be so *good*. He moved back and forth between her breasts, licking them with his tongue, sucking until she wanted to scream. It was amazing and arousing and intriguing.

When he moved them to the bed, she went eagerly, wanting to know what else there could be, what other experiences she could have. He removed the rest of her clothes and she shocked herself by not minding that she was naked. Not when he stared down at her with a fire even she could see in his eyes.

"I want you," he breathed. "All of you. Kayleen, I want to touch you and taste you and be inside of you. But I will not take what isn't offered."

He had her at "I want you." She reached out to touch his hand, then gently tugged until he knelt next to her.

"You are eager?" he asked quietly.

"I'm shameless. I want you to touch me." She couldn't say the other stuff, but she was thinking it. She wanted to know what it was like to be with a man—to be with *him*.

He removed his shoes and socks, then shrugged out of his shirt. His chest was broad and muscled, with a light dusting of hair she itched to touch. Then he stretched out next to her and smiled.

"I will go slowly," he told her, tracing the shape of her mouth with his finger. "Tell me if anything frightens you or hurts you and I will stop."

"I know it's going to hurt when you, um, well, you know."

His smile faded. "It will, for a moment. Do you wish to stop?"

She shook her head.

"Good. Neither do I."

He took her hand in his and brought it below his waist. She felt the hard thickness of him.

"This is what you do to me," he told her. "This is what touching you does to me."

His words and his arousal filled her with a feminine power she'd never experienced before. It hadn't occurred to her that a man could *want* her that way. Or any way. A shiver raced through her as desire and anticipation both grew.

He leaned in and kissed her again. His hand settled on her stomach, an unfamiliar weight. She told herself not to think about it, but then he was moving down her belly to the apex of her thighs.

His touch was light and gentle, more teasing than insisting. When he reached the curls only slightly darker than her hair color, she wasn't sure what to do.

A single finger eased between the curls. It explored her, which was really sort of nice. She wouldn't mind him touching her more if he—

He brushed against the very center of her. She'd heard about that place, of course, but had wondered how she would ever know if she was touched there. Stupid question, she thought happily as delicious, erotic fire raced through her. She knew. How could she not know?

He moved against that place again and her legs fell open of their own accord. She found it difficult to breathe.

He continued to touch her there, moving lightly across that single spot, rubbing it, circling it, making her body tremble and heat and strain. She barely noticed when he stopped kissing her because his touch was so exquisite. She closed her eyes and let herself get lost in the sensation.

Around and around. He moved against her, going faster now. She found herself pulsing her hips in time with his touch. She strained but wasn't sure toward what. He bent down and took her nipple in his mouth. The combination of sensations made her gasp.

It was too much. A direct connection between her legs and her breasts. She grabbed at the sheets, trying to push herself toward…toward…

Her body tensed. She felt every muscle clench, which probably wasn't a good thing, but what he was doing felt too good for her to stop. Then time seemed to pause as she hovered on the brink of—

The wave of sensation caught her off guard. It was unlike anything she'd experienced before. Liquid pleasure poured through her as her muscles contracted. It was frenzied and amazing and she was terrified if she did anything at all, it would end suddenly.

But the moment went on and she lost herself in what she realized was her first orgasm. She allowed herself to breathe and the bliss continued. Tension faded, muscles relaxed, until she felt content and satisfied and more than a little shocked such a thing was possible.

As'ad moved his fingers away. She opened her eyes and stared up at him.

"I want to do that again," she told him.

He laughed. "So you enjoy the lovemaking?"

"Who wouldn't? Can that happen again? Can it happen now?"

He rose onto his hands and knees. "As you wish,

Kayleen. We will try another game. But a gentle one. I don't want you to hurt later."

Later was a long time away, she thought as he settled between her legs and gently parted her curls.

It was obvious he was going to kiss her *there,* which was shocking and something she probably should refuse. Except what he'd done before had been so amazing. Could this be as good?

She sank back onto the bed and closed her eyes. A soft whisper of breath was her only warning, then his mouth pressed against her and his tongue touched her more intimately than she'd ever thought possible.

It was like kissing, but a billion times better, she thought as all the air rushed from her lungs. The steady flick of his tongue was impossible to resist. She gave herself over to the sensation, to the tension that quickly tightened all her muscles. Despite the awkwardness of the position and her lack of experience, she found herself pushing toward the pleasure goal.

She wanted that experience again. She wanted the waves, but this time from his tongue. She wanted him to push her higher and closer and she wanted it now!

She found herself digging her heels into the bed as she pushed her body against him. Impatience battled with arousal. The journey was exquisite, but the destination was—

He slipped a finger inside of her. The action was shocking enough to make her gasp. She waited for pain or pressure, but there was only the need to push down on that finger, to have him fill her.

He continued to lick her, making her body tense more. Then he moved his finger in and out, matching the rhythm of his tongue, taking her up and up and up until she had no choice but to crash back to earth.

The second journey down was even better than the first. She felt herself cry out and tried to stifle the noise. Her body shuddered as her release filled every cell and pleasured every nerve. It was too much. She hadn't known that anything like this was possible.

As'ad straightened, then moved next to her. He touched her all over, caressing, but perhaps reassuring. She stared into his dark eyes.

"I didn't know," she whispered.

"There is more."

That made her laugh. "Not possible."

"I will show you."

Would he? Could they explore this together? "I'd like that."

He stroked her face. "What is your wish, Kayleen? For me to leave now? You remain an innocent."

"Technically," she murmured, although she knew a whole lot more than she had an hour ago. She gathered her courage and put her hand on his bare chest. His skin was smooth, his muscles hard. "Be in me."

"You are sure?"

She smiled. "Very."

He pulled her into a sitting position, then stood beside the bed. After removing his slacks and briefs, he stood in front of her.

She'd never seen a man naked before. Art really didn't count. He was bigger than she'd expected.

She stroked the length of him, liking the velvety smoothness of the skin and the way he felt like a rock underneath.

"You're not going to fit," she told him as she wondered if women did to men what he had done to her. Touching with their mouths. Would that be nice?

He chuckled and reached for his slacks. "It will fit."

He removed a square of plastic, then sat on the bed. She was going to ask what he was doing, then remembered that the act itself had consequences. He was making sure she had nothing to worry about.

She was about to ask him why he had a condom in his pocket, then he eased her onto her back and slipped between her legs.

The position felt a little strange and she didn't know what to do with her feet or her hands. Did she just lie there? Was she supposed to move? Should she keep quiet or did people talk?

"This will hurt a little," he warned. "You are prepared?"

She nodded and braced herself.

He smiled. "Perhaps you could pretend you are excited."

"What? Oh, sorry. I'm just nervous."

"Perhaps I can distract you."

He reached between her legs and began to rub her again. She immediately relaxed as the familiar tension started. If he kept that up for very long, she would come again.

But before she could get far along the path, he stopped and she felt something hard pushing against her. She took a deep breath as he slowly, slowly filled her.

The pressure was unfamiliar and a little uncomfortable, but not bad. There was more and more until at last he said, "I am in."

She opened her eyes and smiled at him. "I'm wild now."

He smiled in return. "It will take a little more for you to be wild, but this is a start. I would like you to touch me."

Oh. "All right," she murmured, not sure where or how.

She stroked the length of his arms, then put her hands on his back. He withdrew and pushed in again. This time she tilted her hips slightly, taking him more easily.

By the fifth time, she didn't have to think about the touching—it just happened on her own. And there was a subtle tension between her legs. Different from what happened before, but still compelling.

She closed her eyes and lost herself in the rhythm of him making love to her, filling her, pushing deep inside of her, making her ache and want. He moved faster and his breathing increased. More and more until he groaned and was still.

He murmured her name as he held her. She wrapped her arms around him, feeling the weight of him, a stretch in her hips, and knew that everything had changed forever.

CHAPTER EIGHT

KAYLEEN SPENT THE following morning not sure what to think. Her evening with As'ad played over and over in her mind like a very naughty movie. Every time she remembered him touching her, she felt all squishy inside.

She hadn't expected to sleep, but after he'd gone back to his room, she'd fallen into her bed and the next thing she knew it was morning. She'd awakened happy and sore and just a little out of sorts. She didn't regret what had happened, but she certainly felt…different.

As'ad had been so great, she thought as she waved to the girls as they climbed into the Town Car that took them to school each day. He'd been gentle and patient and funny and sexy. He'd been everything she could have imagined a man being. More, she reminded herself. He was *better* than anything—or anyone—she could have imagined.

And the whole being together thing had been amazing. Who had thought that up? Why hadn't she understood before? Was this what her Mother Superior had meant about getting out in the world?

Kayleen covered her mouth. She doubted that was exactly what the other woman had meant. Still, she understood now that there were possibilities. Things she'd never known about. Did she want to give up that kind of a relationship forever? Did she want to get married and have a family? Did she—

"Good morning, Kayleen. How are you?"

She looked up and saw Lina walking toward her. Kayleen had the sudden thought that the other woman knew. That everyone knew. It had to be obvious, didn't it? Could they tell? Was her appearance different? Was there something in her eyes?

The crash of guilt was as powerful as it was unexpected. Yes, her night with As'ad had been wonderful and exciting, but what was she thinking, giving herself to a man like that? They weren't in love. She wasn't sure she knew what being in love with a man felt like. So she'd just given herself to him? Why? Because he'd made her feel good? Would she give herself to anyone who asked?

"Kayleen?" Lina frowned. "What's wrong? Are you ill?"

"I'm fine," she said, trying to act normal, which was difficult. She suddenly couldn't remember what normal was.

"What happened? You're flushed. Are you sure you feel all right?"

Kayleen ducked her head. Guilt quickly turned to shame as she realized she was not the person she'd always thought. "I'm not sick. It's nothing. I just… I can't… I have to go. Please excuse me."

She turned and ran, but no matter how fast she went, she couldn't escape herself.

AS'AD FINISHED WITH his tie and reached for his jacket. The door to his suite burst open and Lina stepped inside. He raised his eyebrows.

"I did not hear you knock," he said mildly, in too good a mood to mind the intrusion. Last night he had shown Kayleen the possibilities. She would quickly realize that returning to the convent school was not the right path for her. She would want to stay in the world—in *his* world. All would be well and very shortly she would come and thank him.

Perhaps they could continue to be lovers, he thought absently. He had enjoyed his time in her bed. She had been passionate and responsive. Just thinking about her soft cries made him want her again. They could pleasure each other and—

"I can't believe it," Lina said, stepping in front of him, her expression stern. "I can't believe you did it."

He shrugged into his jacket. "Did what?"

"You slept with Kayleen."

He shrugged. "It is not for you to criticize."

"What?" Her voice was high-pitched and carried a tone that warned him there was danger ahead.

He decided to change tactics. "Kayleen is nearly twenty-five. While it is very kind of you to be concerned about her welfare, she is more than capable of taking care of herself."

Lina put her hands on her hips. "Are you kidding me? That's it? That's all you have to say? As'ad, you are a prince. You defiled a virgin under the king's roof. You don't get to escape by telling me she's an adult and therefore responsible for her decisions."

Defiled a virgin? Did she have to say it like that? He shifted uncomfortably. "I did not take anything that wasn't offered."

"Oh, there's an excuse."

"Lina, you will not speak to me this way."

"Of course I will." She glared at him, her outrage clear. "As'ad, I am Kayleen's friend. I brought her into this house. I'm responsible for her."

"You wanted me to marry her."

"I considered it a possibility. I thought you would be a good match. You weren't supposed to take her virginity. She was raised by nuns. She's nearly twenty-five and has had what, a dozen dates?"

He refused to feel guilty. He was Prince As'ad

and because of that, whatever he chose to do was the right thing. And yet there was a nagging voice in the back of his head that pointed out he hadn't thought things through.

"She planned to return to the convent school," he told Lina. "She was going to bury herself there."

"So you decided to change that? If you don't want her, who are you to destroy her life?"

"Her life is not destroyed." He resented the implication. "I honored her."

"Oh, please. It was never for you to decide what she did with her life. It was never for you to judge. You took the one thing she would want to give her husband. Now she can't go back to the convent school and you'll have no use for her. Then what? She's ruined, As'ad, and you did it. Kayleen isn't the type to take that lightly. She had choices before. You've taken them away from her."

He turned from his aunt and walked to the French doors leading to the balcony. While Lina made things more dramatic than they needed to be, he understood her point.

He'd wanted Kayleen and he'd taken her. It had happened before—dozens of times. Hundreds. Women were always delighted to be with him. But there was a large difference between them and Kayleen. The women he enjoyed were experienced. They understood how the game was played. Kayleen didn't even know there was a game.

She had given herself eagerly, sensually. She'd enjoyed their lovemaking. He'd opened her eyes to the possibilities, but he had also taken something that couldn't be returned.

His aunt's words echoed in his head. That he had defiled a virgin under the roof of the king. There was a time when, prince or not, such an offense would result in his death. Virginity was a prize to be given to a husband. It was a gift of honor. Something she had no more.

He turned back to Lina, intent on explaining, once again, that he'd only had Kayleen's best interests in mind. That it was important that she not lock herself away and ignore the world. But was that his only motivation?

Had there been some part of him that had wanted to be her first time? Some part of him that had wanted to claim her for himself because he knew he could?

"I will marry her," he said firmly, the words surprising him. He paused, waiting for the sense of being trapped to rise up inside of him. Waiting for the protests he must feel, but there was nothing.

It occurred to him that because he did not plan to love his wife, Kayleen was an excellent choice. As good as any other he could think of. He already liked her. She was spirited and beautiful, he enjoyed her company. She was good with children and had a sharp mind. While she knew nothing of the lifestyle of a royal bride, she would learn quickly. She would provide him with strong sons. And just as important, she was not the type to make unreasonable demands. She would be grateful for his proposal and treat him with respect.

Lina stared at him. "You'll what?"

"I will marry her. I accept my responsibility in what has occurred. Kayleen deserves more than having her gift taken in a thoughtless manner. While she gave herself to me willingly, I do not believe she had thought through the ramifications of our night together."

"That's why they call it 'swept away,'" Lina murmured, then nodded slowly. "You are sure?"

"I will speak to her this morning. I have a meeting in fifteen minutes, but after that I will explain what has to be done. She is a sensible woman. She will understand the great honor I bestow upon her and be pleased."

"How I wish I could be there for that conversation."

"Why do you say that?" he asked.

His aunt smiled at him. "I would tell you to phrase things differently, but you won't listen. For what it's worth, I think you have chosen well, As'ad. I hope things work out the way you want them to."

"They will. I am asking Kayleen to marry me. What more could she want?"

Lina's smile widened. "I can't think of a single thing."

KAYLEEN RAN AND ran until she found herself outside. The bright, sunny morning seemed to be mocking her as she wandered through the curving paths. How could everything here be so beautiful when she felt so awful inside?

What had she done? How could she have slept with As'ad? A few kisses and she'd given in? What did that make her?

She found a bench and sat down. The stone was warm to her touch, almost as if it were trying to offer comfort. Her eyes burned as she longed for someone to talk to. Someone to advise her. But who? She didn't feel comfortable discussing something so personal with the other teachers she'd worked with. Especially after moving to the palace. She was too ashamed to call her Mother Superior back home. Normally she would go to Lina, but how to explain to her what she'd done? As'ad was Lina's nephew.

Besides, Kayleen couldn't bear to see disappointment in her friend's eyes.

All the regrets she'd been so happy not to feel seemed to crash in on her. Not regret for what she'd done, but for the consequences, which made her horribly weak. Her regrets were about her future, not her past.

How could she return home now? How could she walk into that place where she'd grown up and had longed to return, knowing she had given in to the first man who asked? It wasn't that she feared punishment, it was that she didn't know who she was anymore.

She stood abruptly and started walking. An odd sound caught her attention.

She turned toward it and saw a large cage filled with doves. They were beautiful, so white and lovely in the sunlight. She watched them hop from perch to perch.

Her dream was gone, she thought. Her plans, her hopes. Now she was trapped here. Nanny to the girls until they were too old to need her or until As'ad replaced her. She was at his mercy. And then what? Another job? Where? Doing what?

She didn't know who she was anymore. What she wanted. What she should do.

Impulsively she leaned toward the cage and opened the door. The doves chirped in excitement, then in a rush, flew out and up, disappearing into the brilliant blue sky.

"Fly away," she whispered. "Fly and be free."

"I do that myself."

Kayleen jumped and turned toward the speaker.

She was stunned to find the king standing on the path.

Horror swept through her. She'd just set free royal doves.

"I... I..."

King Mukhtar smiled kindly. "Don't worry, child. It's difficult to resist setting them loose. There is no need for concern. They always return. It is their nature. This is their home. They can't escape their destiny."

She knew he meant the words to be reassuring, but they cut through her. Yesterday she had known her own destiny, but today she was less sure. What was her place? Where did she belong? What happened now?

"Are you enjoying living at the palace?" the king asked. "You are treated well?"

His question nearly made her laugh. But she was afraid that if she started to laugh, she wouldn't stop and then she would start crying. Hysterics would lead to a lot of questions she didn't want to answer.

"Everything is lovely," she said, doing her best to keep her emotions in check. "The palace is beautiful. I've been studying the history of the building and of your people. There is a long tradition of bravery in battle."

"The desert runs in our blood. We were warriors long before we were rulers."

"It must be difficult to leave the desert," she told him. "The beauty, the wildness, the tradition. The nomads live as they always have."

"With few modern conveniences," he said with a smile. "Much can be endured if one has excellent plumbing."

She gave a little giggle, which seemed to take a sharp turn at the end. She swallowed the sound. "But to walk in the steps of those who have gone before would be a fair compensation."

"So says the woman who has not experienced desert life. Spend a week with my people and then we will have this conversation again."

She nodded. "I would like that."

She spoke the truth. There was something appealing about simplicity right now. About having the rules of one's life spelled out. Too many choices could be complicated.

If she had never left the convent school in the first place, she wouldn't have met As'ad and none of this would have happened. Yet was it equally wrong to hide from the world? To take the safe and, therefore, easy road? To never test herself? Is that what she'd been supposed to learn?

"I just don't know," she said.

The king looked quizzical. "What troubles you, child?"

"Nothing." She felt tears burning in her eyes. "I… I'm sorry. I don't feel well. Please excuse me."

She gave a little bow, then hurried away. When she'd taken a turn in the path and knew she was out of sight, she began to run. The only problem was there was nowhere else to go.

AS'AD WALKED TO Kayleen's suite, knocked, then entered. He found her in her room, curled up on the bed, sobbing as if her heart was broken.

He stared at her for a moment, feeling both compassion and a sense of certainty that his good news would erase her tears. He allowed himself to anticipate her sweet kisses when he proposed. How she would be so excited and grateful. Perhaps they would make love again. He was more than ready, although he would have to be careful so that he did not hurt her. She was new to the sensual world and too much attention in too short a time would leave her sore.

He walked to the side of the bed. "Kayleen."

"Go away."

"I will not. Sit up. I wish to speak to you."

"No. I don't want to talk. This isn't your problem."

"Of course it is. I caused it."

She continued to cry, which surprised him. She'd seemed fine when he'd left her last night. A woman should not be left alone with her thoughts. It only created trouble.

"Kayleen—"

"Go *away.*"

He considered the situation, then sat on the edge of the bed and pulled her upright. She ducked her head, refusing to look at him. He drew her against him.

"It is not as bad as all that."

"Of course it is." Her body shook with the force of her sobs. "I have betrayed everything I believe in. I'm not the person I thought. I gave myself to you without thinking it through. I barely know you. I don't love you. You're just some guy. What does that say about me?"

Some guy? He was Prince As'ad of El Deharia. He was royal and a sheik. Women *begged* him to claim them for just a single night.

"I honored you," he told her curtly.

"It wasn't an honor to me."

What? He pushed away his annoyance. She was emotional, he told himself. She wasn't thinking clearly.

"Kayleen, we share a connection with the girls. You see me as a friend and someone you can trust. It is natural you would turn to me easily."

She looked at him, her eyes swollen and red. "It's not natural to me. I'm supposed to wait until I'm in love and married."

"Sometimes it is difficult to resist the pull of sensual need."

She hiccuped. "You're saying I gave in because

I wanted to do it and you just happened to be there? That's supposed to make me feel better?"

Why was she deliberately misunderstanding him? "Not at all," he said through gritted teeth. "I'm saying that I am an experienced man. I know what to do to awaken that part of a woman."

"So you tricked me? While I appreciate the effort, it's not working. I have a responsibility in this. I have to deal with what happened, what I did and what it says about me."

"I did not trick you."

She shifted away and stood. "Whatever. You can go now."

"I am not leaving," he said as he rose to his feet. "Kayleen, you are missing the point of my visit."

She wiped her cheeks with her fingers. "What's the point?"

Not exactly the opening he'd imagined. He cleared his throat. "It occurs to me that you were not in a position to consider the ramifications of what happened to us. You were lost in the moment, not realizing that by giving in to me you were destroying your most precious gift and—"

Fresh tears filled her eyes. "How could you?" she breathed and ran into the bathroom, slamming the door behind her.

He stared in disbelief. She'd walked away from him?

He followed her to the closed door. "Kayleen, please come out here at once."

"Go away. I have to figure this out and you're not helping."

He opened the door and stepped into the bathroom. "You will listen to me. I am here to make this better. I am here to fix your problem."

She shook her head. "You can't fix anything. I've lost everything I wanted."

"You have lost nothing. You are not a woman to be locked away. You deserve more than that and I am going to give it to you. Think of being married, of having a family to fill your day, children of your own." He paused to give her a chance to brace herself for the honor he would bestow upon her.

"Kayleen, I will marry you."

He smiled at her, waiting for her tears to dry. Instead more fell. Perhaps she did not understand.

"You will be my wife. You will live here, with me. In the palace. I have taken your virginity, therefore I will return your honor to you by marrying you. You will carry my name."

He waited, but she said nothing. She didn't even look at him.

"All right. I see you are having trouble understanding all this. It is unlikely you ever allowed yourself to dream of such a life. In time you will be able to believe this has truly happened. Until then, you can thank me and accept. That is enough."

She raised her gaze to stare at him. Something hot and bright burned in her eyes, but it wasn't happiness or gratitude.

"Thank you?" she repeated, her voice high and shrill. "*Thank* you? I'm not going to thank you. I wouldn't marry you if you were the last man alive."

He was so stunned that when she shoved him, he took a step back. The bathroom door slammed shut in his face and he heard the bolt shoot home.

CHAPTER NINE

"TAKE ANOTHER DRINK of tea," Lina said soothingly.

Kayleen wrinkled her nose. The brew was a nasty herbal concoction that tasted like wet carpet smelled, but her friend assured her it would help. At this point, Kayleen was open to any suggestions.

She finished the mug and set it on the table, then grabbed a cookie she didn't want to get the taste out of her mouth.

"Better?" Lina asked.

Kayleen nodded because it was expected. In truth she didn't feel better, she felt awful. She still couldn't get herself to understand what had happened or how she'd so quickly and easily lost her moral compass. Yes, As'ad was handsome and charming and an amazing kisser, but she should have been stronger than that.

Lina sighed. "I can see by the look on your face that you're still beating yourself up. You need to let it go. Men like my nephew have been tempting women since the beginning of time."

"It's not that I don't appreciate the information," Kayleen murmured. "It's just..."

"It doesn't help," Lina said kindly.

"Sort of. I feel so stupid and inexperienced."

"At least you're more experienced than you were."

Despite everything, Kayleen smiled. "That's true. I won't fall for that again. Next time, I'll resist."

Assuming there was a next time. Her last meeting with As'ad had ended badly. He had to be furious.

"He was serious about marrying you," Lina told her. "Don't dismiss that."

"I didn't have a choice. He didn't propose—he commanded, then he expected me to be grateful. I know he's part of your family and you love him, but that wasn't a proposal, Lina. He's just so..."

"Imperious?"

"Among other things."

And it hurt, Kayleen admitted to herself. That he would talk to her that way. If he'd come to her with compassion, truly understanding what she was going through, she would have been appreciative of what he offered. She might have been tempted to say yes. At least then her world would have been set right. But to act the way he did?

"I understand," Lina said. "As'ad is like most princes—used to being impressive. He handled the situation badly and violated your romantic fantasy at the same time."

Kayleen frowned. "I don't have a romantic fantasy."

"Don't you?"

An interesting question. She'd never really thought about getting married and having a family, so she'd never really thought about a proposal. But if she had, it would have been different. Flowers and candlelight and a man promising to love her forever.

The image was clear enough to touch, she thought ruefully.

"Okay, maybe I did. Maybe I didn't allow myself to believe it would ever happen, but deep down inside, I wanted more than instructions and an order to feel grateful."

Lina winced. "That bad?"

"Oh, yeah. The only good news is I slammed the bathroom door in his face. I don't think that happens to As'ad very much." She touched her stomach, as if she could rub away the knot that had formed inside. If As'ad was angry enough, he could send her away and she might never see the girls again. "How mad is he?"

"He's less angry and more confused. From his perspective, he did a wonderful thing."

Kayleen resisted the need to roll her eyes. "I'll write a thank-you note later."

"His world is a different place," Lina said quietly. "Like his brothers, he has been raised to know that he will be expected to serve his country, that his life, while privileged, comes with a price. Growing up it was difficult for him to know who truly wanted to be friends because they liked him, and who wanted to be friends with a prince. He made mistakes and slowly learned whom he could and could not trust."

Kayleen could relate to the pain of not having real friends, of wanting to find a place that was safe.

"But he had his brothers."

"Yes, and that helped. Still, as he got older, there were many girls, then women, willing to do anything to make him fall in love with them. Or at least sleep with them."

Kayleen felt heat on her cheeks. "Like me."

"Not like you at all. You didn't throw yourself at him or pretend to be interested. You were caught up in circumstances. As'ad shares blame in what happened. I'm simply saying he has a different perspective. While his proposal was meant to be the right thing, he handled it badly. As'ad isn't skilled in dealing with emotion. His father saw to that. He was taught that emotions make a man weak. He avoids them."

Kayleen had heard that from him and still found it hard to believe anyone could think of love as a weakness. Love gave a person infinite power and strength.

"Is there any part of you that wants to marry As'ad?" Lina asked.

The question was unexpected. Kayleen considered her reply. "It seems the easy way out."

"Which does not give me an answer."

Did she want to marry As'ad? In truth, the idea wasn't horrible. He was a nice man and the thought of spending every night in his bed was thrilling beyond words, which probably meant she was in even worse shape than she'd first thought.

But there was more to marriage than the physical, she thought. There was a lifetime of connection. Did she want to have children with As'ad? Be a true mother to the three girls? Live in El Deharia forever?

The swell of longing surprised her. The need to belong—to have roots and a home—swept over her until it was difficult to breathe. She'd been on the outside looking in all her life. To be inside now was more than she'd ever dreamed. But to marry without love?

"I'm tempted," she admitted. "Marrying As'ad would give me so much. But I'm not in love with him."

"Practical marriages are a time-honored tradition," Lina reminded her.

"I'm not royal. He's a prince. Doesn't that matter?"

"The old ways have changed. Now a prince may pick his bride. You have qualities such as honor, intelligence and kindness that make you everything I could want for As'ad."

The gentle praise made Kayleen want to cry again. "Thank you," she whispered.

"There is more to consider," Lina said. "As the wife of a prince, you would be in a position to do good on a grand scale, both here and in the world. You could devote yourself to many worthwhile causes, assuming you have time after you and As'ad start to have children."

Lina painted a picture that was difficult to resist. "Allow me to use some of the intelligence you claim I have to point out you're manipulating me."

Lina smiled. "Perhaps a little, but not as much as I could. If I truly wanted to convince you against your will, I would tell you that As'ad needs you. He needs someone who will love him unconditionally and teach him how important love is."

"I don't love him."

Lina's smile never wavered. "Perhaps you are right, but I'm not convinced. I know you, Kayleen. You wouldn't give yourself lightly to a man. I think you have feelings for As'ad and it won't take much for them to grow. Everyone deserves love. Give him his and in time, he will give you yours."

242 THE SHEIK AND THE CHRISTMAS BRIDE

The idea of being loved was much more powerful than the fantasy of being a princess. Yes, the palace was lovely, but Kayleen would be content to live in a trailer at the ends of the earth if she could be with a man who truly loved her.

Was Lina right? Did she, Kayleen, have feelings for As'ad? Did he need her to care for him?

"What are you thinking?" Lina asked.

"That I don't know what to do."

"Then we are in a good place to start finding that out."

KAYLEEN FORCED HERSELF to go to As'ad's office because it was the right thing to do. She knew that he had only been trying to help and the fact that he'd done it so badly didn't excuse her behavior or take away his intent. Still, it was embarrassing to face him again after her emotional outburst. She'd slammed a door in his face, both figuratively and literally. He might not be so happy to see her.

She walked into his office. Neil, his assistant, didn't immediately throw her out, which she considered a good sign.

"Is he available?" she asked.

"Perhaps. Just a moment." Neil buzzed As'ad and announced her. There was a pause before Neil said, "You may go in."

Kayleen nodded, then braced herself and opened the door.

The prince rose as she entered. He wore a suit, which was typical, yet everything about him seemed different.

Maybe it was because she *knew* him. She'd touched his bare skin, had been as intimate with him as it was possible to be. She knew his heat, his taste, his sound. She knew what he could do to her and how she could make him react. Nothing was as it had been and she wondered if it would ever be the same again.

"Kayleen."

His voice was low, his dark eyes unreadable.

Their last meeting was a blur. She'd been beyond upset, still reeling from the reality of what she'd done. While she'd tried to explain that her feelings were about herself and not him, she wasn't sure he'd understood or believed her. Oddly, she didn't want him to feel bad.

She crossed her arms over her chest, then dropped her hands to her sides. The silence stretched between them. It occurred to her that he might be feeling a little awkward after the way she'd rejected him.

Was that possible? Did a prince get upset when his proposal of marriage was thrown back in his face? She couldn't decide if As'ad was too arrogant to feel rejection or if the lack of it in his life left him unprepared for the sensation.

"I'm sorry," she told him, meeting his gaze.

"You came to me in good faith and made a generous offer. I handled the situation badly. I know you meant well and I should have acknowledged that. You were trying to do the right thing."

"I was," he agreed. "But I have blame, as well. I could have phrased things differently and not been so..."

"Imperious?" she offered.

"That is not the word I would have chosen."

"And yet it fits perfectly."

His gaze narrowed slightly. "Your apology seems to be lacking humility."

"Humility has never been a strength for me. Yet another flaw."

"You have much to recommend yourself, Kayleen. That is what I should have told you before."

Had he always been so good-looking? she wondered as she got caught up in his eyes. His features were perfectly balanced and his mouth...just looking at it made her remember kissing him over and over again.

Weakness invaded her legs, making it suddenly difficult to stand. Fortunately As'ad took her arm and led her to the sofa at the far end of his large office. When she was seated, he settled next to her.

He smiled. "You challenge me."

"Not right now."

"True, but let's give it a minute. You have done well with the girls."

"They mean a lot to me."

He touched her cheek. "I do not want to see you lock yourself behind convent walls. In my arrogance, I chose to make that decision for you. I chose to seduce you so that you couldn't return. It was wrong of me and I apologize."

She opened her mouth, then closed it. He'd planned it? All of it? "You slept with me on purpose? You weren't caught up in the moment?" The information stunned her and hurt quite a bit.

"I was more than caught up," he told her. "You bewitched me."

"I don't think so."

He cupped her chin, forcing her to look at him. "I assure you, my desire for you remains as fiery as ever."

There was a light in his eyes, a need she recognized. Her insides clenched and she found herself wanting to be with him again. The hurt faded.

"I took away your choices," he told her. "I decided for you and that is wrong."

"An apology is enough," she muttered, wishing she could look away from his intense gaze.

"It is not."

"Marriage is a pretty high price to pay for poor judgment."

One corner of his mouth lifted. "I said I was wrong to decide *for* you. I never said there was anything wrong with my judgment."

"What?"

He released her chin only to take her hand in his. "Kayleen, I am a man in need of a wife. I need someone who understands what it is to give with her whole heart, who will love the girls and El Deharia and my people. I need someone who cares more about what is right than the latest fashions or how many pieces of jewelry she has in her possession. A woman I can respect, who will stand up to me and yet be by my side. I need *you*."

She heard the words. Her heart was still beating, she could hear that, too, and feel his hand on hers. And yet it was like she'd left her body and was watching the moment from somewhere else. Because there was no way this was really happening to her. Princes didn't propose to her. Normal guys didn't even want to *date* her.

"But…"

"Do you doubt my sincerity?" he asked. "I cannot promise to be the most perfect husband, but I will try to be all you wish me to be. I need you, Kayleen. Only you."

Need. The word was magic. To be needed meant to never be abandoned. She would have a home, a husband, a family. As Lina had pointed out, she could help people and make a difference in the world. Her—some no-name kid whose only family had dumped her on the steps of an orphanage and left her forever.

"I can't be a princess," she blurted without thinking. "I don't even know who my father is. What if he's in prison or worse? I told you about my mother. She abandoned me. My grandmother didn't want me, either. What if there's something hideously wrong with me?"

"There is not. There never could be." As'ad drew her hand to his mouth and kissed her fingers. "I know *you*," he told her. "That is enough. I know your character and you are more than I could ever wish for. I would be proud to have you as my wife. Marry me, Kayleen. Marry me and adopt the girls. We will be a family together. We need you."

There was only one answer, she thought as her eyes filled with tears. Happy tears, she reminded herself as she nodded.

"Yes," she whispered. "Yes, I'll marry you."

"I am pleased."

He leaned in and kissed her. She started to respond, but then he straightened and removed something from his jacket pocket. Seconds later, he slipped a massive diamond ring onto her finger.

She stared down at the center stone. It was nearly as big as a dinner plate. It glittered and shimmered and was unlike anything she had ever seen.

"Do you like it?" he asked.

"I don't know if I can live up to it," she admitted. "I think the ring is a little too smug for me. What if it calls me names behind my back?"

He chuckled. "This is why you delight me."

"Seriously, As'ad. I own two pairs of earrings, a cross necklace and a watch. I don't think I can wear this."

"What if I told you I picked that stone specifically and had it set for you? The diamond belonged to an ancestor of mine. A queen known for speaking her mind and ruling both her people and her husband with wisdom and love. She was admired by all. She lived a long time and saw many grandsons born. I think she would have liked you very much."

As he spoke, the ring seemed to glow a little brighter. The last of Kayleen's fears faded and she knew she had finally found the place she was supposed to be.

As PLANNED, As'AD went to Kayleen's suite after work that evening. She and the girls were waiting, although only Kayleen knew the nature of the announcement.

He walked in to a domestic scene, with Dana and Nadine both absorbed in their homework and Pepper on Kayleen's lap. The little girl read aloud.

As'ad took in the moment, thinking how it looked like a styled photograph. They were his responsibility now—all of them.

His gaze settled on the woman he would marry. Over the years he hadn't given much thought to his bride and he never would have imagined someone like Kayleen. But now that she was here—in his life—he knew he had made an excellent choice. She would suit him very well.

As for the sisters—he had grown fond of them. With Kayleen he would have sons, but the girls would always be special, for they had come first.

He smiled as he imagined facing Dana's first boyfriend. It would not be easy to meet a prince on a first date, but having to deal with him would be an excellent test of character for any young man.

Kayleen looked up first. "As'ad, you're here."

"So I am."

She took the book from Pepper, then set the girl on the sofa next to her. After she rose, she paused, as if not sure what to do. They were engaged now—some greeting was required. Obviously she did not know what.

He crossed the room to her and pulled her close, then kissed her. Behind him, he heard the girls murmuring. They were not used to such displays of affection, but they would become accustomed to them. He enjoyed being with a woman and having Kayleen in his bed would be one of the perks of married life.

When he stepped back, he kept his arm around her.

"We have something to tell you," he said.

All three girls huddled together, their eyes wide and apprehensive.

Kayleen smiled. "It's a good thing. Don't worry."

"Kayleen and I are to be married," As'ad said. "Nothing has been formally announced so you'll need to keep the information a secret for now, but I wanted you to know."

The girls stared at each other, then back at him. "What about us?" Dana asked, sounding worried.

Kayleen knelt down and held out her arms. "You're staying right here. With us. We'll both adopt you. This will be your home forever."

Nadine and Pepper ran into her embrace. Dana looked at him. Her smile was bright and happy, her eyes wide with excitement.

"I'd hoped this would happen," she admitted. "I wanted you to figure out you were in love with Kayleen. You look at her the way Daddy used to look at Mommy."

Love? Not possible, As'ad thought, dismissing the very idea. Kayleen kept her head down. Dana rushed to her.

"Do you have a ring?" the girl asked.

Kayleen removed it from her pocket and slipped it on her fingers. The girls gasped.

"That's really, really big," Pepper said. "Is it heavy?"

"I'm getting used to it."

As'ad watched in contentment. All had turned out well, thanks to his aunt. She had given him advice on the best way to approach Kayleen. While he didn't usually agree with taking advice from a woman, in this case she was the acknowledged expert.

She had told him about Kayleen's desire to be needed. It was a position he could respect. Having a place to belong was far better than worrying about a fleeting emotion like love.

Kayleen stood. The girls rushed at him and he found himself embracing them all. He bent down and gathered Pepper into his arms, then straightened and settled her on his hip.

"I'm a real princess now," she said. "I want a crown."

"A princess wears a tiara," he told her.

"Then one of those. Does this mean the next time I hit a bully I won't get into trouble?"

"Hitting anyone is never a good idea," Kayleen told her.

Pepper sighed and looked into his eyes. "But you're the *prince*. Can't you change that?"

She was delightful, as were her sisters. He smiled. "I will see what I can do."

"You shouldn't encourage her," Kayleen told him.

Perhaps not, but he suddenly wanted all that was possible for the girls. He wanted to give them everything, show them everything, and always keep them safe.

An odd pressure tightened in his chest. It was a feeling he didn't recognize, so he ignored it. But it was there.

FAYZA ST. JOHN arrived the next morning exactly on time for her prearranged meeting with Kayleen. She was a fifteen-year veteran of the protocol office, something she shared with Kayleen immediately upon their meeting.

"I'll be in charge of the wedding," Fayza said as she stretched her thin lips into what Kayleen hoped was a smile.

Everything about the woman was thin—her body, her face, her legs, her hair. She was well-dressed, but more than a little scary-looking, although elegant. Kayleen had the feeling that the other woman already knew her dress had been bought at sixty percent off at a discount outlet and that the patch pockets had been added after the fact to cover a stain that wouldn't come out.

"You're our first bride in decades," Fayza went on. "Princess Lina was the last, of course. With the princes getting older, we knew it was just a matter of time, so we've been doing a lot of prep work, just in case. Now you'll have to deal with a lot of decisions yourself, but much of the wedding will be handled out of my office. You can request things like colors, but everything will have to be vetted. While this is your happy day, it is also a state occasion." She paused. "Any questions?"

Kayleen shook her head. A question would require a functioning brain, which she didn't have at the moment. Marrying As'ad was unexpected enough, but to find out the event would be a state occasion?

"Obviously no serious work can get done until we have a date," Fayza continued. "The king mentioned a spring wedding."

"Uh-huh."

"With a formal announcement right after the holidays?"

Kayleen nodded.

"All right. That gives us time, which, believe me, we won't have enough of. You'll start working with one of our people right away. She'll help you learn the culture and traditions of El Deharia. You'll need instruction in the language, deportment, current events, etiquette and a hundred other things I can't even think of right now. Oh, I'll need your personal list for the announcements and the wedding. What family are you inviting?"

Kayleen had to consciously not grab her head to keep it from spinning. This wasn't anything she'd imagined. All she wanted was to marry As'ad and get on with her life.

"Does it have to be like this?" she asked. "Can we just go away and get married quietly?"

Fayza laughed. "He's a prince, dear. And the first one to marry. You're going to be on the cover of *People* magazine."

The idea made her want to throw up. "What if I don't want to be?"

"Sorry—this will be the social event of the spring. We'll try to keep the number of guests down. Anything over five hundred is a nightmare."

F-five hundred? Five? As in five hundred?

Kayleen stood and walked to the window. The need to run was as powerful as her instinct to keep breathing. None of this felt right, probably because it wasn't. Not for her. But this was As'ad's world. This was what he expected. If she was to be his wife, she would have to learn his ways. He believed in her and she wouldn't let him down.

"Your family? About how many?" Fayza asked again.

What family? Not her own—they had abandoned her. Why would she want them at her wedding? Would any of the nuns she knew back home make the journey?

"I'm not sure I have any," she admitted.

"Something we'll deal with later. Now, you're

going to have to be a little more careful when you go out. You must be escorted, either by Prince As'ad or Princess Lina. If neither of them are available, you'll have a security person with you. You already have one in the car when the girls go to and from school, so that helps. You will not be allowed to be alone with a man who is not attached to the palace. No friends even. Brothers are fine, cousins squeak in."

"That won't be a problem," Kayleen told her as she stared down into the garden.

She wanted to marry As'ad, she thought. She wanted to be with him, his wife, the girls' mother. But like this? Why couldn't he be a regular man? Even the camel dealer he had joked about on Thanksgiving.

She told herself she was being ungrateful. That her hardships were nothing when compared with those in the world who truly suffered. She should be grateful.

"We won't be making an announcement for a few months," Fayza continued. "It's unlikely there will be any media leaks, but it would be best if you didn't wear your engagement ring outside the palace. Just to keep things quiet."

Kayleen nodded, but she wasn't really listening anymore. Instead she stared at the cage in the garden. The one that had held all the doves.

Even though the door was open, the space was full again. They had all returned home.

Products of their destiny, she thought. Trapped. Just like her.

CHAPTER TEN

"I'M NOT SLEEPING at all," Lina complained as she sat on the stone bench in the garden.

"Thank you."

It took her a moment to realize what Hassan meant. She laughed. "All right. Yes, you're a part of my exhaustion, but not the only part. Playing matchmaker is hard work. I feel guilty in a way. I started all this. I brought them together."

"You introduced them and then removed yourself from the situation. You did not lock them in a room together and insist they become intimate. They chose that course themselves."

"I agree, in theory. But I planned this from the beginning. I thought Kayleen would be good for As'ad and that she secretly longed for more than teaching at the convent school. But what if I was wrong? What if I messed up both their lives?"

Hassan leaned in and kissed her. "You worry too much."

"I'm very good at it."

"Perhaps it is not a gift one should cultivate."

She smiled. "You don't actually expect me to change, do you?"

"Not really."

"Good." Her smile faded. "I just wish I knew I'd done the right thing."

"Why would it be otherwise? As'ad proposed and Kayleen agreed. Now they will be thrown together even more. Who knows what might happen."

He was so confident the outcome would be positive, but Lina wasn't so sure. What if As'ad couldn't open his heart to Kayleen? What if she stopped falling in love with him?

"I can see I do not have your full attention," Hassan complained. "I forbid it to be so."

She laughed. "You are not king here, sir. You are my guest."

His dark eyes brightened with humor. "I have enjoyed being your guest. Spending time with you makes it difficult for me to consider going home. But I must."

She didn't want to think about that. "You have many sons to rule in your place."

"For a time, but the ultimate responsibility is mine. I must also consider my people. I do not want them to believe I have abandoned them."

"I know." She didn't want to think about that. She didn't want Hassan to leave, but couldn't ask him to stay. She looked at him. "I will miss you."

"As I will miss you." He squeezed her hand. "I suppose it would be presumptuous to ask that you could come with me to Bahania."

She steeled herself against hope. "As a visit?"

He smiled. "No, my love. Not as a visit. It has been so long, I'm doing this badly." He kissed her. "Lina, you are an unexpected treasure in my life. I did not think I would find love again. I certainly never expected to find such a beautiful, enticing woman such as yourself. Your physical perfection is only matched by the gloriousness of your spirit and your mind. You have bewitched me and I wish to be with you always. I love you and would be most honored if you would consider becoming my wife."

Kayleen stood frozen on the garden path. She'd been walking as she did each morning, only to accidentally stumble into a personal moment.

At first she'd only heard the low rumble of voices and had thought nothing of them. There were often other people in the garden. Then she'd heard King Hassan say something about his people. The next thing she knew, he'd proposed.

Now she held her breath and looked desperately for a way to escape so they could be alone. She turned slowly, intent on creeping away, when Hassan spoke again.

"Tears are unexpected, Lina."

"They're happy tears. I love you so much. I never dreamed, either, that I could fall in love."

"So you will be my queen."

"Oh, dear. A queen. I never thought of that."

"My people will adore you nearly as much I do. I have the added delight of knowing every part of you."

There was a soft giggle and silence. Kayleen took advantage of their attention to each other and quietly moved away.

So Lina and the king had fallen in love. She was happy for them. The thought of her friend moving to Bahania was a little sad, but also exciting. Kayleen had never known a queen before.

She made her way back to her suite. As she climbed the wide staircase leading to the second floor, she paused, remembering the king's emotional proposal and how happy Lina had been. Even from several feet away, Kayleen had felt the love they shared.

"I want to be in love," Kayleen whispered. "With As'ad."

She wanted to love the man she would marry and she wanted him to love her back. Could it happen? Was it possible? Or was she like a child, hoping to catch the moon?

As'ad walked into the suite Saturday morning. "Are you ready?" he asked.

The girls all called out that they were, while Kayleen hovered behind them. For some reason, she felt shy with As'ad. How strange. She'd never felt awkward with him before. Perhaps it was because they were engaged now. Everything was different, yet it was oddly the same.

"You never said what we were going to do," Dana told him.

"I know. It's a surprise."

He crossed to Kayleen and smiled at her. "You are quiet."

"I'm caught up in the moment."

"You don't know what the moment will be."

"I'm sure it will be wonderful."

"Such faith." He captured her hand in his, then glanced down. "You do not wear my ring."

She pulled her hand free and hid it behind her back. "I, um, thought it was best. After talking to Fayza and all."

"Who is Fayza?"

"From the protocol office. I think that's where she's from. She wanted to talk to me about the wedding and how to behave, now that I'm going to be, you know, a princess."

She could speak the word, but it was hardly real to her. It was the same as saying she was going to wake up an aardvark. A princess? Her? Not possible.

"I see," As'ad murmured. "What were her instructions?"

Kayleen tried to remember them all. "I shouldn't go out by myself. I shouldn't talk to any man who isn't staff or a member of the royal family. I shouldn't wear my ring until the engagement is officially announced. I shouldn't talk to the press, dress inappropriately." She paused. "There's more. I wrote it all down."

He touched her cheek, then lightly kissed her. "It seems there are many things you should not do. Perhaps it would have been easier to give you a list of what is allowed."

"That's what I thought."

His dark gaze settled on her face. "Kayleen, you may do whatever pleases you. In all things. I would ask that you not travel outside of the palace walls without a bodyguard, but you may come and go as you wish. You are my fiancée, not my slave."

She liked the sound of that. "But Fayza was very insistent."

"I assure you, she will not be again. Would it please you to wear your engagement ring?"

She nodded. Somehow wearing the ring made her feel as if she belonged.

"I would like you to wear it, as well."

She went into her bedroom and slipped on the ring. When she turned, she found As'ad behind her. He pulled her close and settled his mouth on hers.

His kiss was warm and insistent, with just enough passion to make her breath catch. She liked the feel of him next to her, the way he held her as if he would never let her go. She liked the taste and scent of him, the fire that burst to life inside of her.

"What are they doing?" Nadine asked in what Kayleen guessed was supposed to be a whisper.

"They're kissin'," Pepper told her.

As'ad straightened. "There are issues with children I would not have guessed," he told her. "Such as privacy."

She smiled. "It's because they're excited about the surprise. You never said what it was."

"You're right. I did not." He led her back into the living room and faced the girls. "We are going shopping. All three of you need new wardrobes, now that you are to be my daughters."

Nadine spun in place. "Pretty dresses and party shoes?"

"Of course. Riding clothes, as well. Play clothes and whatever else Kayleen thinks you require."

"I want a crown," Pepper announced.

As'ad laughed. "I am not sure the store carries crowns, but we will ask."

Kayleen laughed. "Maybe we can make one here." She turned to him. "Thank you. The girls will love getting new things. They're all growing so quickly."

"You will be shopping, as well," he told her.

"What? I'm fine."

"You need a wardrobe that befits your new position." He shook his head. "What you have will not do."

She felt herself flush and tried to tell herself that it made sense a prince wouldn't be impressed by her plain, inexpensive wardrobe.

"I've never been much of a shopper," she admitted. Growing up, she'd made do with hand-me-downs and donations. When she started working, she'd never made a lot of money and her clothing budget had been modest at best.

"You will have to learn," he told her. "You are a beautiful woman and you deserve to wear beautiful things. Silks and lace with jewels that glitter. You will sparkle like the stars in the sky."

She'd never heard him talk like this before, she thought happily. She liked it.

The store was like nothing she'd ever seen before. It was on a quiet street with pale buildings that had striped awnings at all the windows. There was no sign overhead. Just discreet gold lettering on the door.

"I have called ahead," As'ad told her as they got out of the limo. "Wardrobes have been collected for each of the girls."

"How did you know the sizes?" she asked, wishing she'd had something nicer to wear into the store. She felt frumpy.

"Neil phoned the laundry and asked them to check. A selection has been made for each of them but the final decision is yours. If something has been forgotten, it will be ordered."

Kayleen had a feeling this was going to be a different experience than the sixty-percent-off sales at the discount stores she usually frequented.

A tall, slender woman greeted them graciously. She was beautifully dressed and smiled as she bowed to Prince As'ad.

"Sir, you are always welcome here. How delighted we are to be of service."

"Glenda, this is Kayleen James, my fiancée. These three young ladies are my daughters. Dana, Nadine and Pepper, this is Miss Glenda."

The girls smiled shyly and stayed close to him.

"A perfect family," Glenda told him. "Although a son would be a lovely addition."

"You speak as my father does," As'ad told her. "You are prepared?"

"We have dozens of things to show everyone. I think you will be pleased." She turned to the girls. "Come on. I'll show you." Glenda took Dana's hand and introduced her to the clerks who were hovering. Each gathered a girl and led her off. Then Glenda turned to Kayleen.

"Such beautiful hair," she said with a sigh. "And a natural color." She slowly walked around Kayleen. "Good structure, excellent posture, clear skin. Prince As'ad, you're a fortunate man."

"I think so."

"All right. Let the fun begin. The dressing rooms are this way." She glanced back at As'ad. "You will find magazines, drinks and a television waiting for you."

"Thanks." He smiled at Kayleen. "Enjoy yourself."

Kayleen nodded because she couldn't speak. Nothing about this experience was real to her. None of it had any basis in reality. In her world, boutique owners didn't act this way. They weren't so accommodating or friendly. At least, Kayleen thought the woman was being friendly. She could have just been acting nice because of the money that would be spent, but Kayleen hoped not.

She followed Glenda to the dressing room where the girls were giddily trying on clothes.

"I have socks with kittens!" Pepper yelled. "Can I have socks with puppies?"

"Yes," the woman helping her said with a laugh. "We even have giraffes."

"I *love* giraffes."

For Nadine there were dance clothes and frilly dresses, for Dana, clothes that were slightly less girly, but still pretty. Pepper ran to Kayleen and thrust kitten socks in her hand.

"Aren't they the best?" she asked breathlessly.

"They are."

"I love shopping!"

"So you're starting them young," Glenda murmured.

"Apparently."

She was taken into her own dressing room where dozens of items hung. There were dresses and jeans and blouses and skirts and suits. In the corner, three towers of shoe boxes stood nearly four feet high.

"We'll start with the basics," Glenda told her. "The prince mentioned you didn't have much of an appropriate wardrobe." She laughed. "Hardly something he had to mention. Not many of us have clothing fit for royal duty. Of course you'd be starting over. And isn't that the best place to be?"

Kayleen fingered her plain dress. "I've never been into fashion before."

"That is about to change. Fortunately you can learn a lot fairly quickly. Pay attention to what looks good on you rather than what's in style, go with classics and coordinates. And expect to be tortured by pretty shoes on formal evenings. All right, dear, let's see what you've got."

Glenda waited patiently until Kayleen figured out she was expected to undress.

Kayleen reluctantly unzipped her dress and stepped out of it. Glenda nodded.

"Excellent. Not too curvy, so you can dazzle in evening wear. That's good. No offense, dear, but you have very ugly underwear. If you're going to marry a prince, you need sexy and pretty. You want to keep him interested."

She began making notes, then motioned to the rack on the right. "We'll start there."

An hour later Kayleen realized she'd underestimated women who shopped for sport. It was exhausting. Trying on, walking out for As'ad's approval, then getting pinned and poked so everything fit perfectly, finding the right shoes, walking around in them, getting another nod from As'ad, then starting the whole thing over with a different dress.

She was zipping up a simple day dress when Dana walked into the dressing room.

"We're finished," she said. "As'ad said to tell you Aunt Lina is coming by to take us to the movies."

Kayleen smiled. "Are you as tired as I am?"

Dana nodded. "It was fun, but work."

"I didn't get to see half of what any of you bought. We'll have to have a fashion show when the clothes are delivered."

But instead of agreeing, Dana moved close, put her arms around Kayleen's waist and started to cry.

Kayleen sat down and pulled the girl onto her lap. "What's wrong?"

"I miss my mom and my dad," she said as she cried. "I know it's wrong, but I do."

Kayleen hugged her tight. "It's not wrong to miss them. Of course you do. This is all new and different. You want to share what's happening and you want the comfort of what's familiar. I don't blame you at all. You've been so brave, sometimes I forget you're not all grown-up."

"I get scared."

"Because all this is different?"

Dana buried her face in Kayleen's shoulder. "We don't want you to go away."

"I won't."

"Promise? Not ever? No matter what?"

"We will always be together. As'ad and I are getting married. We're going to be a family."

Dana looked at her. "If you leave him, you'll take us with you?"

Kayleen smiled. "I'm not leaving."

"You could. People leave."

"I won't, but if something happens and I do, I'll take all three of you with me. I promise."

Dana wiped her face. "Okay. I trust you."

"Good, because I love you."

Dana sniffed. "Really?"

"Really. You and Nadine and Pepper. I love you

all so much. I always wanted girls and now I have three."

Dana hugged her hard. Kayleen held her, willing her to feel safe, to know she, Kayleen, would always protect her. At last Dana straightened.

"I'm better," she said as she slid to her feet.

"I'm glad. I'm always here, if you need to talk or anything. Just tell me. Okay?"

Dana nodded and left. Kayleen stood and smoothed the front of the dress. "We know it wrinkles," she said to herself.

As'ad stepped into the dressing room. He stood behind her and put his hands on her shoulders.

"I heard your conversation with Dana," he told her, meeting her gaze in the mirror.

"Do you disapprove?" she asked.

"Not at all. You reassured her and she will reassure her sisters." One corner of his mouth turned up. "Perhaps you could have hesitated before agreeing you would probably leave me."

"I never said that. I won't. Marriage is forever for me."

"As it is for me," he told her, then turned her to face him. "You are an excellent mother. That pleases me. For the girls and the sons to follow."

"You do realize that you're technically responsible for the gender of any children we have. That if I have girls, it's your fault?"

He smiled. "Yes, I know. Although I would remind you I am one of six brothers. So the odds are in my favor."

She wanted to mention that a healthy child should be enough, regardless of gender. But what was the point? As'ad was a prince and a sheik. He was arrogant, but he was also kind and charming and she didn't want to change anything about him.

"Are you enjoying shopping?" he asked.

"It's a lot of work. I'm not really used to this level of service."

"You will become accustomed to it."

"Maybe. Do I really need all these clothes? It seems excessive."

"You are my wife."

"I get that, but still…"

"You represent El Deharia. The people have expectations."

Oh. Right. How long would *that* take to get used to? "Then it's fine," she told him.

"So you will do what is necessary for my people but not for me."

"Pretty much."

He bent down and kissed the side of her neck. Her insides clenched in response.

"I see I have to teach you to respect me," he murmured, his mouth moving against her skin.

He wrapped his arms around her waist and drew her back against him. He was warm and hard and she loved the feel of him so close.

She wanted this to be real—all of it. The girls as her family and As'ad as the man she loved more than anyone else. She wanted him to feel the same way. She wanted to make him weak at the knees and be all to him. If only…

He turned her to face him. "When we return to the palace I wish to discuss finances with you," he told her. "You and the girls will always be taken care of. Even if something should happen to me, you will be financially secure. The palace will always be your home, but should you wish to live elsewhere, money would be made available."

He didn't have to do that. She wasn't marrying him for the money. "I don't want anything to happen to you."

"Neither do I. Regardless, you are protected. Now that we are engaged, I have opened a bank account for you. As you spend money, more will be provided. I will give you credit cards, as well." He touched her face. "I want you to be happy, Kayleen. Go shopping as you like."

"I don't need much."

"Then you will be embarrassed by your excesses. Life is different now. You are different."

He kissed her, his mouth moving lazily over hers. When she parted, he slipped his tongue inside, teasing hers until she couldn't catch her breath.

She wanted him to touch her everywhere. She

wanted them to make love. She wanted to know the wonder of a release, his body so close to hers, their hearts beating together.

He pulled back slightly. "Although I would prefer you didn't change too much," he whispered as he lowered the zipper on her dress.

She felt his hands on her bare skin. He pulled the dress down to her waist, then moved aside the cup of her bra. His fingers were warm on her breast. He brushed against her hard nipple, making her gasp, then lowered his head and sucked on her.

Aware they were in a dressing room with a very flimsy door, she did her best to keep quiet, but it was difficult as his tongue circled her. Heat blossomed between her legs. Heat and an ache that made her squirm for more.

"So impatient," he whispered, then unfastened her bra.

She pushed the scrap of lace away and ran her hands across his head, then his shoulders. More. She needed more.

He chuckled before moving to her other breast and teasing it until her breath came in pants.

She felt one of his hands on her leg. The material of her dress was drawn up and up, then he moved between her legs.

She knew she should stop him. The girls were gone, but there were other people out there. Clerks and Glenda and maybe customers. They couldn't do this.

Except she didn't want him to stop. Not when he pushed down her panties and urged her to step out of them. Especially not when he slipped his hand between her thighs and began to rub.

He found her center immediately. Back and forth, back and forth, the steady pressure of his fingers on her slick flesh. She was so ready, she thought as she held in another groan. He eased her backward, then raised her leg until her foot rested on the bench.

"Lean on me," he whispered.

She did as he asked because to do otherwise was to risk him stopping. He supported her with one arm around her waist and eased the other under her dress, back between her legs.

She clung to him as he carried her higher and higher. The pleasure was so intense, she could think of nothing else. He knew exactly how to touch her, how to push her closer and closer until her release was in sight.

She felt the tension in every part of her body. She began to shake, holding on to him to keep from falling. Her breath came in pants. Suddenly she was there…on the edge and aching for him to push her over.

He circled her once, twice, and then she was coming and coming and it was as intense and glorious as she remembered. He leaned in and kissed her, silencing her gasps. He continued to touch her, flying with her, down and down, as the ripples of release eased through her. She was still shuddering in aftershocks when he swore softly and let her go.

"What's wrong?" she whispered.

"This was supposed to be for you," he muttered as he bent down and grabbed her bra. "Here. Put this on."

"I don't understand."

He looked at her, passion flaring in his eyes. "I must take you back to the palace at once. To my bed. We will finish the shopping later."

She smiled. "That's a good plan."

IT WAS NEARLY midnight when Kayleen dialed the familiar number and, when the call connected, ask to speak to the woman in charge.

"Kayleen? Is that you?"

Kayleen smiled. "Yes. It's been too long since I last called. I'm sorry."

"If you've been off having adventures, I forgive you at once. How are you? How is life at the palace? You must tell me everything."

The familiar voice, rich with affection and a life energy that inspired those around her, made Kayleen wish to be back in the convent, sitting in the room with her Mother Superior, instead of half a world away.

"I'm well. Very busy. I... The girls are adjusting well." She'd already called and talked about As'ad adopting the girls and her becoming their nanny.

"I worry about them. There have been so many upheavals. So much pain for those so young. You're with them and that must help."

"I hope so." Kayleen cleared her throat. "I have something to tell you. I'm not sure what you'll think." She drew in a deep breath. "It's about Prince As'ad. He arranged for us to have a Thanksgiving dinner a few weeks ago. It was lovely. But then..."

The Mother said nothing. Kayleen suspected she had long ago learned that silence was powerful motivation for the other person to keep talking.

"It was late and we were alone," Kayleen said, then told her everything. When she'd finished explaining about the proposal, she paused, waiting for whatever judgment might follow.

"He is a good man?" the other woman asked at last.

It wasn't the question Kayleen had expected. "Um, yes. A very good man. A little too used to getting his way, but that must come with being royal."

"He takes care of you and the girls?"

"Yes. Very well."

"Can you love him?"

An interesting question. "Yes, I can. I want to."

"Then I am pleased. I always wanted a husband and a family for you, Kayleen. I know you longed to return here, to the familiar, but sometimes we find our happiness in unexpected places. To love and be loved is a great blessing. Enjoy what you have and know I am always thinking of you."

"Thank you," Kayleen whispered, feeling the words wash over her like a blessing.

"Follow your heart and you will never be led astray. Follow your heart, child."

Kayleen nodded. She could already feel her heart drawing her toward As'ad. As he was the man she would marry, it was a journey she longed to make. To a place where she would finally belong.

CHAPTER ELEVEN

KAYLEEN LOOKED AT all the designs spread out on the large dining room table. "You're kidding," she said.

"This is only from today's mail," Lina told her with a sigh. "I never thought anything I did would make designers notice me. I certainly buy nice clothes, but I'm not that into fashion. Besides, I gave up being trendy years ago. But the second Hassan announced our engagement, I started getting calls." She flipped through the sketches of wedding gowns. "He was supposed to wait, you know. He promised." She sounded more exasperated than actually annoyed.

"He said he couldn't stand to keep his happy news a secret," Kayleen told her with a smile. "I saw the news conference. He was giddy."

Lina grinned. "Don't tell him that. He'll explain that a king is never giddy."

"He was this one time. I'm glad you're so happy."

"Me, too." Lina sighed. "I've really liked my

life. I've been blessed. Even though I lost my husband so early, I had my brother's sons to fill the void. I was okay with that. I was going to grow old taking care of their children. Now, suddenly, I'm in love and engaged. I still can't believe it."

Kayleen glanced at Lina's ring—the diamonds glittering on the platinum band made her engagement ring look like a tiny toy. "You're going to have to start exercising more if you're going to carry that around all day."

Lina laughed. "I know. It's huge. So not my taste, but if you'd seen the look on Hassan's face when he put it on my finger. He was so proud. How am I supposed to tell him I'd like something smaller than a mountain?"

"If it doesn't really matter to you, you don't."

"You're right." Lina picked up a design and studied it. "You're going to have to go through all this as soon as your wedding is announced."

"Hopefully on a much smaller scale," Kayleen told her, knowing being royal was going to take a lot of getting used to. "I only ever wanted to belong to a family. Now I have a whole country."

"There are perks."

"I'm not that interested in the perks."

"Which is why I'm glad As'ad picked you," Lina told her. "I know you're not in it for the money." She set down the design and picked up another. "I'll admit I'm hoping you'll fall in love with him."

Kayleen felt herself blush. "I've thought about it," she admitted. "He's a good man. Thoughtful and kind. He really cares about the girls. He takes care of things. He makes me feel safe. I know I like him, but love? What does that feel like?"

"Like you can hold the stars in the palm of your hand," Lina said, then laughed. "I sound foolish."

"You sound happy."

"I am. Hassan is my world. Oh, I know that will change, we'll settle into something more normal. But for now, I'm enjoying the magic. The way my heart beats faster when he walks in a room. The way he can take my breath away with a simple kiss. I only want to be with him."

"So I'm boring you?" Kayleen teased.

Lina laughed. "Not exactly. But I think about him all the time. It was different before. When I was young. I loved my husband, but I didn't appreciate what I had. Now that I'm older, I understand how precious love is. How rare." She turned to Kayleen. "I think you already know that, because of how you grew up."

"I know it's something I want. It's important to me. I want to love As'ad. I already love the girls."

"Then you're halfway there. Just give things time."

"We have that," Kayleen murmured.

"You have your life. After you're married, you can start having children of your own."

Kayleen touched her stomach. A baby. It had always been her secret dream. The one she wouldn't allow herself to think of very often.

Lina sighed. "I'd love to get pregnant. I'm a little old, but I'm going to try."

"Really?"

The princess nodded. "I always wanted children. While my nephews have been a source of endless delight, I confess I still have the fantasy of my own child. Hassan is willing to try. We'll see. If it is meant to be, then it will happen. If not, I still have the man of my dreams."

"I'M NERVOUS," KAYLEEN told As'ad as they walked into the auditorium at the American School. "I've been working with the girls. I know in my head they'll be fine, but I'm still terrified."

"Yet they are the ones performing."

"I want them to do well so they'll be happy," she said. "I don't want them to feel bad."

"Then you should have faith in them. They have practiced. They are ready."

"You make it sound so logical."

"Is it not?"

"No, it's not. It's horrible. I think I'm going to throw up."

As'ad laughed and pulled her close. "Ah, Kayleen, you delight me."

"By vomiting? Imagine how excited you'll be

when I get a fever." She grumbled, but in truth she enjoyed the feel of his arm around her and the heat of his body next to hers. Not only for the tingle that shot through her, but because the sensation was familiar. She'd leaned against him enough to know it was him. She would be able to pick him out blindfolded—by touch or scent alone. She'd never been able to think that before.

They took seats toward the front, by the aisle. Kayleen was vaguely aware that people were looking at them, but she was too nervous for the girls to notice or feel uncomfortable. A thousand horrible scenarios ran through her mind. What if Dana forgot her lines or Nadine tripped or Pepper decided to teach some bully a lesson?

As'ad took her hand and squeezed her fingers. "You must breathe. Slowly. Relax. All will be well."

"You don't *know* that."

"I know that your panic will in no way influence the outcome and it will only make you more uncomfortable."

"Again with the logic. It's really annoying."

She glanced at him and he smiled. She smiled back and felt something tug at her belly. Something that felt a lot like a connection. It startled her and made the rest of the room fade away. In that moment, there was only As'ad and she didn't want anyone or anything else.

A few minutes later, the orchestra began and the curtains parted. The pageant went from the youngest students to the oldest, so it wasn't long before Pepper appeared on stage with her class. They did a skit about a frog family snowed in for the holidays. Pepper was the mother frog.

Kayleen mouthed the girl's lines along with her, only relaxing when she left the stage at the end of the skit.

"A flawless performance," As'ad murmured. "You worry for nothing."

"Maybe my worrying is what made it perfect."

"You do not have that much power. Nadine is next. I believe she will dance. That will be enjoyable to watch."

Sure enough, Nadine and several of her classmates danced to music from *The Nutcracker.* Kayleen willed her to hold her positions exactly long enough and exhaled when the music ended and the girls were still.

"You will wear yourself out," As'ad told her.

"I can't help it. I love them."

He looked into her eyes. "Do you?"

"Of course. How could I not?"

Something flashed through his eyes—something she couldn't read. "I was most fortunate to find you. Not that I can take total credit." He smiled. "We must send Tahir, the desert chieftain, a gift of thanks."

"Maybe a fruit basket."

"I was thinking more of a camel."

"That can be tricky," she told him. "Don't you hate it when all you get in a year is camels?"

"You mock me."

"Mostly I'm mocking the camel."

Another class took the stage, then Dana's group appeared. Once again Kayleen held her breath, willing the preteen to get through all the lines without messing up.

Partway through the performance, As'ad took her hand in his. "You may squeeze my fingers, if that helps."

She did and felt a little better. When Dana finally left the stage, Kayleen slumped back in exhaustion.

"I'm glad we only have to do that a few times a year," she said. "I couldn't stand it."

"You will grow more used to this as the girls are in more performances."

"I don't want to think about it. I'm not sure my heart could take it."

"Then brace yourself. There is one more surprise yet to come."

She turned to him. "What are you talking about?"

"You'll see. All will be revealed when we leave here."

Kayleen really wanted to whine that she wanted

to know *now,* but managed to keep quiet. She fidgeted until the last song ended, then followed As'ad out of the auditorium. Only to step into an impossible-to-imagine scene of snow.

It fell from the sky, cold and wet and delightful. The children were already outside, running and screaming. Kayleen held out her hands, then laughed as the snow landed on her palms.

"It's real," she said.

As'ad shrugged. "Dana mentioned missing snow, as did the other girls. I thought they would enjoy this."

It was only then that Kayleen noticed the roar of the large snow-making machine off to the side of the parking lot.

"You arranged it?" she asked, stunned by the thoughtful gift.

"Neil arranged it. I simply gave the order."

It wasn't just simple, she thought. As'ad had thought about the girls, about how this time of year would be difficult for them, and he'd done his best to make it better.

Dana came running up to them. "It's snowing! I can't believe it."

She flung herself at As'ad, who caught her and held her. Then Nadine was there and Pepper and he was holding all of them.

Kayleen watched them, her eyes filling with happy tears. It was a perfect moment, she thought.

Her chest ached, but not in a scary way. Instead it seemed that her heart had grown too big to hold all her emotions. Light filled her until she was sure it poured from her body.

The world around them shrank until there was only As'ad and the children he held. She wanted to hold that moment forever, to never forget the image or the feelings.

The director of the school came up to greet them and the spell was broken. Dana crossed to Kayleen and hugged her.

"Isn't this the best?"

"It's wonderful," Kayleen told her. "All of it. You did really well. I was scared, but you didn't seem nervous at all."

"It was fun," Dana said. "I've never been in a play before. I like it. I think I want to go into drama next year." She raised her face to the snow. "Can you believe this?"

Kayleen looked at the tall, handsome prince who had asked her to marry him. The man who spoke of their life together, of children and who made it snow in the desert because it brought a smile to a child's face.

"No, I can't," she admitted, even as she realized she now knew exactly what it felt like to be in love.

As'ad watched the children play in the snow and was pleased with his gift. All was going well. Lina had told him to pay attention to the females in his life—that for a small amount of effort, he would receive much in return. She had been right.

He heard Kayleen's laughter and found her in the crowd. With her hair like fire and her hazel eyes, she was a brightly colored flamingo in a flock of crows. He was proud to have her as his bride. She would provide him with strong, healthy sons and serve the people of his country well. She would keep him satisfied at night and, if the emotions he'd seen in her eyes earlier told the truth, love him.

He knew it was important for a woman to love her husband. That life was much easier for them both when her heart was engaged. He had hoped Kayleen would come around and she had. She would be content in their marriage, as would he. He could not ask for more.

"I'M EXHAUSTED," KAYLEEN said as she slumped in the back of the limo. "All that worrying, then the snowball fight. If this keeps up much more, I'm going to have to start working out."

"I do not wish you to change anything about yourself," As'ad told her.

Words to make her heart beat faster, she thought as he pulled her into his arms and kissed her.

At the first brush of his mouth, her entire body stirred in anticipation. She was eager to taste him, touch him, be with him. Unfortunately the trip back to the palace was only a few minutes.

"Perhaps later," he murmured, kissing her mouth, her cheeks, her jaw.

"Yes," she whispered. "I am very available."

"An excellent quality."

Far too soon, they arrived at the palace. A royal guard opened the passenger door and As'ad stepped out. He held out his hand to her. As she took it, she saw King Mukhtar in the courtyard. He seemed very pleased with himself as he spoke with a woman Kayleen had never seen before.

"Who is that?" she asked.

"I do not know."

The woman was of average height, with platinum-blond hair teased and sprayed into a curly mass. Heavy makeup covered her face, almost blurring her features. She wore a too-tight sweater and jeans tucked into high-heeled boots. Inappropriate clothing for someone visiting a palace.

Kayleen had never seen her before but as she walked toward the king and his guest, she got an uneasy feeling in the pit of her stomach.

King Mukhtar saw her and beamed. "My dear, you are back. Excellent. I have a surprise." He put his hand on his companion's back and urged her forward. "Do you remember when we were walking in the garden shortly after you arrived? You mentioned your family. Specifically how you did not remember your mother and did not know her whereabouts."

Kayleen jerked her attention back to the badly dressed woman and wanted to be anywhere but here. It wasn't possible. Nothing that horrible could really be happening.

"I have found her," the king said proudly. "Here she is. Kayleen, this is your mother. Darlene Dubois."

The woman smiled broadly. "Hi, baby. Why, Kayleen, you're just so pretty. I knew you would be. Let me look at you. You're all grown up. How old are you now? Nineteen? Twenty?"

"Twenty-five."

"Oh, my. Well, don't go telling people that. They'll think I'm getting old. Although I was only sixteen when you were born." She held out her arms. "Come on, now. I've missed you so much! Give your mama a hug."

Trapped by the manners instilled in her by caring nuns, Kayleen moved forward reluctantly and found herself hugged and patted by the stranger.

Could this woman really be her mother? If so, shouldn't she feel a connection or be excited? Why was her only emotion dread?

"Isn't this fabulous?" Darlene asked as she stepped back, then linked arms with Kayleen. "After all these years. You won't believe how shocked I was when that nice man on the king's staff called and invited me to El Deharia. I confess I had to look it up on a map." She smiled at the king. "I had to leave high school when I got pregnant. Since then, I've been pursuing a career in show business. It hasn't left much time for higher education."

Or contact with her family, Kayleen thought bitterly, remembering standing alone on the steps of the orphanage while her grandmother told her that no one wanted her and that she would have to stay with the nuns.

"But what about my mommy?" Kayleen had cried.

"You think she cares? She dumped you with me when you were a baby. You're just lucky I put up with you all these years. I've done my duty. Now you're on your own. You'll grow up right with those nuns looking after you. Now stop your crying. And don't try to find me or your mama again. You hear?"

The memory was so clear, Kayleen could feel the rain hitting her cheeks. She knew it was rain because it was cold, unlike the tears that burned their way down her skin.

"Kayleen, would you like to show your mother to her rooms?" the king asked. "She is on the same floor as you and the girls. The suite next to yours. I knew you would want to be close."

Kayleen was happy that one of them was sure

of something. She felt sick to her stomach and caught by circumstances. She looked at As'ad, who watched her carefully.

"What girls?" Darlene asked. "Do you have babies of your own?"

Darlene sounded delighted, but for some reason Kayleen didn't believe her. The other woman didn't seem the type to be excited about being a grandmother.

"They're adopted," As'ad told her. "My children."

Kayleen introduced them, using the chance to disentangle herself from her mother.

"A prince?" Darlene cooed. "My baby marrying a prince. Does that just beat all." She smiled at the king. "You have very handsome sons, sir. They take after you."

Mukhtar smiled. "I like to think so."

Kayleen couldn't believe this was happening. It didn't feel real. She looked at As'ad and found him watching her. There was something quizzical in his expression, as if he'd never seen her before.

What was he thinking? Was he looking at her mother and searching for similarities? Was he uncomfortable with the living reminder that she didn't come from a socially connected family? That she would be of no use to him that way?

"Your mother must be tired from her journey," the king said. "Let us keep you no longer."

"I'll arrange to have your luggage sent up," As'ad told the other woman. "Kayleen, I'll see you later."

She nodded because she had no idea what to say. Both the king and As'ad left, abandoning Kayleen to a stranger with greedy eyes.

"Well, look at you," Darlene drawled when they were alone. "Who would have thought my baby girl would grow up and land herself a prince. I'm so happy for you, honey." She grabbed a strand of Kayleen's hair and rubbed it between her fingers. "God, I hate that color. Mine's exactly the same. It costs a fortune to keep it bleached, but it's worth every penny. Men prefer blondes. Although you're carrying the color off great and the prince obviously likes it." She looked Kayleen up and down. "You could pass for Vivian's twin."

"Who's Vivian?"

"My sister. Your aunt. You had to have met her before, when you were living with my mama." She looked around at the vast entrance hall. "Did you get lucky or what? I couldn't believe it when that guy who works for the king called and asked if you were my daughter. After all this time, I had no idea what had happened to you." She smiled. "Imagine my surprise to see what you've become. My little girl. Come on. Show me what life is like in the palace."

Kayleen led her down the hallway. Her head

hurt. This couldn't be happening. Not after all these years. Not *now,* when she was engaged to As'ad.

Then she scolded herself for not being happier to see her mother. The woman had given birth to her, after all. Then abandoned her. But shouldn't she be able to forgive that?

Rather than try to decide now, Kayleen talked about the history of the palace. She took Darlene to the room next to hers and walked inside.

The other woman followed, then breathed a sigh of sheer pleasure as she took in the view of the Arabian Sea and the elegant furnishings filling the large space.

"Oh, I like living like this," Darlene said. "How did you get from that convent to here?"

Kayleen looked at her, trying not to notice that under the layers of makeup, they had the same eyes. "You knew about that? Where they sent me?"

"Sure. Mama kept complaining about how much trouble you were. I got tired of hearing it and told her to take you there. I knew, ah, you'd be cared for real well. So how'd you get here?"

"I took a teaching job at the convent school here. I'm a teacher."

Darlene looked amused. "Seriously? You teach children? Interesting."

Kayleen watched her move around the room. "Your last name is Dubois?"

Darlene nodded without looking at her. She lifted up a small Waterford clock, as if checking the weight and the value.

"Is that my last name?"

Darlene glanced at her. "What are you talking about?"

"I never knew. When my grandmother dropped me off at the orphanage, I didn't know my last name. Everyone in the house had a different one. Grandmother wouldn't say which was mine. I had to make one up."

Darlene grinned. "I made mine up, too. What did you pick?"

"James. From the King James Bible."

"I prefer Tennessee Williams myself." Darlene started opening cabinets. "Can you drink in this place?"

"Yes. Right there." Kayleen pointed to the carved doors hiding the fully stocked wet bar.

Darlene found the ice and fixed herself a vodka tonic, then took a long drink. "Better," she said with a sigh. She walked to the sofa and sat down, then patted the seat next to her. "You're going to start at the beginning and tell me everything."

Kayleen stayed where she was. "About what?"

"The story here. You're really engaged to that prince?"

"Yes. There will be a formal announcement in a few weeks and a wedding in the spring."

Darlene took another drink. "So you're not pregnant. I'd wondered if you were."

Kayleen tried not to be insulted. "I didn't have to trick As'ad into marrying me."

"Of course not. I didn't mean to imply you would. Still, you have to be sensible. Do you have a prenuptial agreement? How many millions is he offering? Do you have an attorney? I wonder if you could get one to fly out and help."

Kayleen took a step back. "I don't need an attorney. As'ad has promised the girls and I will be taken care of."

"And you believe him? You're lucky I'm here."

Kayleen doubted that. "Why *are* you here?"

"Because I finally found my long-lost daughter."

"You knew I was in the convent all those years. That's hardly lost."

Darlene shrugged. "You're much more interesting now, honey."

"Because of As'ad." It wasn't a question.

"Partly. Oh, Kayleen, life was hard for me when you were young. I couldn't take care of a baby, I was just a baby myself. You're grown-up. You can see that. Then I lost track of you. But now we're together."

Kayleen found it difficult to believe she would have been so hard to find.

Darlene stood. "I'm your mother. I want what's

best for you. If you really expect this prince to marry you, you're going to have to keep him interested. I can help you with that. Otherwise, some rich socialite will steal him away. We don't want that, do we?"

"I find it hard to believe you care anything about me," Kayleen said, feeling both anger and guilt. What was she supposed to believe? "You never did before."

"Don't say that. Of course I cared. But I had a career. You were better off with those nuns. They took real good care of you."

"How would you know?"

"It's the kind of people they are. Am I wrong?"

"No," Kayleen told her. "They're exactly who you'd think they would be."

"Then you should thank me." She walked to the bar and fixed a second drink. "I'm not leaving, Kayleen. The king thinks he's done you a big favor, finding me and bringing me here. I, for one, agree with him. You're my baby girl and that means something to me. We're going to get to know each other, you and I. Now run along. I need to rest. We'll talk about this more later."

Kayleen left. Not because she'd been told to, but because she couldn't stand to be there anymore.

She didn't know what to think about Darlene. She'd never really allowed herself to imagine what her mother was like—it hurt too much to think

about all she'd lost. But this woman wasn't anyone's fantasy.

Then Kayleen thought about what the Mother
Superior would say about judging someone so
quickly. Maybe Darlene *was* sorry about their
lost relationship. Maybe they could at least learn
to be friends. Didn't Kayleen owe her to give her
a chance to prove herself?

CHAPTER TWELVE

KAYLEEN RETURNED TO her suite, but she couldn't seem to settle down. Not with her mother so close. Just a wall away.

It was her own fault for lying, she reminded herself. If she'd told King Mukhtar the truth, none of this would have happened. But she hated talking about how her mother didn't want her and her grandmother abandoned her. It sounded sad and pathetic. So she'd made up a more comfortable version and now she was stuck with it.

She walked to the French doors and started to open them, then remembered her mother was right next door. She didn't want another run-in with her. She turned back to pace the room when someone knocked.

Kayleen froze, afraid of who would be there. The door opened and As'ad stepped inside.

Without thinking, she ran to him. She wrapped her arms around him, wanting to feel the warmth of him, the safety that came from being close.

"That bad?" he asked as he hugged her.

She nodded.

"I take it my father's surprise was not a pleasant one."

She looked at him. "I don't know," she admitted. "I don't know what to think or what I feel. She's not like mothers on television."

"Few are." He touched her cheek. "Are you all right?"

She sighed. "I will be. It's just strange. I don't know her. I've never known her and now she's here and we're related and I can't figure out what it all means."

"I should probably tell you that getting to know her will take time, that it will get easier, but I am not sure that is true." He smiled at her. "So perhaps I bring you good news."

"Which is?"

"Do you remember your unexpected visit to the desert? Sharif, the chieftain there, has heard of our engagement and invites us to join him and his people for dinner."

"I thought the engagement was supposed to be a secret."

"There are those who find a way to know everything. He is one of them."

"He probably saw light reflecting off my diamond ring. It's like a beacon."

As'ad chuckled. "Perhaps. I have spoken with

Lina. She is pleased to take the girls if you would like to go."

Kayleen bit her lower lip. "Is it too rude to leave my mother on her first night here?"

"I think she will be exhausted from her journey. Perhaps you can leave a message on her phone and see her another time."

Kayleen was more than up for that. She left the message, then changed into a comfortable dress for her evening in the desert and met As'ad downstairs.

They walked out front where a Jeep was waiting. "You will need to learn to ride," he told her. "Eventually you will want to go into the desert with the girls."

"I know." She settled in beside him and fastened her seat belt. "Maybe I'd do better on a camel. Horses and I don't get along."

"A camel is not a comfortable ride. Trust me. You would much prefer to be on a horse."

"Maybe." She would have to try a camel first.

It was late afternoon. The sun sat in the west, giving everything a rosy, golden glow. The air was warm with the promise of a cool night to follow.

"I wonder what it's like to live in the desert," she said as she stared out the window. "Traveling with a tribe, connected to the land."

"No plumbing, no heat or air-conditioning, no closet."

She laughed. "I can't see you worrying about a closet."

"I would not, but what about you?"

"I like plumbing and closets." She didn't have a lot of things, but she did like to have her few treasures around her.

"My brother Kateb lives in the desert," he said. "He has always preferred the old ways, when life was simple and a man lived by his wits and his sword."

"You're serious? He's a nomad?"

"It is how he prefers it. When each of us reached the age of thirteen, my brothers and I were sent into the desert for a summer. It is considered a rite of passage—a test of manhood. The tribes were not cruel, but we were shown no preference because of our stature. I enjoyed my time, but had no interest in changing my future because of the experience. No so Kateb. He spoke of nothing else when he returned. Our father insisted he complete his education and Kateb agreed. But when he graduated from university in England, he returned here and went into the desert."

It sounded romantic, Kayleen thought, if she didn't think about the reality of the life. Weren't there sand fleas? And the heat in summer would be devastating. Still, the wilderness had some appeal. Not answering to anyone. Except one would have to answer to the tribe. There would have to be rules for the greater good.

"Will I meet him?" she asked.

"Not tonight. Kateb lives deep in the desert. Once or twice a year he returns to the palace, to meet with our father."

As'ad watched as Kayleen stared out into the desert. "It's all so beautiful," she said. "I can see why your brother would want to make it his home. Even without running water."

She spoke almost wistfully, as if she meant what she said, which she most likely did. He had learned that Kayleen's word was truth—an unusual trait in a woman. But then Kayleen was not like other women he'd known.

Now that she had a wardrobe of designer clothes, she dressed more like someone engaged to a prince, but there was still an air of…freshness about her. She blushed, she looked him in the eye when she spoke, she never considered hiding her emotions. All things he liked about her. He hoped she would not develop a hard edge of sophistication. He enjoyed her candor and down-to-earth ways.

A surprise, he thought, knowing he had always preferred women of the world. Of course, those women had been companions for his bed, not anyone he would consider to be the mother to his children. He remembered a conversation he'd had years ago with his aunt. Lina had told him that there were different women in this world. That he should have his fun but save his heart for someone unlike his playthings.

She had been right—not that he would give her the satisfaction of telling her. At least about marriage. His heart remained carefully unengaged, as it should in situations as important as these.

He pulled up by the edge of the camp and parked. Kayleen drew in a deep breath.

"They are so going to laugh at me," she murmured.

"Why would they do that?"

She looked at him and said, "Good evening. Blessings to you and your family," in the old tongue of El Deharia. Then added in English, "My pronunciation is horrible."

"You are learning our language?"

"It seemed the right thing to do. Plus, last time almost no one would talk to me in English. It's their country, right? One of the maids is teaching me on her lunch hour. She's taking night classes and I'm helping her with her calculus."

He stared at the hazel-eyed beauty who sat next to him. In a few months, they would be married and she would be a princess for the rest of her life. Her blood would mingle with his and their children would be able to trace their lineage back a thousand years.

She had a vault of jewels to wear whenever she liked, a bank account that never emptied; she lived in a palace. Yet did she expect humble people of the desert to speak her language? Did she hire a tutor? Have a linguistic specialist summoned? Not Kayleen. She bartered with a maid and learned an ancient speech not spoken outside the desert.

In that moment, as he stared into her eyes and saw their future, he felt something. A faint tightness in his chest. A need to thank her or give her something. The feeling was fleeting and unfamiliar, therefore he ignored it.

Or tried to.

There could be no softer emotions. With them came weakness, and strength was all. But he could be grateful that she had stumbled into his life and changed everything.

He reached for her hand. "I am glad we are to be married," he told her.

Happiness brightened her eyes and her whole face took on a glow. Love, he thought with satisfaction, knowing all would be well.

"I am, too," she whispered.

SHARIF AND ZARINA greeted them as they arrived, then the other woman pulled Kayleen aside.

"I see you managed to keep him all to yourself," Zarina teased as she picked up Kayleen's left hand and stared at the ring there. "You have chosen well."

"I think so."

Zarina laughed. "I recognize that smile. You are pleased with As'ad."

"He's wonderful."

"What every bride should think about her groom."

She led Kayleen toward a group of women and introduced her. Kayleen recognized a few of them from her last visit and greeted them in their native language. There were looks of surprise, then two of them started talking to her, speaking so quickly she caught about every tenth word.

"I have no idea what you're saying," she admitted in English. "I'm still learning."

"But you are trying," Zarina said, sounding pleased. "You honor us with your effort."

"I was hoping we could be friends," Kayleen told her.

Zarina smiled. "We are. But we will have to remember our places. Once you are a princess, things will change."

"Not for me." Kayleen wasn't interested in position or money. She wanted more important things.

"Then we will be good friends," Zarina told her. "Come. We are fixing dinner. You can keep us

306 THE SHEIK AND THE CHRISTMAS BRIDE

company. We will teach you new words. Perhaps words of love to impress your future husband."

"I'd like that."

Kayleen settled in the open cooking area. The women gathered there, talking and laughing. She couldn't follow many of the conversations, but that was all right. She would get more fluent with time.

She liked the way the women all worked together, with no obvious hierarchy. How the children came and went, dashing to a parent when they felt the need for attention. How easily they were picked up and hugged, how quick the smiles.

The tribe was an extended family—in some ways similar to her experiences in the orphanage. The group pulled together for the greater good. The difference was one would always belong to the tribe.

Roots, she thought enviously. Roots that traveled along. What would that be like?

She thought about her mother, back at the palace. They were supposed to be family, but Darlene was a stranger to her. Kayleen only had vague memories of her aunts and her grandmother, but then she'd forgotten on purpose. What was the point of remembering long days of being left alone, of being hungry and frightened?

She heard giggles and saw Zarina whispering to one of the young women. There were gestures and the next thing Kayleen knew, she was being pulled into a tent.

"We don't do this very much," Zarina told her. "It is only to be used on special occasions. With power comes responsibility."

"I have no idea what you're talking about."

Zarina opened a trunk and dug around, then pulled out several lengths of sheer veil.

"The trick is to maintain the mystery," Zarina told her as she passed over the fabric. "It's about confidence, not talent. No man can resist a woman who dances for him. So you can't feel self-conscious or worry about how you look. You must know in your heart that he wants you with a desperation that leaves him weak. You are in charge. You decide. He begs and you give in."

Kayleen took a step back. "If you're saying what I think you're saying…"

"After dinner, we will send As'ad to a private tent. You will be there. You will dance for him." Zarina smiled. "It's a memory he'll hold on to for the rest of his life."

As much as Kayleen wanted to be accepted by the women of the tribe, she was terrified at the thought of trying to seduce As'ad.

"I don't know how to dance. I'm not good at this."

"You are the woman he wishes to marry. You

know all you need to. As for the dancing…it is easy. Come, I will show you."

Zarina tossed the fabric onto a pile of pillows, then shrugged out of her robes. Underneath she wore a sleeveless tank top and cropped pants. A simple, modern outfit that would work perfectly in the desert.

"Lower your center of gravity while keeping your back straight. Rock your hips until you feel the movement, then begin to rotate them."

Zarina demonstrated, making it look easy. Kayleen tried to do as she said, but felt awkward.

But she didn't give up and after a few minutes, she had the hip movement down. Next she learned to hold her arms out to the side, moving them gracefully.

"Very good," Zarina told her. "Now turn slowly. You want to dance for a minute or two, turn, then remove one of the veils."

Kayleen skidded to a stop. "I can't dance naked."

"You won't have to. No man can resist the dance of the veils. You will remove two, maybe three, then he will remove the rest."

"What if he thinks I look stupid?"

"He won't. He'll think he's the luckiest man alive. Now let us prepare you for the evening."

Unsure she was really going to be able to do this, Kayleen followed Zarina to another tent where there were several women waiting. She was stripped down to her underwear and sat patiently as henna was applied to her hands and feet.

"It's the temporary kind," Zarina told her. "A sugar-based dye that will wash off in a week or so."

Kayleen stared at the intricate design and knew she wouldn't mind if it lasted longer.

Next she was "dressed" in layers of veils. They were wound around her, woven together until they appeared to be a seamless garment. They were sheer, but in enough volume to only hint at what was below.

Zarina applied makeup, using a dark pencil to outline Kayleen's eyes and a red stain on her lips.

"Better than lipstick," the other woman told her. "It won't come off."

Her hair was pulled back and up through a beaded headpiece. Dozens of bracelets fit on each wrist. The final touch was a pair of dangling earrings that nearly touched her shoulders.

When they were finished, Zarina led her to a mirror. Kayleen stared at the image, knowing it couldn't possibly be her. She looked *exotic*. She'd never been exotic in her life. She also looked sexy and mysterious.

"I will leave you here for a few minutes to practice, then come for you," Zarina told her. "Believe in yourself. With this dance, you can snare As'ad's heart so that he can never be free again. What wife doesn't want that?"

Good question, Kayleen thought when she was alone. Nerves writhed in her stomach, but she ignored them. Having As'ad respect her wasn't enough. She wanted more—she wanted him to love her.

He had to see she was more than just someone to take care of the girls or an innocent he'd slept with. Their engagement might have begun due to circumstances other than love, but it didn't have to stay that way.

She'd already given him her heart—now she had to claim his. Which meant being equal to a prince.

Could she? Kayleen had spent her whole life in the shadows, lurking in the background, not making waves, desperate for what she wanted, but afraid to step up and take it. It was time to be different. If she wanted to love a prince, she would have to claim him. She would have to show him she was so much more than he imagined. Her upbringing had given her an inner strength. She would use that power to achieve her heart's desire.

With a last look at herself, she walked to the front of the tent to wait for Zarina. She wasn't afraid. She was going to bring As'ad to his knees and make him beg. And that was just for starters.

WHILE AS'AD ENJOYED the company of Sharif, he was disappointed in the evening. He'd brought Kayleen to the desert so they could share the experience. But she had been whisked away and a polite guest did not ask why.

As the strong coffee was served at the end of the meal, he glanced at his watch and calculated how long he would have to wait until they could politely take their leave. Perhaps he and Kayleen could go into town for a couple of hours. There were a few nightclubs that were intimate and had small, crowded dance floors. He liked the idea of holding her close.

Zarina approached and bowed. "Prince As'ad, would you please come with me?"

As'ad looked at his host. "Do I trust your daughter?"

Sharif laughed. "As if I know her plans. Zarina, what do you want with the prince?"

"Nothing that will displease him."

As'ad excused himself and followed her. Night had fallen and the stars hung low in the sky. He thought briefly of his brother Kateb, and wondered when he would next return to the palace. If he came in time, he could attend the wedding. As'ad would like to have all his brothers there for the ceremony. And to point out that he would no longer have to listen to their father's complaints that they had yet to all find brides.

Zarina wove her way through the tents, pausing at one in the back, almost on its own.

"In here, sir," she said, holding open the flap. "I wish you a good evening."

As'ad ducked inside. The tent was dim, with only a few lights. There was an open space covered with rugs, and a pile of cushions in front of him.

"If you will please be seated."

The request came from a dark corner. He recognized Kayleen's voice. A quiet tent, seclusion and the company of a beautiful woman, he thought as he lowered himself to the cushions. The evening had improved considerably.

Music began. The melody was more traditional than contemporary, as were the instruments. An interesting choice, he thought, as Kayleen stepped out of the shadows. It was his last rational thought for a very long time.

She wore veils. Dozens and dozens of sheer lengths of fabric covered her body. Yet there were flashes of skin—her waist, her legs, a bit of arm.

Her face looked the same, yet different, with her eyes suddenly dark and intriguing. Jewels glittered from her wrists and her ears; her skin shimmered in the dim light. She was the woman he knew yet a woman he had never known. Even before she began to move, he wanted her.

She moved her arms gracefully. He saw the henna on her skin and dropped his gaze to her bare feet. It was there, as well. The patterns were oddly erotic on her fair skin.

She moved her hips back and forth, turned and a single veil dropped to the rug.

It showed him nothing more. She was too well-wrapped. But when it hit, his chest tightened. Blood heated and raced through him, heading to his groin, where it settled impatiently. The desire was instant, powerful and pulsing.

He knew of the dance, had heard it described, but had never experienced it himself. He'd heard men talk of the power of being seduced in such a way by a woman and had privately thought them weak. But now, as Kayleen danced in time with the music, he knew he had been wrong. There was something primal in her movements, something that called only him.

She turned again and another veil fell.

It was all he could do to stay seated. He wanted to jump to his feet, pull her close and take her. He wanted to be inside of her, feeling her heat, pleasuring them both. Heat grew until he burned. And still she danced.

Her hips moved back and forth, her arms fluttered. This time when she turned, he knew the veil would fall, anticipated it, looked greedily to see more of her. A tug and it fluttered to the ground.

She turned back. He saw a hint of curve, the lace of her bra, and he was lost. He sprang to his feet and crossed to her. After he grabbed her around the waist, he pulled her against him and kissed her.

He told himself to hold back, that she wouldn't appreciate his passion, but despite his forceful kiss, she met him with the same intensity. She plunged her tongue into his mouth, taking as much as she gave.

Kayleen was shaking, both from nerves and from need. Zarina had been right. Despite her uncertainty, she'd managed to bring a prince to his knees. Or at least his feet, which was just as good.

She'd seen the need in As'ad's eyes, had watched him get aroused. He was already hard and straining. Even as they kissed, he pulled at the veils covering her, swearing with impatience when one tangled and would not budge.

"How many are there?" he asked, his voice thick with frustration and sexual arousal.

"A lot."

She reached for his shirt and began to unbutton that.

"Too slow," he told her and ripped the shirt open, then shrugged out of it. Seconds later he'd removed the rest of his clothes. Then he was naked and reaching for her.

His eagerness thrilled her. She was already damp and swollen, ready to be taken. To show him, she reached between them and stroked his arousal. He groaned as his maleness flexed in her hand.

"I want you," he breathed in her ear. "I want you now."

His words turned her to liquid. "Then take me."

He stared into her eyes. "Kayleen."

"I am to be your wife, As'ad. Take me."

He lowered her to the cushions and pushed the veils aside. After pulling down her panties, he slid his fingers between her legs.

"You want me," he told her as he rubbed against her swollen center.

"Always."

He smiled, then continued to touch her. She pushed his hand away.

"Be in me," she told him. "Claim me."

His breath caught, then he did as she asked. He settled between her knees and pushed inside of her.

She always forgot how large he was, how he filled her and made her ache with need. Normally he was slow and gentle, but tonight he pushed inside as if driven. The passion excited her.

He thrust deeply, groaning, his arousal moving her in a way she'd never experienced before. Her muscles began to tense and she closed her eyes to enjoy the ride.

He took her hard and fast, as if daring her to keep up. She accepted him easily, letting each plunging, rubbing pulse take her higher and higher.

She pulled her knees back, then locked her legs around his hips, drawing him in deeper.

Faster and more, pushing and straining until her release was only a heartbeat away.

He spoke her name. She looked up and saw him watching her.

"You are mine."

Three simple words, but they were enough to send her spiraling out of control. She lost herself in her release, screaming as the pleasure claimed her. He pushed in twice more, then groaned the end of his journey.

The waves of their pleasure joined them and they clung to each other until the earth stopped moving and their bodies were finally at rest.

KAYLEEN LET HERSELF into her suite shortly after midnight. She felt happy and content and as if she could float. Or do the whole veil dance again!

Rather than turn on a light, she crossed to the balcony and stepped out into the night. The air had a slight chill, but she didn't care. All she had to do was think about how much As'ad had wanted her and she got all hot inside.

The evening had been magical and she didn't want to forget any part of it. If there were—

The sound of a chair moving caught her attention. She turned and saw something sitting in the shadows. The light from a cigarette glowed briefly.

"Well, well, aren't you a bit of surprise." Her mother's voice was low and tight with something Kayleen didn't recognize. "I thought you were just a silly girl who'd gotten lucky, but I was wrong. You just have a different game you play."

Kayleen faced her. "I don't know what you're talking about."

"That innocent, country-mouse act is a good one. I'll bet your prince fell for it in a heartbeat."

"I'm not acting. All of this is real."

Darlene laughed. "Don't try to play me. I invented the game. I'm saying I respect your tactics. They wouldn't work for me, but they obviously work."

"I have no idea what you're talking about. It's late. I'm going to bed."

"You've already been to bed. What you're going to do this time is sleep. Am I wrong?"

"I'm not discussing this with you." She wouldn't allow the other woman to turn her amazing evening into something ugly.

"You made one mistake, though. Falling in love with him makes you vulnerable and that means you can make a wrong move. It's better to stay detached. Safer."

"I'm marrying As'ad. I'm supposed to love him."

Her mother laughed again. "Just don't go expecting him to love you back. Men like him don't.

Ever." She inhaled on her cigarette. "That's my motherly advice to you. A little late, but no less valuable."

"Good night," Kayleen told her and walked back into her room.

Her good mood had faded, which she hated, but worse were the doubts. Was her mother right about As'ad? Kayleen needed him to love her. She hadn't realized it mattered, but it did. And if he couldn't...

She walked into her bedroom and sank onto the mattress. If he couldn't, how could she marry him?

CHAPTER THIRTEEN

KAYLEEN HUDDLED IN the chair in Lina's living room and did her best to keep breathing. She'd recently discovered that terror and anxiety tended to make her hold her breath. Then she ended up gasping, which was not attractive or likely to make herself feel better.

"She's hideous," she moaned. "Isn't it enough that she abandoned me when I was a baby? Does she have to show up now?"

Lina patted her hand. "I am so sorry. My brother thought he was helping. Truly."

"I know. I've already mentally flogged myself for not telling the truth, but I just hate talking about my biological family. It's pathetic to be abandoned twice. What does that say about me?"

"That you rose above your circumstances. That you have great character and inner strength. That we are lucky to have you marrying into our family."

Kayleen smiled. "You're good."

"Thank you. It's a gift. Now about your mother…"

Kayleen's smile faded. "I don't want to think about her, but I have to. She's everywhere. Lurking. She constantly shows up without warning. She has totally terrified the girls. Last night she made Pepper cry when she told her she was going to have to be smart in life because she wasn't that pretty. Pepper wanted to hit her and I almost let her. Who says that to a little girl? Pepper's adorable. I can forgive her being mean to me, but to little kids? Never."

"Do you want me to tell her to leave the country?" Lina asked. "I will. I can be very imperious. We can ship her back on the next plane."

Kayleen was tempted. Very tempted. "I can't tell you how much I want to say yes. It's just…she's my mother. Shouldn't I try to have a relationship with her? Don't I owe her?"

"Only you can answer that. Although I must ask what you owe her for. Giving birth? You didn't ask to be born. That was her choice. And with having a child, comes responsibility. If she didn't want to be bothered, she should have given you up for adoption."

"I wonder why she didn't," Kayleen said. What would her life have been like if she'd been raised by a couple who wanted a child? She couldn't begin to imagine.

"Who knows. Perhaps the paperwork was too complicated for her tiny brain."

Kayleen grinned. "I like that. But it still leaves me with the issue of what to do with her. While I appreciate your offer to get rid of her, that doesn't feel right to me. I think I have to try and make a real connection with her, no matter how different we are. I'll deal with her for another week. If we can't find some common ground and she's still acting awful, then I'll take you up on your offer."

"You're giving her more chances than I would, but you have a kinder heart."

"Or more guilt." She sighed. "You don't suppose As'ad thinks I'm anything like her, do you?"

"Of course not. We can't pick our relatives. Don't worry—he doesn't blame you for your mother."

"I hope not." She rose. "All right. I need to go make good on my word and try to spend time with Darlene."

"Let me know how it goes."

"I will."

Kayleen walked down a flight of stairs to her suite. She paused at the door, then moved to the next one and knocked.

"Come in."

She walked into her mother's suite and found her at the dining room table, sipping coffee. There was a plate of toast and some fruit in a bowl.

Breakfast, she thought, trying not to judge. It was after eleven.

"Oh, there you are," Darlene said by way of greeting. "I just received the most delightful note from the king. I'm invited to a formal party. Something diplomatic. It sounds fabulous. I'll need something to wear. Can you take care of that?"

Kayleen sat across from her at the table. "Sure. One of the boutiques is sending over some dresses. If you give me your size information, I'll have them send over some for you."

Darlene smiled. "I like the service here."

Despite the fact that she hadn't been up very long, Darlene was perfectly made-up, with her hair styled. She wore a silk robe that clung to her curves. She looked beautiful, in a brittle sort of way.

"I thought maybe we could spend some time together," Kayleen told her. "Get to know each other. Catch up."

Darlene raised her eyebrows. "What do you want to know? I got pregnant at sixteen, left you with my mother and took off for Hollywood. I landed a few guest spots on soaps and a few prime-time shows, which paid the bills. Then I met a guy who took me to Las Vegas. You can make a lot more money there. Which I did. But time isn't a woman's friend. I need to secure my future. I wasn't sure how that was going to happen, when I heard from your king. Now I'm here."

Kayleen leaned toward her. "I'm your daughter. Don't you want to at least be friends?"

Darlene studied her for a long time. "You have a very soft heart, don't you?"

"I've never thought about it."

"You took in those girls. Now you're adopting them. You're going to be exactly the kind of wife As'ad wants."

"I love him. I want him to be happy."

Darlene nodded slowly. "You like it here? In El Deharia?"

"Of course. It's beautiful. Not just the city, but out in the desert. I'm learning the language, the customs. I want to fit in."

Darlene lit a cigarette. Her gaze was sharp, as if she were trying to figure something out. "The king is nice."

"He's very kind and understanding."

"Interesting. Those aren't the words I would have used." Her mother sipped her coffee. "Yes, Kayleen, I *would* like us to be friends. I just showed up here, which had to have been a shock. I've only been thinking of myself. I'm sorry for that."

"Really?" Kayleen was surprised, but pleased to hear the words. "That's okay. You've had a difficult life."

"So have you. But a better one than you would have had if you'd gotten stuck with my family. I

know you probably don't believe that, but it's true."
She rose. "Let me shower and get dressed. Then,
if you have time, you can take me on a tour of the
palace. It's a beautiful building."

"It is. I've been studying the history. I want
to know everything about As'ad and his people."

Darlene's expression tightened. "I'm sure he
appreciates that."

AS'AD TOOK KAYLEEN'S hand in his and kissed her
fingers. "What troubles you?"

They were having lunch together in his office.
She smiled at him. "Nothing. I'm just thinking."

"Obviously not about how you consider yourself
blessed above all women for being engaged to me."

She laughed. "No. Not that. I'm thinking about
my mother."

"I see."

She looked at him. "You don't approve of her?"

"I do not know her. What matters to me is your
feelings."

"I'm not sure of anything," she admitted, wondering when everything had gotten so complicated. "I told her I thought we should get to know
each other and try to be friends."

"And?"

"It's better," she said slowly. "I just don't know
if I believe her. Then I feel horrible for saying that.

I asked, she agreed and now I'm questioning that? Shouldn't I trust her?"

"Trust must be earned. You have a biological connection, but you don't know this woman."

"You're right. I'm so uncomfortable about everything." Especially Darlene's statements that she was in El Deharia to find a rich man to secure her future. Kayleen was torn between keeping her emotional distance and wanting to have family.

She'd always been taught to see the best in people, to believe they would come through in the end. So thinking her mother was using her violated what she knew to be right and what she felt in her heart. But assuming all was well violated her common sense.

She glanced at him. "You know I'm not like her, right?"

He smiled. "Yes, I know."

"Good."

DARLENE HUMMED AS she flipped through the dresses on the rack. "I could so get used to this," she murmured as she picked out a low-cut black gown that glittered with scattered beads. "The work is incredible. The details are hand-done. Have you looked at these prices? Twenty-three thousand dollars. Just like that." She put the black dress in front of her and turned to the full-length mirror set up in Kayleen's living room. "What do you think?"

"It's beautiful." Kayleen thought the dress lacked subtlety, but what did she know about fashion?

Darlene laughed. "Not your thing?"

"Not exactly."

"You're young. You'll grow into black." She carried the dress over to the tray of jewelry on the dining room table. "I'm thinking the sapphire-and-diamond-drop earrings and that matching pendant. Or the bracelet. As much as I want to wear both, less is more. Are you wearing that?"

Kayleen held up a strapless emerald-colored dress. The style was simple, yet elegant. It wasn't especially low-cut, but it was more daring than anything she'd ever worn. Still, she wanted to be beautiful for As'ad.

"I love it," she admitted. "But it makes me nervous."

"It's all in the boning. That dress is couture. It should have the support built right in. Don't worry—you'll stay covered." Darlene put her dress back on the rack, then returned to the jewelry tray. "Something surprising. Young, but sophisticated. Let's see."

She picked up an earring, then put it down. She handed another to Kayleen. "Here."

Kayleen took the piece and studied the curving

shape. The free-form design was open and sparkled with white and champagne diamonds.

"Really? Not the emeralds?"

"Too expected with the dress," Darlene told her. "And just the earrings. No necklace or bracelet. You're young and beautiful. Go with it. When you start to fade, you can add the sparkle. Someone's going to do your hair, right? You'll want it up, with long curls down your back. And you don't wear enough makeup. It's a party. Use eyeliner."

Kayleen put in the earring, then held her hair away from her face. "You're right."

"Thanks. I've been around a long time and I know what men like. Now let's see how I look in this black dress."

She stripped down to her lingerie and then stepped into the black gown. Kayleen helped with the zipper.

"Perfect," Darlene said as she stared at herself in the mirror. "I've already met the Spanish ambassador earlier in the garden. He's very charming. A little older, but that's good. I can be his prize."

Kayleen didn't know what to say to that. "Have you ever been married?"

Darlene held her hair up, as if considering the right style. "Once, years ago. I was eighteen. He was nobody. But I was in love and I told myself money didn't matter. Then the marriage ended and

I had nothing. I learned my lesson. Something you should learn."

"What are you talking about?"

"As'ad. You get starry-eyed when he's around. It's embarrassing for all of us."

Kayleen flushed. "We're engaged."

"I don't see how that matters." Darlene stepped out of the dress and put it back on the hanger, then reached for her own clothes. "I know this sounds harsh, but believe me, I have your best interests in mind. Men like As'ad don't have to bother with love. You're setting yourself up for heartache. Take what you can get and move on."

"So no one matters. No one touches your heart."

"Life is easier that way," her mother told her.

"You're wrong," Kayleen said. "Life is emptier that way. We are more than the sum of our experiences. We are defined by our relationships. The people we love and those who love us in return. In the end, that matters more than money."

"So speaks the girl who has never been hungry and without a home."

Kayleen stiffened. "I *have* been without a home. My grandmother dumped me at an orphanage because she couldn't be bothered. But then why should she when my own mother walked out on me?"

Darlene pulled on her shirt and buttoned it.

"Here we go," she said, sounding bored. "Poor you. Nobody loves you. Get over it. Life is hard, so make the best of it."

"You mean use other people to get what you want."

"If necessary." Darlene seemed untouched by the comment. "Maybe it seems cruel to be tossed aside, but sometimes it's worse to be kept. Your grandmother wasn't exactly a loving parent. There's a reason I left."

"I was your daughter. You should have taken me with you."

"You would have only dragged me down."

"So you left me to the same fate?"

Darlene shrugged. "You got lucky. She didn't bother with you. Trust me, if she had, it would have been a whole lot worse."

Kayleen didn't want to believe the words, but it was impossible not to. "You don't care about me at all."

"I'm proud of what you've accomplished."

"Catching a rich man?"

"Every woman's dream."

"Not mine," Kayleen told her. "I only wanted to belong."

"Then consider the irony. You have what I want and I've turned down a thousand of what you want. Life sure has a sense of humor."

The battle between Kayleen's head and her

heart ended. She walked over to the tray of jewelry and shook it. "This is why you're here. This is why you're pretending we can be friends. Let me guess—if you land the Spanish ambassador, you'll be gone and I'll never hear from you again. Until you need something."

Darlene shrugged. "I didn't come looking for you, honey. I was living my life, minding my own business. You're the one who set all this in motion. I'm just taking advantage of the ride."

Kayleen had always tried to hate her mother. It had been easier than being disappointed and heartbroken over being thrown away. But it was impossible to hate someone so flawed and unhappy.

"It won't matter if you end up with the Spanish ambassador," Kayleen told her mother. "You'll never feel like you have enough. There's not enough money in the world to fill that hole inside of you. It's going to take more. It's going to take giving your heart."

"Spare me." Darlene waved her hand dismissively.

"I can't. You can only spare yourself. But you won't listen to me because you think you already know everything you need to. You can't use me anymore. You can stay for the party, but then you have to leave."

Her mother glared at her. "Who the hell are you to tell me whether or not I can stay?"

Kayleen drew herself up to her full height. "I'm As'ad's fiancée."

KAYLEEN WAS DETERMINED to enjoy her first formal event despite feeling uneasy about her mother. Darlene had been friendly, as if nothing had happened. As if she wasn't planning on leaving. Kayleen was determined to handle the situation herself, so she didn't mention anything to As'ad.

He came to her door a little past seven, looking tall and handsome in a black tuxedo and white shirt.

Dana let him in after insisting Kayleen needed to make an entrance.

"You're so pretty," the girl told her. "He needs to see all of you at once."

Kayleen did her best not to fidget as As'ad walked toward her, his dark eyes unreadable. He paused in front of her.

"You are perfection," he murmured as he lightly kissed her. "I will have to keep you close or you will be stolen away."

"Not likely," she told him with a laugh. She turned in a slow circle. "You like the dress?"

"Yes, but I adore the woman who wears it."

Her heart fluttered.

She'd taken Darlene's advice on her hair, asking the stylist to put the top part up and leave the rest in long curls. The gown fit snugly and seemed secure enough for her to relax. She wore the champagne-and-white-diamond earrings, along with a simple diamond bracelet. Her high-heeled sandals gave her an extra four inches and would be excruciating by the end of the evening, but they looked fabulous.

"When do *we* get to go to formal state parties?" Pepper asked with a whine. "I want a new dress and fancy hair."

"When you are thirteen."

"But that's forever away."

He touched her nose. "You will get there soon enough."

"I only have to wait a year and a half," Dana said happily. "Then I can go."

"Three pretty girls," As'ad told Kayleen. "We're going to have to watch them closely. There will be boys at these parties."

"Am I pretty, too?" Pepper asked. Her eyes were big and she sounded doubtful, as if expecting a negative answer.

Kayleen remembered Darlene's harsh assessment and wanted to bonk her mother on the head for it.

As'ad crouched in front of the little girl. "You are more than pretty. You are a classic beauty. Never doubt yourself. You are to be a princess."

Pepper smiled widely. "When I'm a princess can I chop off people's heads if they're mean to me?"

As'ad choked back a laugh and straightened. "No, but you will have other powers." He took Kayleen's hand. "We must leave. Be good tonight."

"We will," Nadine told him.

Kayleen waved as they left. This being a palace, there was always someone to babysit.

They walked the length of the long corridor, then went down a flight of stairs. Once on the main floor, they joined the milling crowd walking toward the ballroom.

While Kayleen had toured the palace many times, she'd never seen the ballroom anything but empty. She was unprepared for the thousands of lights glittering from dozens of massive chandeliers or perfectly set tables set around a large dance floor.

The room was like something out of a movie. Well-dressed couples chatted and danced and sipped champagne. She'd never seen so many jewels in her life. Each dress was more beautiful than the one before, each man more handsome. As they walked into the ballroom, she waited for the sense of not belonging to sweep over her. She waited to feel awkward or out of place. Instead there was only contentment and the knowledge that she belonged here.

The burst of confidence bubbled inside of her, as if she'd already had too much champagne. She enjoyed the sensation, knowing this was her world now. She would marry a wonderful man and together they would adopt the girls. In time she would have children of her own.

As'ad led her to the dance floor, then pulled her into his arms. "Now what are you thinking?" he asked.

"That I'm Cinderella and I've finally arrived at the ball."

"So you leave me at midnight?"

She stared into his eyes. "I'll never leave you."

He stared back. "Good. I do not wish you to go. I need you, Kayleen. I will always need you."

Happiness filled her until she felt as if she could float. The music was perfect, as was the night. They danced until the king arrived, then As'ad led her around and introduced her to several of the guests.

The sound of loud laughter caught her attention. She turned and saw Darlene leaning against a much older, heavyset man. The man's attention seemed locked on her barely covered chest.

"The Spanish ambassador?" Kayleen asked As'ad.

"Yes. Do you wish to meet him?"

"Not especially."

He watched Darlene. "So that is who she has chosen?"

"Apparently."

"He's very rich, but alas, he is married. His wife does not accompany him when he travels."

Married? Kayleen looked at her mother. Did Darlene know?

"I should tell her," she said.

He frowned. "Why?"

"Because she's looking for security in her old age and he's obviously not the way to find it."

"Do you care what happens to her?"

"She's my mother. I can't not care." Which didn't mean she'd changed her mind. She still wanted her mother gone. Not that she'd figured out how to make her go.

"I think it is time I dance with my new sister."

Kayleen turned and saw Qadir, As'ad's brother, standing next to her.

"Assuming you don't mind," Qadir told As'ad.

"One dance and don't flirt."

Qadir laughed. "I flirt as easily as I breathe. Are you so worried that I will steal her away?"

"A man always guards what is precious to him."

Kayleen held in a sigh. "Flirt away," she told Qadir. "My heart belongs to your brother."

"Then he is a lucky man." Qadir led her to the dance floor. "You are beautiful tonight."

"Just tonight? Am I usually a troll?"

He laughed. "So this is what has charmed my brother. There's a brain."

"I have all my organs. Unusual, but there we are."

He laughed again. They chatted about the party and the guests. Qadir told her outrageous stories about several people, including a rumor about an English duchess who complained about not being allowed to bring her dog to the event.

When the dance was finished, Kayleen excused herself. Qadir was nice enough, but not the person she wanted to spend the evening with.

She walked around the edge of the room, and saw As'ad speaking with her mother.

"That can't be good," she muttered to herself and crossed the room to where they were standing.

"You will leave," As'ad said as Kayleen approached.

"I'm not so sure about that," Darlene told him. "The girl is my daughter. Who are you to come between her and her family?"

"A man who is willing to pay you to leave."

Kayleen caught her breath. No. As'ad couldn't do that. It wasn't right. She moved forward, but neither of them noticed her.

"You will not see her again," he continued. "If she contacts you herself, that is fine, but you will not have contact with her directly without her permission."

"So many rules." Darlene smiled. "That'll cost you."

"I would think a million dollars would be enough."

"Oh, please. Not even close. I want five."

"Three."

"I'll take four and you'll consider it a bargain."

The room went still. Oh, sure, people were dancing and talking and Kayleen was confident the orchestra kept playing, but she couldn't hear anything except the conversation of the two people in front of her.

"I'll wire the money as soon as you get me an account number," he said.

"I can give it to you tonight." Darlene patted his arm. "You really care for her. That's sweet."

"She is to be my wife."

"So I hear. You know she's in love with you."

Kayleen's breath caught.

"I know." As'ad spoke quietly, confidently.

"I'll bet that makes things real easy for you," Darlene said.

"It does."

Her mother tilted her head. "You think she's foolish enough to think you love her back?"

"You are not to tell her otherwise."

"Of course not." Darlene smiled again. "But I

think I should be allowed to keep the dress and the jewelry then. As a token of goodwill."

"As you wish."

"Then she'll never hear the truth from me."

CHAPTER FOURTEEN

KAYLEEN DIDN'T REMEMBER leaving the party, but she must have. When she finally looked around, she was in the garden—the one place she always seemed to retreat to. It was mostly in shadow, with lights illuminating the path. She wandered around, her body aching, her eyes burning, neither of which compared to the pain in her heart.

As'ad didn't love her. While he'd never specifically said he cared, she'd allowed herself to believe.

"I'm a fool," she said aloud.

He'd dismissed feelings as nothing more than a convenience. He'd admitted that their marriage would be easier for him, because of her feelings. He was using her. Nothing about their engagement mattered to him. *She* didn't matter to him.

She hurt. Her whole body ached. Each breath was an effort. She wanted to cry, but she was too stunned.

Her hopes and dreams continued to crumble around her, leaving her standing in a pile of dusty "what could have been." She'd thought she'd found where she belonged, where she could matter and make a difference. She'd thought so many things. But in As'ad's mind, she was little more than a comfy ottoman, where he could rest his feet. Useful, but not of any great interest.

She turned, trying to figure out where to go, what to do. Light caught her engagement ring and made it sparkle. She'd been such a fool, she thought bitterly. So stupidly innocent and naive about everything. Her mother had been right— why on earth would a man like As'ad be interested in a country mouse like herself? She'd wrapped herself in the fantasy because it was what she wanted to believe. Because it was easier than accepting the truth.

She heard a sound and looked up. One of the doves shifted in its cage. Willingly trapped because they either didn't understand they could be free or weren't interested. They took the easy way out, too.

Anger joined a sadness so profound, she knew it would scar her forever. Because whatever mistakes she'd made, she truly did love As'ad. She always would. But she didn't belong here. She couldn't stay and marry a man who didn't love her.

That decided, she made her way into the palace. Her mother's door stood partially open. Kayleen stepped inside without knocking to find her mother supervising two maids who were packing her suitcases. Darlene had already changed out of her evening gown into an elegant pantsuit. When she saw her daughter, she smiled.

"Oh, good. You stopped by. That saves me writing a note. Look, I'm leaving—just like you said I should. I've had a great time. I'm sorry we didn't get a chance to get to know each other better. Next time you're back in the States, you'll need to look me up."

Everything about her was false, Kayleen thought emotionlessly. From her bleached hair to her fake smiles.

"You're leaving because As'ad is paying you four million dollars," Kayleen told her. "I heard the conversation."

"Then you know I got what I came for. A secure future. It's not a fortune, but I know how to invest. I'll live well enough and maybe find someone to supplement my excesses. It doesn't compare with your haul, of course, but we can't all be that lucky."

Lucky. Right. To fall in love with a man who didn't care about her.

"When do you leave?" Kayleen asked.

"There's a plane waiting at the airport. I love the truly rich." Darlene frowned. "You're not going to want an emotional goodbye, are you?"

"No. I don't want anything from you."

With that, she left and returned to her own suite. The babysitter greeted her.

"They were all so good tonight," the young woman said.

"I'm glad. Thank you."

The other woman left and Kayleen was alone.

Despite the pain, she felt almost at peace. Maybe it was finally seeing the world as it was, and not as she wanted it to be. Maybe it was knowing the truth.

The truth was she would never have the kind of relationship with her biological family that she wanted. She could keep trying and maybe in time, things would improve, but there was no rescue there. There was no happy ending.

The same was true with As'ad. He'd proposed out of duty and maybe with the belief that she would be a good wife. He'd told her he didn't believe in love and she hadn't listened. She'd created a different story because it was what she wanted to believe.

But he didn't love her and he had no intention of loving her. So her choices were clear. She could stay and marry him, live life as a princess, or she could walk away. Darlene would tell her the money, the prestige, the palace, were worth nearly everything. But Kayleen remembered reading once that when a woman marries for money, she earns every penny.

She didn't want to marry for money—she wanted to marry for love. She wasn't like the doves—trapped even though the door was open, she was free to leave.

After looking in on the girls, she returned to her own room. She undressed and pulled on a robe, then sat in a chair by the French doors and stared out at the night.

The only part of leaving that bothered her was knowing how much she would miss As'ad. Despite everything, she loved him. Would she ever be able to love anyone else?

Because that's what she wanted. A real life, with a family and a man who cared. She wasn't going to run back to the convent school. She was going to make her way in the world. She was strong— she could do it.

As'ad found Kayleen in her suite. She'd changed out of her ball gown and pulled on a robe. She sat in the living room, a pad of paper on her lap.

He walked in and stared at her. "You left the party. I looked everywhere and you were gone."

She glanced up at him. "I didn't want to stay any longer."

That didn't sound right, he thought warily. She'd left without talking to him? "Are you ill?"

"I'm fine."

"You came back here to make notes?"

"Apparently." She set the paper and pen on the coffee table, then stood. "Have you transferred the money to my mother?"

He swore silently. "You spoke with her?"

"Not about that. Don't worry. She didn't tell me anything, so she gets to keep the dress and jewelry, right? I mean, that *was* the deal. Along with the four million. A generous offer. I'd already told her to leave, but you didn't know that. She made out well."

"I do not care about the money," he said, trying to remember exactly what he and Darlene had discussed. Obviously Kayleen had been in a position to overhear their conversation.

He felt badly—he guessed she was hurt and his intent had been to avoid that.

"I know," Kayleen said. "But she does, so it works out well for both of you."

He tried to read her expression, but he had no idea what she was thinking. Was she angry?

"Once she is gone, all will be well," he said, willing it to be so.

"I'm not as sure." She stared into his eyes. "This is just a marriage of convenience for you. I'm surprised you'd pick me. I'm sure there are women with better pedigrees out there. Women who understand what it's like to be a princess and who won't have foolish expectations."

"I am pleased to be marrying you. I want you

to be the mother of my sons. I respect you, Kayleen. Isn't respect and admiration more important, more lasting, than a fleeting emotion like love? I will honor you above all women. That must have value."

"It does. But love has value, too. Maybe it's a peasant thing."

She was calm and he didn't like it. Screaming and crying he could understand, but not this quiet conversation. What did she want from him?

"I take a lot of the blame," she said, her gaze steady. "I took the easy way out. You told me that after we slept together, and you were right. I want to hide, first at the convent school and then here, with you. I was never willing to really strike out on my own. I was afraid and I let that fear rule me. I thought by staying close to what I knew, I would be safe and belong. Even when I went halfway around the world to your country, I huddled in the orphan school, terrified to take a step."

Her reasoning sounded correct, but he had a bad feeling about what she was saying.

"Now you have chosen a different path," he pointed out. "So you are making changes. That is as it should be."

"I am making changes, As'ad. Big ones." She removed her engagement ring and held it out to him.

"No," he told her, shocked by her actions. "You

have agreed to marry me. Changing your mind is not permitted."

"*You* don't get to decide that. I won't marry a man who doesn't love me. I'm worth more. I deserve more. And so do you. I know you believe love makes you weak, but you're wrong. Love makes you strong. It is powerful and the reason we're here. To love and be loved. You need that, As'ad. I love you, but that's not enough. You have to be willing to love me back. Maybe I'm not the one. Maybe there's someone else you can love."

She gulped in a breath and tried to smile. Her lips trembled. "It hurts to say that. It hurts to think of you with someone else. But I can't make you love me."

She didn't mean this, he told himself. It was the emotion of the moment. She would get over it.

"I will not accept the ring back."

"That's your choice." She put it on the coffee table. "Either way, I'm leaving."

"You cannot go. I won't permit it. Besides…" He prepared to say the one thing that would change her mind. "I need you."

She nodded slowly. "You do. More than you realize. But that's not enough."

He frowned. It had worked before. Lina had told him Kayleen wanted to be needed above all. "I need you," he repeated.

"Maybe, but you can't have me." She sighed. "It's late, and you should go."

Somehow he found himself moving to the door. Then he was in the hallway. He stood there a long time, fighting the strangest feeling that he'd just lost something precious.

No, he told himself. Kayleen wouldn't leave him. She couldn't. She belonged here. To him and the girls. She would be fine. In the morning they would talk again. He would make her understand that she belonged here. With him. It was what he wanted. And he was Prince As'ad of El Deharia. He always got what he wanted.

As'ad gave Kayleen plenty of time to think about what she was considering, which turned out to be the one flaw in his plan. For when he returned to her suite close to midday, she and the girls were gone.

Their closets were empty, the toys missing, the dining room swept clean of homework and books. The only thing lying there was the engagement ring he'd given her.

He had expected a fight or tears or even an apology, but not the silence. Not the absence of life. It was as if they'd never been there at all.

He walked through the rooms, not truly accepting the truth of it. She had left him.

Him! A prince. After all he'd done for her, all

he'd given her. He'd rescued her and the children, started the adoption process for the girls. He'd given them a home, had proposed to Kayleen. What more did she want?

He burst into his aunt's office and glared at her. "This is all your fault," he told her sternly. "You created the problem and you will fix it."

Lina's office was small and feminine, overlooking the garden. Normally he would tease her about the frills and ruffles, but not today. Not now when she had ruined everything.

Lina poured herself some tea from a pot on a silver tray. "I have no idea what you're talking about."

"Of course you do. Kayleen is gone. She left and took the girls. Those are my children. El Deharian law states royal children cannot be taken from the country without their royal parent's permission."

"You're not the royal parent yet. Your petition for adoption has not been approved, nor is it likely to be. Custody will be given solely to Kayleen. She's already spoken to the king."

As'ad stared at her, unable to believe what she was saying. "That is not possible."

"It's very possible. You only took the girls because I suggested it as a way to solve the problem with Tahir. You never actually wanted them."

This was *not* happening, he told himself. "I did

not know them. I know them now and they are my daughters."

"Not really. Kayleen is the one who loves them."

"I provided snow for their pageant."

"Which was great and I know they enjoyed it. I'm not saying you didn't care about them, As'ad. But love? You don't believe in it. You've told me yourself. Your father understands completely. Don't forget, these aren't royal children who grew up like you did. They expect their parents to love them. Kayleen will. They're leaving El Deharia. All four of them."

Leaving? Permanently?

"I will not allow it," he told her. "I insist they stay."

"They will through the holidays, then Kayleen is taking the girls back to the States. It will be easier for them to start over. Your father has offered to help financially. Kayleen is being her usual sacrificing self. She will allow him to help her with the girls until she gets established, but then she'll handle things. She's going to let him pay for college, though. Especially for Dana. Apparently she wants to be a doctor."

"I know that," As'ad said through ground teeth. "And Nadine will dance and Pepper has yet to decide, but she's only eight and why should she? This is ridiculous. My father will not support my children. It is my responsibility and my right.

You have meddled, Lina. You have ruined everything."

"Actually, you did that all yourself. Kayleen is a wonderful woman. She adored you and would have made you very happy. She was yours to lose and you did. But don't worry. She'll find someone else. I'm a little more worried about you."

He wanted to rant and yell. He wanted to throw her antique desk through the large window. He wanted to crush her teapot with his bare hands.

"None of this is acceptable," he growled.

"I'm sorry you see it that way, but I think it's for the best. Kayleen deserves a man who will love her. Or don't you agree?"

He glared at his aunt. "You seek to trap me with your words."

"I seek to make you understand that you don't deserve a woman like Kayleen."

Her words cut him in a way no words had before. He stared at her for a long moment as the truth settled into the wound. She was right—he did not deserve Kayleen. All this time he had assumed he was doing her a favor when, in truth, the situation was reversed.

He left Lina's office and retreated to his own. He told Neil he would not be disturbed. Then he stood alone in the silence and wondered what had gone wrong.

TWO DAYS LATER he understood the real meaning
of the words *living in hell*. Only there was no living for him, only reminders of what he had lost.

He had always enjoyed life in the palace, but
now every room, every corridor, was a reminder
of what was missing. He turned, expecting to see
one of the girls. But they weren't there. He thought
of a thousand things he should tell Kayleen, but
she wasn't around to listen. He ached to hold her,
touch her, kiss her, and there was no one.

She had left him. Willingly, easily. She had
walked away and not come back. She, who had
claimed to love him.

While he knew in his heart her affection for
him had not had time to fade, in his mind he grew
angry. But she was not there to fight with.

He spent the night in her rooms, wandering,
sitting, waiting, remembering. He arranged to go
to Paris to forget her, then canceled his plans. He,
who had never allowed himself to care, to need, to
love, had been broken. Prince As'ad of El Deharia
reduced to a shell of a man because his woman
had left.

He hated that. Hated to be weak. Hated to need.

He hurried to see his father, walking in on the
king without knocking. His father looked up from
his morning paper. "As'ad, what is wrong? You do
not look well."

"I am fine. Kayleen has left."

"Yes, I know."

"You must not give her permission to leave the country, or take the girls with her. Those are my children. The law is clearly on my side."

His father frowned. "Kayleen said you did not love the girls. That they would be better off with her. Was she wrong? What do you wish?"

Love. Why did it always come back to that? As'ad walked to the window and stared out at the horizon.

What *did* he wish?

"I want her back," he said quietly. "I want her here, with me. I want the girls to return. I want..."

He wanted Kayleen smiling at him, laughing with him, close to him. He wanted to see her stomach swell with their baby, he wanted to ease her discomfort when she was sick. He wanted to see the girls grow and learn and prepare for college. He wanted to walk each of them down the aisle, only after terrifying any young man who would claim one of them as he had claimed Kayleen.

What if Dana was in a love with a man who did not love her back? What would he do?

Kill him, he told himself. He would kill the suitor in question, then take his daughter home where she belonged. He would insist she not be with anyone who did not love her desperately. Because that was what she deserved. What they all deserved. He could not let them go under any other circumstances.

Didn't Kayleen deserve the same?

He already knew the answer. He believed it. But if it was true, then shouldn't he let her go to find such a man?

No!

The roar came from deep within him. He faced his father. "No. She is to have no one but me. I am the one who first claimed her and I will not let her go."

His father sighed. "We have let go of the old ways. You will not be allowed to claim a bride who is not interested in marrying you."

"I will convince her."

"How?"

"By giving her the one thing she wants."

The king looked doubtful. "Do you know what that is?"

As'ad finally did. "Where is she?"

Mukhtar hesitated. "I am not sure…"

"I am. Where is she? I know she has not left the country. Lina told me. Where is she hiding?"

And then he knew that, as well. "Never mind. I'll find her myself."

KAYLEEN DID HER best to smile. The puppy was adorable, as was Pepper as the two of them tumbled together on the rug by the fire. Dana and

Nadine were off with the older girls. Despite the sudden change from a palace to a desert camp, the sisters had adjusted well. They thought they were on a fun adventure.

Kayleen wished she could share their excitement and flexibility. While she appreciated that Sharif and Zarina had taken them in, she longed to be back at the palace. While life under the stars offered a level of freedom she'd never experienced before, it was difficult to even breathe without thinking of As'ad.

She ached for him every minute of every day. She knew she had to stay strong and she was determined not to give in to the need to see him, but there were times when the pain overwhelmed her.

Zarina hadn't asked any questions when Kayleen had shown up with the girls. Instead she'd offered a comfortable tent and acceptance by the villagers. But it was a temporary situation—in a few days the tribe would return to the desert and Kayleen would have to find temporary housing until she could leave El Deharia.

Perhaps in the city somewhere. A small house. Lina had promised it would only take a couple of weeks for her paperwork to be pushed through the legal channels. There were advantages to a royal connection.

Thank goodness As'ad hadn't been interested in hurrying the adoption. If he had she wouldn't have been able to leave. Royal children could not be taken from El Deharia without the royal parent's permission.

She touched her belly and remembered the last time they'd made love. If she was pregnant, she would be trapped forever. Imagine the irony if she at last had the baby she'd long desired.

"I will not think of that," she whispered to herself. "I will stay strong."

She might not know the future, but she was confident she could handle whatever life threw at her. She'd stood up for what she believed, she'd faced As'ad and turned down the half life he'd offered. She'd been willing to lose everything to gain her heart's desire. There was some peace in knowing she'd been true to herself. Unfortunately peace did not seem to ease pain.

She stood and walked to the fire, where tea always boiled. After pouring herself a mug she stared up at the clear sky. Only two days until Christmas. They would celebrate out here, under the stars, then return to the city.

She turned back to the tent, only to stop when she saw a man riding toward the camp. For a moment her heart jumped in her chest, but then she realized he wore traditional clothes. One of the young men who came and went, she thought, looking away. Someone's husband.

Several of the tribespeople called out to each

other. Kayleen tried to figure out what they were saying, but they were speaking quickly, yelling and pointing. Was there a problem?

Then she looked back at the man and recognized him. As'ad. But he was unlike she'd ever seen him before. He looked determined, primal. This was no prince in a suit—this was a sheik.

She stood her ground, reminding herself she had nothing to fear. He couldn't hurt her worse than he had when he'd admitted he didn't love her and that her love for him was a well-timed convenience. She shook out her long hair, then raised her chin. Pride and determination stiffened her spine. She didn't move, not even when he rode his horse right up to her.

Their eyes locked. She had no idea what he was thinking. Despite everything, she was happy to see him, happy to drink in the male beauty of his hard features. She wanted to touch him and kiss him and give herself to him. So much for being strong.

"I have claimed you," he told her sternly. "You cannot escape me."

"You can't hold me against my will. I'm not your prisoner."

He dismounted and handed the horse off to one of the young boys who had run up. Then he stalked over to her.

"You're right, my heart. I am yours."

She blinked. What had he called her? And what did he mean that he was her prisoner? What?

He touched her face with his fingertips. "I have missed you. Every second of every day since you left me has been empty and dark."

She swallowed. "I don't understand."

"Nor do I. My course was set—the plan clear. I would marry appropriately, father sons, perhaps a daughter or two, serve my people and live my life. It was arranged. It was my destiny. Then one day, I met a woman who leads with her heart, who is fearless and giving and kind and who bewitched me."

She couldn't breathe, but that didn't seem to be such a big deal. This was all good, right? He was saying good things. Maybe, just maybe, she could hope.

"Kayleen, I was wrong," he told her. "Wrong to think I knew so much more, that I was in charge. You swept into my life and nothing was the same. It was better—so much better. I miss you desperately. You and the girls. I need to see you smile every day. All of you. I need to hear your voices, your laughter. You cannot take my daughters from me and you cannot take yourself."

She ached for him. Giving in seemed the only option. But how could she?

"I won't live in a loveless marriage," she told

him, fighting tears, fighting the need to surrender. "I deserve more."

"Yes, you do. I was wrong to suggest such a thing before. You deserve to be loved, to be worshiped. To be the best part of your husband's life."

He took her hands in his and kissed her knuckles, then turned her wrists and kissed her palms.

"Let me be that man," he said quietly. "Let me show you all the ways I love you. Let me prove myself again and again, then, when you are sure, continue to test me." He stared into her eyes. "I will not fail, my heart. I will never fail. Because I love you. Only you. I did not think it was possible, yet here I stand. Humbled. Needing. In love. Can you find it in your heart to forgive me? To give me another chance?"

"Say yes."

The words were whispered from behind her. She sensed all three of the girls standing there, willing her to give As'ad the second chance he asked for.

"Yes," she whispered, then threw herself into his arms.

He caught her and pulled her close, saying her name over and over, then kissed her and held her as if he would never let her go.

He felt so right, next to her, she thought, nearly bursting with happiness. Then there were more arms and he pulled back only to let the girls into their circle of love.

He picked up Pepper and put his arm around Nadine. Kayleen pulled Dana against her and they held on to each other…a family at last.

"I'm so happy," Kayleen told him.

"As am I. Perhaps not as quick a learner as you would like."

"You figured it out."

"Only because you had the strength to leave me. You will always do the right thing, won't you?"

"I'll try."

He kissed her again, then frowned. "Why do you cry?"

"I'm not."

She touched her cheek and felt wetness. But it was cold, not warm and wasn't a tear.

Pepper shrieked. "It's snowing. As'ad, you brought the snow machine to the desert!"

"I did not. There is no way to power it out here."

Kayleen looked up. Snow fell from a clear sky. Perfect snow. Miracle snow. Christmas snow.

He set Pepper on the ground. She joined her sisters and the other children, running around, trying to catch snowflakes in their hands and on their tongues. As'ad pulled Kayleen close.

"You must promise to never leave me again," he said. "I would not survive it."

"As you will never leave me."

He laughed. "Where else would I want to be? I have you."

"For always," she told him.

"Yes," he promised. "For always."

Love burned hot and bright in his eyes. Love that filled the empty space inside of her and told her she had finally, *finally* found her way home.

* * * * *

New York Times bestselling author

SUSAN MALLERY

brings you a heartwarming tale for the holidays!

$16.95 U.S.

The unrelenting cheer in Fool's Gold, California, is bringing out the humbug in dancer Evie Stryker. She learned early on that Christmas miracles don't happen, at least not for her. Even when she's recruited to stage Fool's Gold's winter festival, she refuses to buy in to the holiday hype. Not even when sparks begin to fly between her and hunky lawyer Dante Jefferson...

A Fool's Gold Christmas

Add it to your collection today!

$1.50 OFF

Susan Mallery's A FOOL'S GOLD CHRISTMAS

Offer Valid: October 23rd to November 9th, 2012

Redeemable at participating retail outlets. Limit one coupon per purchase.
Valid in the U.S.A. only.

5 65373 00078 6 (8100)1 18200

HARLEQUIN® HQN™
www.Harlequin.com

BESTSELLING AUTHOR COLLECTION

™ CLASSIC ROMANCES IN COLLECTIBLE VOLUMES

New York Times **Bestselling Author**

SUSAN MALLERY

When military expert Quinn Reynolds defeats defense instructor
D. J. Monroe in a martial arts match, she agrees to give him
whatever he wants in exchange for teaching her to be a better
fighter. But she promised herself never to be vulnerable again…
and the one thing Quinn wants is *her.*

QUINN'S WOMAN

Available December 18 wherever books are sold!

**Plus, enjoy the bonus story *Home for the Holidays*
by Sarah Mayberry, included in this 2-in-1 volume!**

New York Times bestselling author

DIANA PALMER

**rings in the holidays with two enthralling stories
of undeniable passion and unexpected love.**

Add it to your collection today!

"Palmer knows how to make the sparks fly."
—*Publishers Weekly* on *Renegade*

HARLEQUIN® HQN™

™ www.Harlequin.com

PHDP718

REQUEST YOUR FREE BOOKS!

2 FREE NOVELS FROM THE ROMANCE COLLECTION PLUS 2 FREE GIFTS!

SUSAN MALLERY

77694	ALL SUMMER LONG	___ $7.99 U.S.	___ $9.99 CAN.
77687	SUMMER NIGHTS	___ $7.99 U.S.	___ $9.99 CAN.
77683	SUMMER DAYS	___ $7.99 U.S.	___ $9.99 CAN.
77601	ONLY HIS	___ $7.99 U.S.	___ $9.99 CAN.
77594	ONLY YOURS	___ $7.99 U.S.	___ $9.99 CAN.
77588	ONLY MINE	___ $7.99 U.S.	___ $9.99 CAN.
77533	SWEET TROUBLE	___ $7.99 U.S.	___ $9.99 CAN.
77532	SWEET TALK	___ $7.99 U.S.	___ $9.99 CAN.
77531	SWEET SPOT	___ $7.99 U.S.	___ $9.99 CAN.
77529	FALLING FOR GRACIE	___ $7.99 U.S.	___ $9.99 CAN.
77527	ACCIDENTALLY YOURS	___ $7.99 U.S.	___ $9.99 CAN.
77520	DELICIOUS	___ $7.99 U.S.	___ $9.99 CAN.
77519	SIZZLING	___ $7.99 U.S.	___ $9.99 CAN.
77510	IRRESISTIBLE	___ $7.99 U.S.	___ $9.99 CAN.
77490	ALMOST PERFECT	___ $7.99 U.S.	___ $9.99 CAN.
77468	FINDING PERFECT	___ $7.99 U.S.	___ $9.99 CAN.
77465	SOMEONE LIKE YOU	___ $7.99 U.S.	___ $9.99 CAN.
77452	CHASING PERFECT	___ $7.99 U.S.	___ $9.99 CAN.
77384	HOT ON HER HEELS	___ $7.99 U.S.	___ $9.99 CAN.
77383	STRAIGHT FROM THE HIP	___ $7.99 U.S.	___ $8.99 CAN.
77372	LIP SERVICE	___ $7.99 U.S.	___ $8.99 CAN.

(limited quantities available)

TOTAL AMOUNT	$ _____
POSTAGE & HANDLING	$ _____
($1.00 FOR 1 BOOK, 50¢ for each additional)	
APPLICABLE TAXES*	$ _____
TOTAL PAYABLE	$ _____

(check or money order—please do not send cash)

To order, complete this form and send it, along with a check or money order for the total above, payable to Harlequin HQN, to: **In the U.S.:** 3010 Walden Avenue, P.O. Box 9077, Buffalo, NY 14269-9077; **In Canada:** P.O. Box 636, Fort Erie, Ontario, L2A 5X3.

Name: _____

Address: _____ City: _____

State/Prov.: _____ Zip/Postal Code: _____

Account Number (if applicable): _____

075 CSAS

*New York residents remit applicable sales taxes.
*Canadian residents remit applicable GST and provincial taxes.

HARLEQUIN® HQN™
www.Harlequin.com